HARRISON HYDE AND THE RUNAWAY BRIDE

THE TEXAS BRAND: GENERATIONS
BOOK ONE

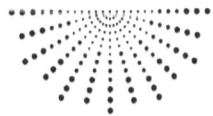

MAGGIE SHAYNE

OLIVERHEBERBOOKS

Harrison Hyde and the Runaway Bride Copyright 2024 © Margaret S. Lewis

Cover art by Dar Albert at Wicked Smart Designs

Published by Oliver-Heber Books

0 9 8 7 6 5 4 3 2 1

PRAISE FOR MAGGIE SHAYNE

"Readers will love this novel, which twists Shayne's usual combination of sharp wit and awesome characters with a killer who could have leapt right off of a television screen." ~**RT Book Reviews** on Sleep With the Lights On

WINNER: Paranormal Romantic Suspense of the Year
FINALIST: Book of the Year

"Maggie Shayne's books have a permanent spot on my keeper shelf. She writes wonderful stories combining romance with page-turning thrills, and I highly recommend her to any fan of romantic suspense." ~*New York Times* bestselling author **Karen Robards**

"In this thrilling follow-up to Sleep With the Lights On, Shayne amps up both the creep factor and the suspense." ~**RT Book Reviews** on Wake to Darkness

CHAPTER ONE

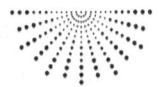

"My life's work is done," said Harrison Hyde. He was driving his reliable ten-year-old Volvo westward across Texas, on his way to New Mexico. He'd started out in Florida.

He glanced at the oval photo charm that dangled from his mirror. "I don't know how I can keep my promise, Mom. You said to keep the family together, and I couldn't even do it for a year. Dad wants to move to that retirement community in Florida where a bunch of your old friends are. It's a nice place. His asthma's getting worse all the time. He shouldn't be alone, but he says they have care-givers there."

He sighed and looked at the horizon. There was a church steeple way off in the distance, and as he drew nearer, he spotted the other rooftops of a dusty West Texas town.

"Lily passed the NCLEX, got her pin and put in applications at every hospital within driving distance of

Ithaca, based on the assumption I'd still be at Cornell. But what do I do about Dad, if he wants to move?"

He was speaking toward the passenger seat, as if his mother were riding with him. He pictured the window rolled down and her long platinum hair blowing in the breeze, and he tried to imagine what she would say.

The words that floated into his mind in his mother's voice were, "What do *you* want, Harrison?"

What *did* he want? Well, that was the question, wasn't it? And that was why he was driving to the demo site in New Mexico instead of flying out like the rest of the team. To give himself time to think about what he wanted, and what came next. He'd been devoted to his research for seven years. And now it was done. The result was sitting in a padded black box that looked like it ought to hold a large piece of jewelry, in the passenger seat, with his mother's ghost.

She'd been gone a year. She hadn't lived to see his life's work accomplished. And while Harrison believed in science, not ghosts, he found comfort in talking to her and imagining her replies. They'd been so close, he could pull up an accurate approximation to what she might say in any given situation, based on all the years they'd spent together. He often worked through problems that way.

Returning his attention to the road, he saw a brown and yellow trailhead sign beside a green metal highway sign that said, "Quinn: 1 mile."

"What I want," he said with a burst of clarity, "is to take a break from driving and stretch my legs. I haven't moved in too many hours."

The pull-off was small and surrounded in scrubby brush. A little stream ran through it, which surprised him, as close as he was to the desert.

He got out, closed the door, and stretched his arms way up over his head, arching his back until it cracked. He was wearing light khakis, a blue, short-sleeved, button-down shirt, and a pair of canvas slip-ons. Everything lightweight and easy. Perfect for a short walk.

It felt good to move. The air was warm and dry as he hiked out along the trail. It would be hot later in the day, it being June in southwest Texas. But it was only ten a.m., and not yet unbearable.

It was weird, not having work to think about or problems to solve. He'd solved them all. Well, he and his team: Carrie, Solomon, and Robert.

The dry air carried the scent of some flower that must be in blossom nearby. He started up the trail, over red-brown dirt and fine red pebbles that hadn't quite made it to dirt yet. He felt them shifting under the soles of his flimsy canvas shoes. Not exactly hiking shoes. He'd brought hiking shoes, but he hadn't thought to change, and he was already too far from the car to warrant going back. Besides, the terrain didn't look too rough. It wound slightly uphill amid squatty trees, and stands of aromatic brush that gave off a scent like pepper and spice. There were boulders every kid ever born would want to climb. He'd climbed boulders just like them as a kid on family camping trips to places like this.

Around the next curve in the trail, he spotted a lean

gray jackrabbit. The rabbit froze, motionless except for his twitching nose.

"Yeah, that's right, buddy. You're invisible." To cut the nervous little guy a break, he turned away, looking elsewhere. As soon as he did, the rabbit scampered off, throwing up dirt in his wake. Harrison laughed.

It was nice, not thinking. Just being. He focused on the moment, something he hadn't done since work on the solar tile had begun. There was nothing left to do but the big demonstration in New Mexico for an audience of potential investors; in private, he'd been referring to the demo as the "Silver City Shark Tank." That was what it felt like.

He had to be there by noon on Wednesday. By the time it was over, he might be a wealthy man. It was only Saturday. He was going to take his sweet time. He'd never thought about what he would do after the solar tile. But he intended to figure it out on this road trip. He had hours of quiet time, driving across Texas with nothing to do but think.

The steady thud of his footsteps in the dry red substrate were like a drumbeat, and they brought a memory. Horse hooves on similar ground. His mom had found a trail-riding outfit not far from their Ithaca home when he was very young and Lily was just a toddler. From that year on, every autumn when the foliage peaked, they'd take a family trail ride amid the vivid colors of New York State. The clip-clop of hooves would eventually soften, cushioned by a lemon-yellow, pumpkin-orange, and scarlet-red carpet of fallen leaves.

He topped a low rise and stopped walking to take in the view. Off in the distance, the white steeple was closer than he'd seen it from the road. He turned to resume his walk just in time to see a speeding, red-headed missile in tattered white satin right before she hit him.

His breath gusted, and he went over backwards, feet up. His back hit the ground hard, his keys and water bottle flying in opposite directions. The woman who'd crashed into him was down, too. He could see white lace portions of her in his peripheral, but his view was mostly of the sky. It took him a second to get a breath, and that second was filled with the woman not-quite-cussing a blue streak

"Golddern, mother lovin' *tourists!*"

He sat up. She got upright, and he took note of her torn wedding dress, the twigs in her wild red hair, and the anger in her doe-brown eyes. She looked right back at him so intently it made him wonder what he looked like through her eyes. Then she looked away from him, snatched up the duffel bag she'd dropped when they'd collided. She continued looking around the ground, so he did, too. All he saw were her cute bare toes, peeking out from the shredded hem of the gown.

She saw something else, though, because she crouch-lunged, snatched his dropped car keys, then raced back down the trail in the direction of his car.

He blinked as reality hit him. The bedraggled bride was about to steal his car!

"Hey!" He sprinted after her. "Hey, what do you think you're doing with my keys?"

"Gettin' away from my family for a few hours," she

shouted. "Keep up, or I'll leave without you." Her bare feet pounded over the trail, making him wince in pain on her behalf, but she didn't even seem to notice. The trail spilled into the parking spot, and the woman threw her duffel into the back of his car and dove behind the wheel.

"No," he shouted. "Just wait a minute now, come on!" He ran up to the Volvo and grabbed the driver's door before she could close it.

She shrugged and started the engine. "I'll drive away with the car *and* your arm. Don't think I won't. I'm not a fan of your gender, right now."

"Just… fine, I'll take you wherever you want, but you have to let me drive."

She looked in the direction of that little town then back up the trail, and he realized she was afraid someone was coming after her. Then she said, "Okay, just, hurry it up." She gathered the white fabric all the way up around her waist and climbed over the console into the passenger seat. On the way, she picked up the black box— his life's work— and tossed it into the back while he reached for it, making noises that weren't quite words.

"*Nah-bah-gah*—" The box landed safely near his dad's tackle box, and he lowered his hand and sighed in relief.

"Come on!" she twanged. She turned around, providing a glimpse of lacy underpants before lowering her skirts and sitting in the passenger seat.

He got in, closed the door, reached for his seatbelt—

She reached over and pulled the shift lever into reverse, and the car jerked, startling him so much he let the seatbelt go and grabbed the wheel.

"Go!" she shouted.

"Going!" He went.

Jessi Brand left her front row pew and walked back down the aisle and around a corner toward the dressing room where her only daughter was getting ready to get married. Her heart was torn right down the middle. On the one hand, she wanted Maria Michele to have the perfect wedding day. On the other hand, if she was having second thoughts about marrying Billy Bob Cantrell, that was probably a good thing. Jessi'd never felt he was good enough for her girl, and she'd had a feeling since sunup that Maria had realized it, too.

Her notion was confirmed when she saw her two nieces, who were serving as bridesmaids, outside the dressing room door, wringing their hands and looking worried in their flouncy red dresses and cowboy boots. Her nephew Bubba was standing in front of the door like an unofficial country-church bouncer. Bubba was as big as his dad, Jessi's big brother Garrett, even though he was adopted. She figured it had to be the food.

"Sorry, Aunt Jess," Bubba said. "Maria Michele wanted a few minutes alone, and I promised I'd give 'em to her."

"She needs us and you're a *dick* for keepin' us out here," Drew said. She was as golden-blond as her parents, Ben and Penny, and only twenty-two.

Willow put a calming hand on her youngest cousin's

shoulder. "It's probably just pre-weddin' jitters. If she needs a few minutes alone, we leave her alone." But when she shifted her dark brown gaze to Jessi's, it said more. Something was wrong.

Willow would know. She and Maria were more like sisters than cousins. It was good that Willow still lived with her parents, Wes and Taylor, out at Sky Dancer Ranch. If she ever moved away from Quinn, it would break Maria's heart.

But she was firmly planted now that she'd been hired as her Uncle Garrett's newest deputy.

Jessi acknowledged Willow's dark look with a nod then refocused on Bubba, who was far too tall to be her nephew. "You're not fixin' to try and keep me from goin' in there, are you, Bubba?"

"It's Ethan," he replied. "You know I go by Ethan."

Jessi rolled her eyes. "It might be Ethan to the honky tonk honeys at your shows, rockstar, but when you're home— no matter how seldom— it's Bubba. It's always *been* Bubba and it'll always *be* Bubba. Now get the hell outta my way before I have to move you." She added a smile to soften her words.

Bubba, all six feet and four inches of him, stepped aside. He even leaned across to open the door for his little aunt. The door swung wide, revealing an empty dressing room. The rear exit stood wide open, a rectangular view of blue Texas sky over a grassy lawn, a scrubby lot, and a stand of woods. There was no sign of the bride.

"Holy smokes, she's run off!" Drew said, shouldering past her aunt and into the small room.

"Thank God," Willow whispered, and maybe no one else heard her, but Jessi did.

"Bubba, go get your uncle Lash." Jessi turned as she said it, but Bubba was already gone.

Jessi lowered her head and walked back into the main part of the church, where the whole clan and half the town had gathered, dressed to the nines for the first wedding of the Brand clan's youngest generation. Everyone looked worried, and they leaned into each other, talking in loud whispers, wondering what the heck had happened.

Jessi walked up the aisle, her strides strong and deliberate, and met the right Reverend Wayland Wheeler's bespectacled eyes with a little head shake to tell him it was off. Then she took the groom by one arm, and leaning close enough to smell the cigarette smoke and cologne blend of him, spoke near his ear. "I'm real sorry, Billy Bob. Maria's gone, and we don't know where. I think we have to call this off."

He pulled back a little to stare into her eyes. His were blue and bloodshot from the bachelor party. She wouldn't know, since none of the Brand men had been invited. Then again, it seemed Billy Bob had been drinking more than he ought to for at least a month. Maybe he'd been having second thoughts, too.

His eyes showed shock first, and just when she started to feel pity for the guy, it turned to anger. Then he pushed past her, almost knocking her down. Would have, except that Lash had appeared beside her without a sound, and caught her shoulders before she could fall.

Billy Bob stormed down the aisle and out the church's

front doors. After making sure she was okay, her husband strode after him. He elbowed Garrett on the way by, and then he *and* her big brother left the church right behind Billy Bob.

As the red double doors swung closed behind them, Jessi stepped up beside the minister, facing the crowd, and cleared her throat. "There's not gon' be a weddin' today, folks. I'm real sorry."

Then she headed for the exit herself, but kept getting waylaid by one person after another, either saying they were sorry or asking if there was a way to help. Quinn was that kind of a town. They filled the pews, and there would be twice as many at the reception. Or would've been. Lord, what would they do with all the food?

Still, she had no time to worry about that, nor to chitchat. She gave short answers, that flash of anger in Billy Bob's face just before he'd taken off, giving her rocket fuel. She got to the doors, threw them open, and ran outside just as Billy Bob's pickup roared away, leaving rubber on the road.

Jessi ran over to join her whipcord-lean husband, Lash, and bear-sized big brother Garrett. "He'd best not get anywhere *near* Maria Michele when he's that teed off," she said.

From behind her, Willow said, "I think we'd better get to her first, to make sure."

Jessi turned to see six out of seven of the youngest generation of Brands standing together. Wes and Taylor's daughter Willow was three quarters Comanche, and looked it. Beside her, blond, blue-eyed Drew and her older brother Orrin stood close together, looking like younger versions of their parents, Ben and Penny. Elliot and Esmeralda's son Trevor had his father's wiry build and his Mexican mother's brown skin and ebony eyes. His dark-brown hair had hints of his dad's auburn. Second cousin Baxter, the oldest of them all at thirty, with his shaggy golden hair and black-framed glasses, stood alone until Bubba came up beside him and clapped his shoulder.

They were all looking down the road in the direction taken by the angry groom.

An old blue import with New York plates passed, heading the same way as Billy Bob's truck.

Then the six youngsters— as the elder Brands called them— piled into Bubba's oversized pickup, some of them in the bed, and they headed off in the same direction, windows down. Willow shouted out the passenger side, "Don't worry, Aunt Jess. We'll find her!" And from the back, Trevor gave a whoop.

"Well, shoot. This isn't gonna go well, is it?" Jessi asked as the rest of her family gathered around.

"If he lays one finger on my girl—" Lash began.

His five brothers-in-law made growly comments of agreement.

"I think the youngsters are takin' this one," Jessi said. "Dang, things sure do change."

Lash put his arm around her shoulders. "And yet, they stay the same," he said.

Maria Michele said, "You're drivin' me right past the church where I was s'posed to marry Billy Bob freakin' Cantrell!" They rounded a curve in the road, and she saw her whole family gathered outside in the churchyard. "Jeeze-Louise!" She ducked way down low in the seat. "You had to go *this* way?"

He slowed down even more. "Sorry. Should I turn around?"

"Just go! Stomp it!"

He did not stomp it. He did speed up a little, though.

"You said you didn't care which way I went," he reminded her in what she thought was a calm tone for a guy who'd been sort of car-jacked by a tattered bride in smeared makeup. "You said just keep going whichever way I was going."

"I didn't mean this way!" She crouched lower.

"But there were only two ways."

"Are we past them yet?"

He adjusted the rearview mirror with his long fingers. An artist's hands, she thought, or a musician's. He hadn't answered, so she looked up at his face. He was still looking into the mirror, and his sky-blue eyes were worried.

"What?" she asked.

"I think they're coming after us," he said.

"*What?*" She rose up out of her seat. Her cousin Bubba's pickup was behind them and gaining. "Go faster!"

The little blue car picked up speed, and the driver's hand landed on top of her head and nudged her gently. "Maybe stay down," he suggested. Then he asked, "What should I do? Should I just pull over?"

"No, don't pull over! Can't you outrun them?"

"Their engine is three times the size of mine." He took a deep, noisy breath, then said, "There's no way they could know you're in this car. I have New York plates; they'd never imagine you in here with me. It doesn't make sense."

He let off the gas a little more, which made her want to slam her foot over his on the pedal.

"Maybe they're after that guy," he said, pointing ahead.

"What guy?" She popped her head up again, face-front this time.

"That guy." He nodded toward a black pickup ahead of them.

"Shoot, that's Billy Bob!" She ducked again.

"The jilted groom?" The driver looked down at her with his eyebrows bent into worried S-shapes. He had nice eyebrows, she noticed. Full and dark. His sable hair was close-cropped and curlier than her own, which was saying a lot.

"Yeah," she said. "Might say we're in between a rock and a hard place. And the hard place has a temper way worse than I ever knew."

He looked at her quickly, a flash of temper she hadn't expected in his eyes. "Did he *hit* you?"

"If he'd hit me, he wouldn't be *capable* of drivin'," she said.

He smiled at her when she said that. Hoo-boy. He was

handsome, for a yank. He let off the gas a little more. She didn't gripe about it this time.

"Is that why you left him at the altar?" He asked the question softly, like he was tiptoeing over a minefield.

She met his eyes. Hemsworth blue was what they were, she decided. "You really want to know why I left?"

"I do," he said.

She rolled her eyes. "You just said 'I do' to a gal in a weddin' gown."

He looked alarmed. Then he glanced into the rearview and looked even more alarmed. "They're coming on fast."

"Tell you what," Maria said. "You get me out of this spot I'm in without havin' to deal with either pickup full of rednecks, and I'll tell you why I left Billy Bob at the altar *and* buy you the best taco in Texas. Deal?"

He glanced at her, at the rearview, and then he kind of winced and crouched lower in the seat, like he was ducking, and he let off the gas even more.

Bubba's big pickup truck grew louder, then sped by them, passing the little Volvo like it was standing still.

For Maria Michele, the world shifted into ultra-slow motion as the jacked up, bright-red F-250 rolled by. She was still crouched low in the seat but looking up. And that truck was up high with a clear line of sight down. The truck's passenger-side window was open, and long jet-black hair she'd braided a hundred times was whipping in the wind. And then that head turned, and Willow looked right down at her, and her eyes widened.

Maria pressed a finger to her lips and tried to make her eyes urgent. Willow looked from Maria to the driver, and crooked one eyebrow, and then the world shifted back to its normal speed, and the truck blasted by.

"I thought they were going to run us off the road," the driver said. He sounded relieved.

"They wouldn't do that. Although, they might do it to Billy Bob, if he got outta line at the church once he realized I was gone."

He looked her way again. "You have to tell me about that temper now. A deal's a deal." Then he tipped his head to one side. "And maybe you could throw in your name."

She looked at him in surprise then shook her head. "We did kinda skip that part. I'm Maria Michele Brand Monroe-almost-Cantrell. But you can call me Maria."

"My mother's middle name was Maria," he said, glancing at the photo hanging from the mirror. She looked at it, too. Beautiful woman, brilliant smile, platinum hair, and those same blue, blue eyes. There was a flash of hurt in the son's set, but he blinked it away and said, "Harrison Hyde."

"Nice to meet you, Harry."

"Harrison."

"That's what I said. Now, Billy Bob's most likely headin' for my favorite spot, so he'll stay on the main road for another few miles, then take a right onto Bluebonnet Lane."

"Your favorite spot's on Bluebonnet Lane?"

"Pretty, right? My house is right on top. Well, it was gonna be my house. It's everything you could want in a house, really. We were gonna buy it right after the weddin'. Wasn't time before. I just finished vet school in May."

"You're a veterinarian?"

"Like my mamma before me," she said. "If we take the next left, we can hopscotch dirt roads all the way to the highway and be in Mad Bull's Bend eatin' Manny's tacos before Billy Bob and my cousins finish checkin' all my usual haunts."

"Heading west? Because I need to be going west."

"Yes, we'll be headin' west." She plucked at her white skirts. "I'm gon' change clothes. Don't look at me."

"I won't." He tipped the rearview mirror upward.

Maria climbed between the seats into the back and unzipped her duffel bag. She'd packed it for a honeymoon at a resort in Silver City, New Mexico that Billy Bob had chosen because there was a rodeo nearby that he wanted to see.

She dug out a pair of jeans, and pulled them on underneath her tattered gown. Such a shame about the dress. It had been pretty, sweetheart neckline, nipped in at the waist, with a skirt that puffed out thanks to crinoline slips. The tiny buttons up the back were false, with a delicate zipper tucked cleverly underneath. She tried to unzip it herself and darn near pulled her shoulder out of the socket.

She looked up front at Harry again. He was rigid, staring straight ahead. A gentleman, huh? Well, she'd lucked out then, hadn't she? "I need your hand back here. Don't look. Just reach back."

"I have no idea what to expect right now," he said, but reached his arm back, hand open. She noticed his hands again. They were attractive to her. She'd never been attracted to a fella's hands before.

"I can't get my zipper. I'm gon' push my back up against your hand. You can feel around enough to find the zipper and not one bit more, you hear?"

"I hear."

"Okay." She angled her back toward him, while he drove with one hand. She tried to aim the zipper, which she'd lowered partway, toward his hand, but her aim was off, and his palm pressed flat to her back, just above the low-slung zipper.

His hand was warm, and it rested against her bare skin for a heartbeat longer than it ought to, but before she could smack him, he moved it, sliding it lower. Oh, Lord, that was worse. It sent a tingle all the way down her spine. The naughty kind.

"Sorry," he said, even though he hadn't done anything. His nimble fingers found the zipper and got hold of it. He tried to pull. She reached behind her to hold the fabric together, to give him something to pull against, and the zipper slid down easy as apple pie. His knuckles brushed over the small of her back, all the way down to the crease of her butt, and then he gasped and pulled his hand away like he'd been bee-stung. The car veered. He righted it.

"Sorry," he said again. "Is that… good?"

"*Real* good," she said. Maybe teasing him just a little bit. "Thanks."

Then she pulled the dress over her head. Quickly, she put on her top, a baby-blue tank with a shelf bra built in. Then she added a thin flannel button down, brown plaid. Finally, she put on some socks and her favorite boots, and climbed into the front seat.

"He punched a stripper," she said without preamble.

Harry looked at her so suddenly and so sharply that he jerked the wheel with the motion. She put her hand over his to straighten it back out. He blinked, and refocused on the road. "Take this left, right here?" he asked.

"Yeah." So, he turned the car, and she clarified. "Billy Bob had a bachelor party last night, to which none of my relatives were invited."

"That doesn't seem very friendly."

"No. But he has his own friends, and it was his big night, so I figured, let him do it his way. He barely knows my cousins, anyway. But he drank too much, which he's been doing a lot lately, and he got all handsy with the stripper his boys hired for him. When she objected, he laid her out."

"Holy..." He kept sending her quick looks. "How did you find out?"

"I knew her in college. When she got the gig, she recognized Billy Bob's name and texted me to ask if I was okay with her dancing at his stag party. I mean, I knew that's how she was workin' her way through school, no judgement here. A gal's gotta do what a gal's gotta do, you know?"

"I do." He closed his eyes. "Shoot, I did it again."

"You did. Anyway, I knew she didn't go in for extracurricular stuff, so I told her to go for it and let me know if he didn't tip her enough. Well, then, this mornin' while I'm fixin' to marry that son of a sidewinder, I get another text from her." She located the text with the photo on her phone and showed him. She knew the image by heart. Her friend Serena with a black eye that covered half her face was burned into Maria's mind. The video that she'd sent with it was considerably worse. But Harry didn't need to see that.

Harry looked away from the road at the phone. "My God." He glanced her way again and said, "I'm really sorry."

"I'm not," she said. "That's the weird part. Soon as I ran out the back door of that church, I felt like a hen freed from the coop. Kinda like I'd just woke up from a long-ass dream."

"A long-ass dream," he repeated.

"Yeah. Next right."

He made the turn. The little blue car threw a cloud of dust behind it on the dirt road. Things got quiet until she said, "You have to tell me your story now. Why were you walkin' around in the middle of nowhere? You have luggage in the back. You on some kind of road trip?"

"Yeah. I'm heading for Silver City, New Mexico."

Well, that was a coincidence, she thought. Her honeymoon was supposed to be in Silver City. She and Billy Bob were going to see the Wild West Rodeo that was in town every June. Yippy ki yay, she thought. She looked Harry up and down. Khaki pants, no belt. A shirt with buttons, not snaps. Canvas shoes, not boots. And there wasn't a hat in sight. "You don't look like a rodeo cowboy to me."

Harry's smile came out like a beam of sunlight. "I'm not any kind of a cowboy. I'm a scientist. I'm going to Silver City to demonstrate my project to a bunch of potential investors."

"Oh. Like a Silver City Shark Tank," she said. He looked

at her in surprise, and she shrugged. "Sorry. Go on. What did you invent?"

"It's uh— in that box you tossed out of your seat, earlier."

She frowned, spotting the box in the back, just lying there loose. She reached back, leaning up over the seat to do so, and brought it up front. "Jeeze, I didn't hurt it, did I?"

"It's pretty well-cushioned in there."

"Can I look?"

"Sure."

She opened the box, and he said, "It's a solar tile. It can process as much energy as a four-by-four-foot panel."

She looked at him, then back at the inch-square glass object nestled in foam inside the box. Its frame and backing were bright yellow, its glass center black. She said, "Wait. What?"

"It's a—"

"I heard you. I understand, I just— I mean, that's pretty huge, isn't it?"

"It is."

"I don't know much about renewables," she said. "But I do know solar doesn't have a very efficient space-to-power ratio." She didn't miss the quick flash of surprise in his eyes. "It's a hot topic down here. Oil country, you know."

"Ah. Well, yeah. You're right. It's been a major issue. A ten-acre lot full solar panels can only power about a hundred homes with today's technology."

"Right."

"So, it's controversial down here? Solar power?"

"A fifty-acre solar farm in our county was sabotaged a few weeks ago," she said.

"Really?"

She nodded. "Explosives. A fire. And two weeks before that, a wind farm, about thirty miles north, same thing."

"That's awful."

"My dad and uncle will get to the bottom of it," she said. "Uncle Garrett's the sheriff, and Dad's his chief deputy. Willow's even a deputy now. My cousin."

"That's a lot of family in law enforcement."

"It's a blessin' and a curse," she said. "Sounds to me like there's a far better thing to replace that solar farm with, though, or soon will be." She replaced the box's lid. "I'm gonna put this somewhere safe." She looked around the back of the car.

"You can tuck it into my dad's old tackle box, for luck," Harry suggested.

She climbed back and opened the tackle box, admired a few of the lures, then tucked the black box into the bottom. "Fits like a glove." She closed it up and returned to her spot in the front. "That's pretty amazin', Harry. I didn't know I'd carjacked a genius."

"I don't deserve all the credit," he said. She thought it was cute that he blushed. "I worked with three other scientists at Cornell."

"They goin' to the Shark Tank, too?"

"Yeah. They're flying out. I'm meeting them there. I had to travel to Florida with my father, to look at a retirement community he's considering. And I thought driving out would give me some time to... well, it doesn't matter." He glanced her way quickly then turned on the radio.

She reached up and snapped it off again. "You drove because you wanted a long, solitary journey."

He looked at her sideways. "Yeah."

"Sorry I ruined it," she said.

"That's okay. I can just drop you off in the next town and resume my—"

"Drop me off? You're gonna drop me off? What am I, a stray dog? You're just fixin' to dump me someplace to fend for myself in my torn-up weddin' dress on my destroyed weddin' day?"

"I— you changed clothes."

"I don't *want* to be dropped off. I *want* to go to Silver City."

"To the demo site?"

"No, not to the demo site. To my honeymoon destination, the Silver Springs Resort and Spa. I have the tickets right in my bag. I'm not fixin' to let 'em go to waste. And you're headin' right there anyway! Now quit gawkin' at me. You're fixin' to miss the turn."

He looked at the road again and made the turn in time.

"We hit the highway in five miles," she said. "Then, tacos, as promised. I'm starved."

"Okay."

"Okay." She reached up and turned the radio back on. An old country song was playing, and she nodded. "At least you have good taste in music."

"That's the only station I've been able to pull in for the past forty miles."

CHAPTER TWO

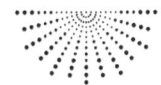

*T*he place with the best tacos in Texas was a Cantina called Manuel's. Harrison knew that because it was painted on a big wooden sign atop the brown adobe building. CANTINA MANUEL, it said in green lettering outlined in black.

They entered through batwing doors. The place wasn't busy in the middle of a Saturday afternoon, but it was open. The inside was painted with green, white, and red, the familiar colors of the Mexican flag. A lone man sat at a table with a nearly empty bottle and a half-full glass in front of him. He was white, his bushy beard was blond, and he wore a sombrero and a woven poncho. He sat so low in his chair, Harrison wondered if he was going to slide onto the floor. He looked as if he was melting in extreme slow motion.

A middle-aged Mexican couple sat at another table eating quesadillas. Regulars, he'd bet. They were dressed down, comfortable, making themselves at home. The happiness between them was palpable in the way they smiled into each other's eyes. Harrison watched them for a moment. Maybe that was what he wanted.

For some reason he looked at Maria then shook his head. Not here, and not her, but that *kind* of thing, like that couple had, and his mom and dad.

The fellow behind the counter had to be Manuel. "Hey, there, Maria Michele," he said, not with the accent Harrison had expected. "I thought you were gettin' hitched today."

"Didn't go to plan, Manny. Didn't go to plan." Maria leaned over the bar, her cowboy boots on tiptoe, accentuating the curve of her backside, and said, "What I need to heal my broken heart are your amazing tacos for two." She glanced over her shoulder at Harrison and winked.

He flinched as if the wink had struck him physically. What did *that* mean? That wink? Did she think he'd been looking at her backside? He *had* been, but did she think it?

"Grab us a table," she said. "I need the restroom."

"Okay, sure."

He found them a table and waited for her to come out of the restroom, feeling like a real jerk, because he was thinking about leaving her there. He wouldn't ditch her without a word, of course, not after what she'd been through. He would just tell her flat-out that he had to continue this journey on his own. She could call someone to come and get her, or book a room for the night in the motel across the street. She'd be okay. She certainly *seemed* okay.

Actually, he kept wondering *why* she seemed so okay.

Surely, most women who'd found out on their wedding day that their intended was a violent waste of oxygen would be devastated. Wouldn't they?

He thought the question toward his mother and waited for his brain to process the data and spit out an answer. Instead, he heard her soft laughter. And then she said, *In your experience, sweetheart... how long was I sick?*

"About nine weeks," he said under his breath. He knew precisely the amount of time from when his mother had taken to her bed, unable to get up, to when she'd passed.

Eighteen months floated through his mind. *You only knew I was sick for those final nine weeks, when I couldn't hide it anymore. Some of us don't share our suffering.*

"They say sharing it lightens the load."

And I was going to lighten my load by shifting some of it onto my kids? Come on, Harrison. You know me better.

Manuel delivered a huge platter of tacos surrounded by sour cream and three bowls of salsa; green, yellow, and red. He set down a second platter full of celery, carrot sticks, and cherry tomatoes. "She okay?" he asked with a nod toward the restroom.

"Fine." The answer was automatic, but the question made him wonder, and he looked that way, too. "Then again, I've only known her for an hour or so. You know her better. Do *you* think she's okay?"

Manny shrugged. "She locked the door. There are four stalls. I'm thinkin' she might not be okay."

Hell. The concerned proprietor walked away. Harrison glanced toward the couple at the corner table, and the woman was looking his way. By the bend of her brows, he thought she was also concerned about the beautiful redhead in the restroom.

Okay, okay. He got up and went to the door, tapped gently. "Maria? Are you all right in there?"

"Why the heck wouldn't I be?" The response came immediately, and he thought her voice was about an octave lower than the last time she'd spoken to him. He heard water running, and then she unlocked and opened the door. "Impatient much?" She didn't meet his eyes. That didn't stop him from noticing that they were red, puffy, and makeup-free.

Hell, she'd been in there crying, hadn't she? She wasn't fine at all.

Of course she's not. This was supposed to be her wedding day.

His stomach growled. Maria sent him an amused look, and he wondered how she could be amused after probably sobbing her heart out alone for the last twenty minutes.

"Well, that explains why you're so impatient," she said. "You're as hungry as I am. You get us a table?"

"Food's already on it." He led her to the table where the food waited, pulled her chair out for her, and wondered why he'd done that. He didn't make a habit of pulling out chairs for women. It wasn't common practice anymore.

Maria bent her eyebrows a little bit, but she sat down, and then he did. And then they started loading tacos onto their individual wooden plates. Some of her filling dropped into her lap. His gaze followed naturally, but he shifted it to her face again. Her eyes were red.

He couldn't stand to see a woman cry.

Now he noticed that her hair was tamed down and

braided all around on one side. It hung down across her shoulder, and copper curls were already springing free here and there. He reached for the yellow salsa bowl. She reached for the red one. "Red's hotter than yella," she said. "Yella's hotter than green."

Her accent made him smile. He liked listening to her talk. It was musical, the rhythm of her voice, the softening of tone that came with her subtle twang.

"You never told me why you're running away. Seems like a big, supportive family back there, no? Or are they pressuring you to marry that guy?"

"Oh, heck no. None of 'em wanted me to marry that guy," she said. "But I feel awful. They spent a buttload of money and time helpin' me plan a weddin', even though they all thought it was a mistake. They let me decide. And I just…" She shook her head slow. "I'm embarrassed, I guess. Ashamed."

"I think you should be proud. It took a lot of courage to walk away like that."

"That's kind of you to say."

"Why do you think…" He wanted to flat out ask her if she'd been in love with the jerk, but didn't know how to ask without making it sound like he was interested for personal reasons— which he was not.

"Why was I so determined to marry Billy Bob?" She finished his question for him. "I been askin' myself the same thing. I just… I had a plan. I had a plan, and nothing was gon' stop me once I got it underway. I was fixin' to become a vet, work in my mom's clinic, gradually take it over, buy that cute little house on Bluebonnet Lane, get married, have a couple of kids, and step into my place in the Brand family dynasty, fully integrated into the community of Quinn as the town veterinarian."

"It's a perfectly valid plan," he said when she paused as if awaiting a reaction.

She shrugged. "I was so focused on the first part, getting my degree, I didn't think much about the second. I didn't date, like other gals. I worked my tail off to get through school, and all of a sudden, I was at the end, and I realized I hadn't finished the plan. And time was short. The house I wanted came onto the market. But the husband part didn't come so easily."

"They don't just appear out of nowhere, do they?" he asked.

"Not generally, no. But I was home from school, and Billy Bob was here to sell off his parents' place when they passed. We'd gone to high school together, so I knew him. He was easy, interested, and comfortable. He seemed like the most efficient way to move ahead with the plan."

"Not exactly a sweeping love story."

She shrugged. "My family is full of sweepin' love stories. But I don't think they happen for everybody. I'm not sure I'm even capable of feelin' that way for someone, and if I were, I'm not sure I'd want to."

"I've thought that before, too. My parents had that great big kind of love. And then my mom died and left Dad just… bereft."

She nodded. "I noticed her photo in the car. She looks like an angel."

"Thank you."

She slathered salsa onto her taco, topped it with a liberal squirt of hot sauce, picked it up, and took a huge bite, her eyes widening in direct proportion to her mouth. He'd taken a bite, too, tried not to laugh, and choked.

She dropped her taco onto her plate and came around the table behind him to pound his back three times, way harder than he expected. "You okay?"

"I'm good, ow, I'm good." He wiped his mouth then sipped his water for good measure.

"Good?"

"I'm good." He cleared his throat. "Thanks."

"That'll teach you to laugh at the way I eat."

"You saw that?"

"I saw that."

"It wasn't ridicule. I thought it was cute."

"That might be worse," she said, returning to her seat. She dug into her food. After a few bites, she wiped her lips, took a drink of water, and said, "How about you? Now that you're probably about to become rich off your invention, what's next for you?"

"I haven't got a clue," he said. "What do you do after you've finished your life's work? That was supposed to be the topic of contemplation on my long, solitary road trip."

"Sorry," she said, with a twinkle in her eye that said she wasn't.

"Not your fault. I was driving myself crazy worrying about it, to be honest."

"Well, what are the options for a guy in your situation?"

He finished the last bite he thought he could hold, and used the damp towels on the table to wipe his mouth. "I could consult for whatever company buys the rights, or I could teach at a university. I imagine myself living in the complementary mansion of an ivy league department head."

"Sounds borin'."

"Exactly."

"You need to keep inventin' things, that's all."

"That's very wise," he said.

She shrugged. "I bet most inventors take a break in between projects. Maybe think of this summer as your break time. It's not your decidin'-the-rest-of-your-life time. Maybe it's more of a settlin'-into-yourself time. You aren't the same person you were before you finished what you call your life's work. Also, maybe you should start thinkin' of it as your first project."

He stared at her, and maybe his mouth wasn't quite closed. For just an instant, he heard his mother's soft voice in his mind, laughter in her words. *I like this girl!*

He shook his head to clear it then took a drink of water to cover his momentary shock. "That's good advice. Maybe I'll do that. Take a break and… settle into myself."

They ate for a while, and then he paused, and said, "I'd like to go on to Silver City without you."

She stopped with her third taco in front of her lips and locked her big brown eyes onto his.

"This is a good place for you to find another option," he said. "There's a motel across the street. You're only thirty miles from home. And you have your phone, right?"

Her paralysis ended. She set her taco down with care,

chewed, swallowed, and took a drink of water. "You're ditching me?"

She was angry. Maybe a little bit hurt, too, but mostly ticked off.

"It's nothing personal, I just— the whole reason I drove instead of flying was to give myself time to—"

"I just got left at the altar, man."

"Um, you did the leaving. But I need this time. Not the summer, just this week. I can't stand being in limbo like this, not knowing, and then there's my dad, and my sister Lily." And my promise, he thought.

She frowned at him and tipped her head slowly to one side, and then, of all things, she reached across the table and covered his hand with hers. "Dang, Harry, you're as messed up as I am, aren't you?"

His smile was wide and involuntary, and he lowered his head to hide it. Nobody, he thought, was as messed up as she was. And then his smile died when a loud, male voice yelled.

"Hey! What the *hail*, Mister! Git yer hands off my woman!"

"Oh shoot," Maria said, looking toward the entrance. "Billy Bob, what the hay are you doin' here?

The guy, who was packing about thirty pounds of excess weight that might've all been muscle, strode across the room and Maria got up and faced him.

Harrison stood up, too, because the raging bull's bloodshot eyes were focused on him. To his surprise, Maria stepped in front of him, right into Billy Bob's path.

"Hey," she said. "You leave him outta this. I hitched a ride with him, is all."

"I'll deal with you later," he growled, and then he clasped her shoulder and shoved her sideways so hard she crashed into the table, tipped it over, and landed on the floor with the remaining tacos. The red salsa bowl broke in half. And for some, suicidal reason, Harrison grabbed the angry groom by the shirt and shoved him away from Maria. He was frankly surprised he'd managed to move the guy at all. Maybe he'd had one of those fight-or-flight adrenaline surges that enable mothers to lift cars off their babies.

In his peripheral, Harrison saw Manual leap the bar with a baseball bat in hand. Dead ahead, all he could see was Billy Bob's fist.

Harry went down hard. Then Billy Bob straddled him, pulled him up by the front of his shirt, and punched him again. Maria scrambled to her feet, grabbed the big glass water pitcher from the table next to hers, and smashed her ex-intended right over the head with it.

Billy Bob howled and spun toward her, furious.

The unmistakable sounds of multiple gun-hammers went *clickita-clickita-clack*, and Billy Bob froze. So did Maria Michele, for that matter. Poor Harry was on his back on the floor, not moving, maybe unconscious. His face was a mess. Some of it was probably salsa. Lord, please let some of it be salsa.

Cautiously, she turned her head to look behind her. The sleepy sombrero-wearing gringo was pointing a long-barreled black revolver. The husband and wife held a pair of shiny silver .38s with pearl handles— a matched set, which was kinda cute, when you thought about it.

Manuel had a baseball bat, and was the only one still moving. He strode, right up to Billy Bob, bat raised. "You git on outta here. G'on, git!"

Billy Bob raised his hands and backed away.

"Wait," Maria said. "First tell me what you're even doin' here?"

"You walked out on our weddin'. You didn't think I'd come after you?" Billy Bob seemed genuinely perplexed.

"I saw what you did to the dancer at your bachelor party last night. I didn't know you were violent, Billy Bob. I want no part of a man who'd hit a woman."

On the floor, Harry moaned. He needed help, but she needed answers.

"I was drunk! You cain't blame a man for what happens at his stag party, anyway."

"Yeah, is the party still goin'? You drunk right now?" She glanced down at Harry. His eyes were too messed up to tell whether they were open. "Look what you did to him, and you knocked me for a loop, too. I don't think I know you at all."

"When a man takes your woman—"

"I ain't your woman, and you'd better thank your lucky

stars for that, Billy Bob, because if I'd married you and you'd ever put a hand on me, they'd never find your body."

He met her eyes defiantly.

"You know me," she said. "You know I don't lie. And you know my kin."

Manuel snort-laughed. He knew 'em, too. Everyone in this place likely knew her family.

"That girl you hit was a friend of mine, workin' her way through college dancin' for pigs like you. And you put your hands on her. You *hit* her."

She took a step sideways, toward Manuel, reaching out her hand, taking the baseball bat from his.

"Hey!" Billy Bob took a step backward. "What do you think you're—"

"How'd you find me, anyway?" she asked.

"I just drove. I—"

"Bull." She swung the bat hard, taking Billy Bob right across the kneecap. He howled, hopping on one foot, holding his knee in both hands. "Gimme your phone right now, Billy Bob, or I'll crack your other knee. And I'll bust this one!"

"Awright, awight!" He wrestled his phone from his jeans pocket, handed it to her. She swiped then held it toward his face to unlock. Then she tapped to the "Find my device" app, and sure as all get out, her phone was listed on there.

"You tracked my phone! How'd you do this?"

He lowered his eyes. "Shared location from your phone to mine when you weren't lookin'."

Rolling her eyes, Maria said, "I wouldn't have thought you were smart enough." She deleted her phone from his finder, then her info from his contacts, then threw the phone back at him. "Git your sorry, phone-spyin', woman-beatin', beer-swillin' carcass outta here, Billy Bob. I never want to see you again." She raised the bat and advanced as she spoke, and he hobbled toward the exit. He made it through and tumbled down the three front stairs to land on the small parking strip in front.

She stopped in the doorway. "If I were you, I'd never set foot back in Quinn. There's nothin' for you here. You been warned."

He scrambled backward, and she backed inside and closed the door. And then finally, she turned to poor Harry.

He was sitting up. Manuel was crouching nearby, holding an ice pack out in offering.

"I had no idea he would do that," she said, and she took the ice pack herself, crushed it to activate, and pressed it to the worst-looking side of Harry's face.

"Ow." He took the ice pack from her. Then he started to say something more, and winced. "Hurts to talk." He let her help him stand. There was salsa dripping down his face and onto his shirt.

The couple from the corner table had put away their weapons. The husband went to the counter to pay up, and Manuel joined him there to take his cash. The Gringo in the corner had put his gun away, drained his glass, and resumed his nap.

Manuel set a first aid kit the size of a toolbox onto the bar. She said, "Jeeze, Manny, you do surgery on the side or what?"

"Saturday nights get rough."

"Thanks. I'll tend to the worst here, and then take him back home for the rest." She got busy with disinfectant wipes.

"We're going back to Quinn?" Harry asked. He was looking around, confused as hell. One eye was swollen, but once she'd cleaned off the salsa, his face wasn't as bad as it had looked.

She helped him to his feet, but he was none too steady. "You think you can make it to a chair?"

He nodded, took a step in the wrong direction, sagged.

"Shoot!" Maria snapped an arm around his waist and helped him stay upright as he shuffled determinedly toward the batwing doors, saying, "I can make it to the car," while trying to use his ice pack to wipe the salsa off his shirt. She didn't think his head was working right. "You might have to drive."

He stepped into the parking lot, and then stopped and looked left and right, seeming even more confused. But this time, so was she. Because Harry's little blue Volvo was no longer there.

Then Harry passed out cold at her feet.

"Well, shoot," Maria said. "This day just keeps gettin' better."

The couple had left while she'd been tending to Harry, but Sombrero remained. Maybe he lived there. Manuel picked

Harry right up off the ground, carried him over to the bar, and laid him there. Then he returned to the door and put up the closed sign. He grabbed the first aid kit, placed it near Harry's head, and opened it up. "I'll get water," he said, heading into his kitchen.

"You look rough, Harry," Maria said softly. "I'm real sorry you got dragged into my mess. You're prolly gonna be mad as a hornet at me when you wake up. I am sorry, though." She unbuttoned his shirt, spread it open. The blood from his nose had soaked through onto his chest, the poor guy. Nice chest, though, bare and lean, defined but not in a bulgy, braggy way. Just right for running one's hands over or resting one's cheek upon.

What strange thoughts to be running through her mind at a time like this.

She pushed his shirt sleeve down one arm, and had to move him around quite a bit to do it. Manuel came back with the water as she got the shirt completely off, and she took her phone out of her pocket, tapped it, and told it to call Bubba. Then she set the phone nearby on speaker, took the wet, soapy cloth from the water basin, and started washing the blood and salsa off Harry's chest.

Bubba answered on the first ring. "Maria Michele? Where the hell are you, cuz? You okay?"

"I'm fine, but I need your help. You still have a truckful of my cousins?"

"He does," Willow said. Apparently, Bubba's phone was on speaker, too.

"I'm at Manny's." One of the cuts on Harry's brow line was still bleeding. She used saline in a hypodermic to clean it more thoroughly, and he moaned through his stupor. Good thing he was out.

To Bubba and Willow, she explained, "I hitched a ride with a stranger and Billy Bob tracked my phone here, beat the tar outta the poor guy, and stole his car to boot. So we're stranded and he's hurt. Hand me the Neosporin, Manny."

"We're on our way," Bubba said.

"From where?" She was pinching the eyebrow cut together, deciding whether to apply butterfly bandages in tight formation or stitch it up. She'd have killed for a stitch-stapler but decided to make do with the butterflies.

"We were headed back to the ranch. The uh... reception is happenin'."

"There was no point in wastin' all the food," Drew called.

"We'll be there in thirty minutes," Willow said. "Are you safe? Do you think Billy Bob will come back?"

"If he does, he won't be walkin' outta here upright, I'll tell you what," she said. "Thanks, you guys." She disconnected, pocketed her phone so she wouldn't forget it, and moved on to the next cut, this one high on Harry's cheekbone, opposite side from the eyebrow. His left eye was swollen and a little bit purple. The right one seemed okay. She laid a cold pack over the eye then ran her thumb and forefinger down the side of his nose. He moaned, but the nose didn't feel broken. She noticed the tiny cut on his nose and the strong, straight shape of it. She liked his nose, and even more, the prominent line of his jaw. He had a strong jawline, softened somewhat by his blue eyes, when they were open. She used a warm cloth to clean more of the salsa from his hair. It was soft beneath her fingers, his hair.

Manuel handed her a T-shirt. She had no idea where he'd got it. Lost and found maybe? She took it, and maneuvered it over Harry's head then wrangled his arms through and pulled it down over his chest, where her fingers brushed skin, when she straightened the shirt fully. It had a longhorn bull on the front, with words above and below it.

Some of y'all weren't raised in Texas...
And it shows!

CHAPTER THREE

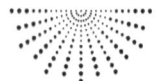

*H*arry was still out cold, and Maria was getting worried.

Tires crunched over gravel, and she went to the window. Bubba's shiny red pickup had pulled in. It had never seen a day's work, that jacked-up truck. It was flawless, not a hoof-shaped dent or a barbed-wire scratch on it. Bubba got out one side, and Willow the other. The four remaining Brand cousins who'd been riding in the back when the truck had passed them earlier, must've stayed behind.

Maria crossed the room and opened the door to greet them. "Thanks for comin'."

Willow hugged her. "You okay?"

"Yeah, but Harry's not." She hugged Bubba in turn and then looked across the room at Harry, still prone atop the bar. "I think we'd better take him to the ER," she said.

"No. I'm... okay," said Harry, and he sat up.

They all hurried over there. Harry's blue eyes were

open, the right one was swollen and bruised. "I just need... a bed and some... maybe some uh... pain reliever."

"We got the bed covered," Bubba said.

"I have pain reliever!" Manuel went into the back, returned in seconds, and handed Harry three white tablets and a glass of water with a straw.

Harry took the pills, removed the straw, and drank deeply from the glass.

"Ibuprofen?" Maria asked as Harry swallowed.

"Sure," Manuel said, which made her frown.

"Manuel, what did you just give him?"

"What he said. Pain reliever."

"I'm gon' need to see that bottle, Manny."

He crooked a finger, and she followed him through the doors into the kitchen in back. He opened a cabinet and took out a brown prescription bottle. The label said, Hysingla ER.

"This is hydrocodone."

"It's what they gave me when I broke my hip last fall. I never used 'em. See? 'For pain.'" He pointed at the instructions on the bottle, which said to take as needed for pain to a maximum of two tablets per day. He took the bottle back, turning it to peruse the label. "Oh," he said. "Uh, did I give him too much?"

"Well, you gave him plenty." She closed her eyes. "But he won't be hurting for awhile. Thank you for the help, Manny."

"Any time, Maria Michele."

"You tally up the damage. My family'll take care of it."

"They always do," he replied.

She returned to the front room. Bubba was already helping Harry out to the truck. Poor Harry was limping along across the parking strip, head down, but Bubba had hold of him.

Willow stood by the batwing doors, waiting for her, her eyes all sympathetic and soft. "He'll be okay," she said.

"He'll be feelin' okay, for sure," Maria replied. "Manny's pain meds were the real deal. Harry's gon' think I'm tryin' to kill him." Then she sighed. "Maybe it'll buy me some time before I have to tell him Billy Bob stole his car outta spite after beatin' him bloody."

"Billy Bob stole Harry's car?"

"He must've. It's gone. And his whole life's work is in that car, in a little black box in the back. Come on, I'll fill you in on the way home."

They walked outside. Willow stopped and looked around. "Maria, if Billy Bob took Harry's car, then where's Billy Bob's truck? He had to drive here in something."

Maria frowned. "I don't know. Maybe he had somebody with him."

"Didn't have anyone with him when he left the church," Willow said.

Maria could see the wheels turning behind her cousin's eyes. Any minute now, she'd be in crime-solving mode and they'd never get out of there. Sleuthing ran in the family. Her youngest cousins, Orrin and Drew, had inherited it from both sides. But she clasped Willow's shoulder and said, "We need to get Harry back to the ranch. You can do your deputy thing later, okay?"

"Yeah," Willow said. "Sure, okay."

Things got very cloudy for Harry. He was in a vehicle, lying sideways, on a narrow back seat. It was not his own car. That worried him. There were strangers in the front seat, a big guy in a big hat was driving, and a woman with long, dark hair rode in the passenger seat. Then he realized his pillow was a set of warm, denim-clad thighs, and immediately sat up.

Maria was beside him. He'd been lying with his head in her lap.

"Hey, no, it's okay," she said. "Here, relax."

"My car—"

"Willow's got folks takin' care of that," she said, nodding toward the woman in the passenger seat. "She's the newest deputy at the Quinn County Sheriff's Department, you know. And don't you worry, cause like I told you, the sheriff's my uncle and the chief deputy's my dad."

He didn't know what her uncle being sheriff had to do with them picking up his car for him, but he appreciated it. He couldn't have driven it himself. "Make sure... the solar—"

"I will."

He closed his eyes in relief.

When he opened them again, he was in a big, soft bed, in a bedroom with flowered wallpaper. Sheer curtains danced in the breeze that came through an open window, beyond which was darkness. It was nighttime. An old man in a red plaid shirt with pearl snaps was standing over him on the other side of the bed. He had a thick head of white hair that fell in waves to his neck and a white mustache to match. If he'd had a goatee, he'd have looked like General Custer.

"No skull fracture," he was saying, and nearby the runaway bride and several strangers sighed in apparent relief. "He should sleep off the hydrocodone by morning. You tell Manuel to turn that in at the pharmacy, Maria?"

"Uh, sure," the beautiful redhead replied, but her compassionate brown eyes were on him.

"Good girl," the doctor said. "Nice job on the butterflies. Can't believe Billy Bob would do something like this."

"Well, let's keep that between us, for now."

"Pssh. 'Round here? Good luck with that, little lady. Thank your mamma for bringing the portable X-ray over from the vet clinic."

"I will."

"Call me if there's any change. But I think he's fine."

"He has to be in Silver City by noon on Wednesday," she said.

"Well, it's only Saturday. He should be okay to make that trip. He won't be pretty, but he'll be up and around."

Harry felt himself relax. His head sank into the soft pillows underneath him. The floral wallpaper and the people standing before it all blurred and faded. Maria, the most vivid figure in the room, faded last of all.

When he woke again, it was morning. He knew it was morning by the way the birds were singing outside the open window. The breeze pushed the curtains so they swelled and floated up, then lowered again. He was in a bedroom with blue wallpaper that had yellow roses all over it. The curtains were white and so was the bedding. Beside the bed, a rocking chair, and a nightstand that held a half-empty coffee cup, a tall glass of water with a straw, a brown prescription bottle, his cellphone and wallet, and an open, face-down paperback called *Love on Bluebonnet Lane*.

He lifted the covers and found himself dressed in light blue cotton pajamas that were not his own. He tried to piece together what had happened and came up with a series of jigsaw puzzle pieces, most of which featured a spunky, brown-eyed redhead.

It was surreal not knowing where he was or how he'd got there. He got out of the bed, his bare feet greeted by soft carpet. He was a little dizzy, but he stood there for a moment, and it passed. Then he shuffled to the open window and pushed the gauzy curtains aside.

There were green lawns, split-rail fences, a large barn, and several smaller ones, all of them white and trimmed in red. Horses grazed in a meadow that bordered a long building that must be their stable. Beyond the barnyard was rolling land, all kinds of land. Parts were brown and brushy, other parts were covered in woods, and still others were green and dotted with grazing longhorns. The land unfurled all the way to the widest, bluest horizon he'd ever seen. Off to the right, an arch rose over a ribbon of driveway, with the words TEXAS BRAND carved into its curve. The X was bigger than the other letters and had circle around it.

"Beautiful, isn't it?"

Her voice made him turn around. The redhead had entered the room bearing a plate full of food and a cold pack. She smiled brightly. "Nice to see you're awake. And up, even. But here, settle back in and relax. When's the last time you had breakfast in bed?"

"When I was ten, I think." He scuffed back to the bed, stacked the pillows high, then got in sitting up, but leaning back against them. "No, eleven. Had strep throat. Mom brought me chicken noodle soup and orange Jello."

"I bet it cured you, too."

"Is this where you live? It's incredible."

"Oh Lord, no, this is the ranch."

"The ranch."

"The Texas Brand. It's kind of the family headquarters. My mom grew up here with her five big brothers. Most have their own places now, though us kids spent endless time here growing up. Uncle Garrett and Aunt Chelsea still live here. My cousins and I all moved in for the week of the weddin'." She set the plate of food on the crowded nightstand and offered Harrison the cold pack. "Even Bubba came home, and it's been a while. Anyway, Uncle Garrett thought you and I would be safer here. You know, until he and his crew find Billy Bob and throw him into a jail cell."

She talked a lot. Used ten words where three would do. He liked it. He liked listening to her. Her accent was as soothing as a full body massage.

"You gon' put that on your head, or just chill your hand with it?" She nodded at the cold pack, and he realized he'd been looking at her a little bit too long. He touched his face with his other hand and felt bandages. His right eyebrow and forehead had the biggest one. There was a tiny one on the bridge of his nose.

Maria took the cold pack from him and laid it across his left eye. It had a little strap attached that she stretched around his head to hold the cold pack in place. "Your eye's still swollen, but I've been puttin' ice on it for ten minutes every little while, and it's improving."

"Is it?"

"You can see through it now, can't you?"

He lifted the cold pack to peek out then nodded and put it back in place.

"It's Sunday," she said. "You still have plenty of time to make your Silver City Shark Tank thing by Wednesday. You don't need to worry. We'll drive you ourselves if we don't find your car by then."

"*Find* my car?" He sat straight again, got a little dizzy, and put a hand on his head.

Maria bent over him, hands on his shoulders, her face near his bent head. She smelled like fresh air and sunshine. "Easy now, easy. Just be still a minute, it'll pass." She moved one hand to his head and somehow it helped.

"It's really not that bad." As the dizziness eased, he lifted his chin. It didn't return. Carefully, he said, "What happened to my car?"

"Billy Bob stole it, after he kicked the stuffin' outta you. Did you leave the keys in it, do you remember?"

He tried to think back. His memory of having his face pounded had returned the minute she'd uttered the name Billy Bob, but what had come before that was still cloudy. "We stopped at a cantina," he said. "For tacos. God, all this for a taco."

"They *were* amazin'," she reminded him. "I was right about that."

He closed his eyes. "We have to get the car back. The prototype is in the car," he said.

"Right, I know. I guess— I was hopin' you'd have a backup."

"In a safe, in my lab two-thousand miles from here, yeah. But still—"

"Billy Bob'll have no interest in pawing through your dad's tackle box. And he wouldn't know a solar tile from a floor tile. We'll find the car and your project will be there safe and sound." Maria handed him his plate of food. "Chelsea's famous flapjacks," she said.

The plate held a foot-tall stack of blueberry pancakes, with a tiny pitcher of syrup that was warm to the touch and home fries on the side. He picked up the fork and his stomach growled.

Maria paced to the window, gazed out and said, "I'm real sorry, Harry. I've brought disaster rainin' down on you."

"I don't blame you for what that guy did," he said. "And

I suspect this breakfast is about to make the whole thing worthwhile."

She let the curtains fall and faced him. "Take your time in here. There's a change of clothes waiting in the bathroom, right there. When you're all set, c'mon downstairs. Willow wants to get the full story from you, while Dad and Uncle Garrett are trackin' down your car. I figured a tour of the ranch would make the time pass faster, if you feel up to it."

"Okay. That sounds good to me."

She bit her lip then her eyes turned intense. "I'm gon' get your tile back and make all this right, Harry. You tried to help me out, not that I gave you much choice, but I'll be danged if you ought to suffer for it. I'm gon' make it right. You have my word as a Brand."

She left the room before he could come up with a reply.

Harrison sighed, glanced at the plate. He loved home fries in a way he loved few other things. He should call his sister and dad to check in. He talked to them both daily, and they'd worry if he didn't.

But he figured it could wait until after breakfast.

With his bandages off for a morning shower a short while later, Harrison got his first good look in a mirror. There was a cut across one eyebrow, expertly taped up. His eye was swollen and the eyelid was slightly purple, and there was a tiny cut on the bridge of his nose. That was all the damage that showed, but his head hurt like hell, and his back was none too limber.

The dizziness seemed to ease the more he moved around, though. He put on the clothes he found in the bathroom attached to the bedroom he occupied— his own jeans and a borrowed T-shirt. His own shirt had been laundered and folded and returned to him, too, but it was bloodstained and torn. He put it into the lined wastebasket beside the sink. Then he took the time to send three texts. One to his father, saying their daily phone call would be a couple of hours late and that everything was fine; one to his sister, saying he'd run into some trouble, but everything was fine, and he'd explain when they talked later; one to Carrie Sayre, the most reliable member of his research team, asking her to get the backup prototype from the safe at Cornell and bring it with her to the upcoming demo in Silver City.

She texted back immediately, saying sure and asking why. His sister was also responding with questions, so he told Carrie he would explain later, and focused on Lily, answering in brief as best he could while heading down the stairs in search of Brands to thank.

> Harrison: Picked up a runaway bride

Lily: What?

> Harrison: The groom caught up. Punched me out and stole my car.

Lily: WHAT?

> Harrison: I'm fine. Staying with friends near Quinn, Texas. I'll Call you ASAP to explain.

> Lily: What friends?

> Harrison: The runaway bride and her family.

> Lily: Huh. What's she look like? This runaway bride?

> Harrison: What's that supposed to mean?

> Lily: Nothing. Call soon. Dad's asthma is worse.

> Harrison: Is he okay?

> Lily: For now. Fill you in when we talk. Love you.

> Harrison: Love you back.

At the bottom of the stairs, he followed voices through a big living room with a fireplace and a long-eared blood-hound lying in front of it, even though there was no fire at the moment. He went out the front door onto a wide front porch with a swing on one side and two rockers on the other all facing that same view he'd glimpsed from upstairs. A warm breeze wafted over him, and horse scent came with it. In front of the porch, Maria stood with people he might or might not know. A twenty-something young man had dark curly hair under his cowboy hat. The Native American woman beside him was wearing a badge.

Willow, from the ride back, he recalled. She was a rookie deputy.

Behind them, four saddled horses nibbled at the grassy lawn. Two were thoroughbreds, one was a prancing black mare with as much nervous energy as a certain runaway bride he knew, and the fourth was a docile chestnut mare with age in her eyes.

He realized his tour of the ranch was going to take place on horseback. Sure, he thought. Why not give the redhead another chance to kill him?

The cousin with the badge and the long black hair extended a hand as he approached. "Hi, again, Harry. I'm Willow. We met in Bubba's truck, but you were kinda out of it."

"Harrison," he said. "I remember you."

"And this is my cousin Trevor," Maria said. She gestured toward her younger cousin, who was as darkly complected as Willow.

Trevor sent him a wave and a friendly smile. "Good to meetcha. Sorry about your... uh... face. You sure you're okay to ride?"

"Um..."

"Have you ever ridden?" Deputy Willow asked with concern in her eyes.

He nodded. "When I was a kid, we took a family trail ride every fall to see the foliage. My mom was nuts about the foliage. She even made us take riding lessons the first summer."

Maria said, "You'll do fine, then."

"Yeah, it's like riding a bike," Trevor said. "But more like riding a horse."

"Adaline is the gentlest mare you'll ever meet." Maria moved to the horse as she spoke and as he suspected, it was the elder chestnut mare. She took the reins and stroked the mare's muzzle. The horse closed her eyes in a slow blink of appreciation. "She's not gonna spook and she won't misstep. You can trust her. If you feel up to it, I mean."

"Sure," he said. "It'll be fun."

He saw the disapproving look Willow sent to Maria, and not wanting to be the cause of strife between cousins, walked right up to the chubby mare, pet her nose, and said, "I'm Harrison. Is it okay if I ride you?"

The horse blew as if answering him, and he said, "I hope that was a yes." Introducing yourself to the horse and asking permission had been step one, according to his mom, though he'd never seen the riding instructor do that part. Just the rest. He stepped into the stirrup and swung his leg on over. The mare didn't move at all the whole time. He patted her neck. "Good girl," he said and when he glanced Maria's way, he saw that he'd impressed her. His chest swelled a little bit. Dumb.

Maria got on the fiery black mare. Willow and Trevor mounted the thoroughbreds, and as one, they turned around, and started off at an easy walk. Maria led the way out past the barns, through gates opened for them by ranch hands who touched their hats as the group rode by. They crossed a wide meadow behind the larger barn, moving among grazing cows, through another gate, and then picked up a trail through a wooded area.

Willow said, "Harry, just so you know, I'm not goofin' off here. Uncle Garrett has an APB out on your car, Billy Bob's truck, and Billy Bob himself. He and Uncle Lash— Maria's dad— are checking his known haunts, his friends. And I'm keepin' an eye on you, here, just in case." She glanced at Maria. "We got the guest list from his stag party, so we're startin' there."

"He punched the stripper, you know," Maria blurted.

"He did *what?*" Apparently, Willow hadn't heard.

"The dancer at Billy Bob's stag party. I knew her from college. I'll send you the video."

She pulled out her phone and did so.

"Either way," Willow said to Harrison, "I expect we'll find Billy Bob and your car before the day's out." Her phone beeped, so she pulled it out and tapped it to watch the video Maria had sent her. Trevor, who rode beside Willow, leaned over in his saddle to watch as well.

Harrison had not seen any video. He leaned up in his saddle to get a glimpse. Maria took pity and handed him her phone. He watched as Billy Bob tried to sexually assault an exotic dancer then punched her in the face when she resisted, in much the same way he'd punched Harrison the day before.

The impact made him wince. "What a jerk!" He looked up from the phone.

On the horse ahead of him, Willow's face was as angry as a storm cloud. "Is the dancer okay?"

"Yeah. She sent me that yesterday mornin'."

"At the weddin'?" Willow asked. Maria nodded and Harrison thought it had been way worse than he'd known.

Some cave-man DNA sent up the desire for another shot at that woman-beating thug Billy Bob. Not that he'd fare any better, but the notion of landing a punch or two felt good.

Willow said, "Aw, shoot, hon, I'm sorry. You'd better believe Uncle Garrett's gonna charge his ass with every bit of it when he catches up to him."

Trevor was quietly fuming.

"Anyway, Harry," Willow went on after a moment, "I expect we'll have your property back by the end of the day. Meanwhile, I've been assigned to keep an eye on you until we have Billy Bob in custody. My personal theory is he blames you for bustin' up the weddin'." She winked at Maria. "You should *hear* some of the speculation around town. It'd make those books you read blush."

Maria rolled her eyes, nudged her horse, and moved in between the two thoroughbreds to cut ahead of them again. They rode in companionable silence for a little while. Soon, Harrison heard the burbling of a little stream that ran alongside the path and eventually spilled into a large pond.

"Swimmin' hole," Maria said, turning to call back to him. "Best place to cool off on a hot summer day." But they didn't stop.

"So, are you two siblings?" he asked Willow and Trevor, mainly for something to say.

Trevor laughed. "We get asked that a lot, but no," he said. "I'm half-Mexican and Willow's three-quarters Comanche."

Willow said, "My parents raise thoroughbreds on nearby Sky Dancer Ranch. These are two of them. Butch and Sundance." She patted her horse as she spoke. "I have my own house on the property."

"Her parents are Wes and Taylor," Trevor said. "My dad's Elliot, youngest of the Brand brothers. My mom is Esmeralda. She immigrated from Mexico, lost all her ID to coyotes on the way, and had to start fresh here. But before this was Brand land, it belonged to her ancestors. So my connection to it is twice as strong." He said it with pride.

Willow rolled her eyes. "And it belonged to my ancestors, before any of them," she reminded him.

"Sorry, Will," he looked sheepish. Then he grinned at Harrison and said, "You aren't expected to learn all the names. Not just yet, anyway." Then he winked.

Willow nudged her horse into a trot and rode off the trail to the pond. She paused there to let her horse drink.

Maria slowed until Harrison was once again riding beside her with Trevor close behind. Quietly, she said, "We all inherit the ranch jointly, when the time comes. Willow thinks it should be given back to the tribes."

"And our cousin Baxter thinks it should switch from raising cattle to raising crops," Trevor said. "And Bubba wants to build a honky tonk on his share."

"We all have very different ideas about what to do with it."

"What do *you* want to do with it?" Harrison asked.

He was talking to Maria, but Trevor thought otherwise and answered the question before she could. "Rodeo!" he said. "We put in three show rings, huge stands, concessions, the whole nine."

"I guess you *do* have different ideas." He glanced Maria's

way, met her eyes and knew she didn't want to talk about her own thoughts on the matter. He read her look, gave a subtle nod, and didn't ask again.

The ride took nearly two hours, and Maria assured him they hadn't put a dent in the property. He was shown pastures, the prettiest family burial ground he'd ever seen, and a large chunk of woodland near the stream that was fenced off for no apparent reason. As he frowned at it, Willow rode up beside him. "My mother is an archaeologist," she said. "She discovered some pottery on this site, and did some informal digging. She's sure a native village thrived here once, so we don't let anyone in."

"Is she planning to excavate it?" Harrison asked.

"No," Willow said. "We just leave offerin's and let it be."

Harrison nodded, understanding her position on what should become of the land in a way he hadn't before. Willow's phone pinged, she glanced at it. "Uncle Garrett says they just picked up Billy Bob. We'd best get to the station." She sent Harrison a smile. "That was even faster than I predicted!" Then she gave a little whoop and kicked her horse into a gallop.

CHAPTER FOUR

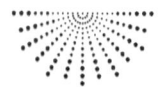

"*I* did not steal any goldern car!" Billy Bob slur-shouted from somewhere in the back of the small adobe building.

Maria rolled her eyes, leaned up closer to the man beside her, and said, "Sounds like he's drunk again." Harry wore a light denim shirt with the sleeves rolled up to his elbows, and she found her eyes kept getting stuck on his forearms. Had she ever found a man's forearms sexy before? His were. They had the finest dusting of light hairs, and she wanted to touch them and see what they felt like.

She and Harry were standing just inside the double doors with the words SHERIFF'S DEPARTMENT on the glass. The public-facing portion of the department was a large beige room with orange plastic chairs for waiting. A plexiglass partition with slots for speaking, separated the waiting area from the rest of the building. Behind the glass was a tall counter, and beyond it, desks, computers, and deputies going about their business. Beside the partition stood a single locked door.

"My dad's the one who brought him in," Maria said.

"Your dad, Lash, the chief deputy," he repeated, as if to remind himself of the details.

"Right. He got a tip. Caught up with Billy Bob at a bar just over the county line. It was a few miles outside his jurisdiction, but Dad hauled his carcass back here anyway. "C'mon, this way." She quickly texted her father to let him know they'd arrived.

Seconds later, her father popped out from the door beside the partition. He hugged Maria then turned to Harry. "I'm Lash, Maria's father."

"Harrison. Good to meet you, Deputy Monroe," Harry said.

"Lash," Lash repeated. "You can come on back."

"Thanks for getting the guy."

"Thank me after we recover your car. It's not goin' well."

"Why not?" Maria asked, noticing the worry that appeared immediately in Harry's eyes. "Billy Bob bein' difficult?"

"Full on denial, and his lawyer's on the way."

They traversed a narrow hallway, passed the first door, marked INTERROGATION and entered the second door, which was right beside it. Inside, there was glass separating the two rooms. On the other side of the glass, Billy Bob sat at a table with his hands still cuffed behind him. Willow stood in front of the table with her back to the glass. Her hair was bundled up, her uniform shirt tucked into her uniform pants. She'd left her weapon behind.

"They can't see us out here," Maria explained.

Harrison nodded. "I figured."

Lash pushed a button on the wall, and the sound came on. Then he said he had to take a call and left them.

"I'm tellin' you, Willow—" Billy Bob slurred. His hair was a mess, and his eyes were bloodshot. Apparently, his buzz was fading, and the aftermath just getting underway.

"That's Deputy Brand to you from now on," Willow told him. "You ain't family." She pulled out the chair opposite him and sat down. "It'll serve you well not to forget it. Now, tell me what happened at Manny's."

"I'll tell you for a beer."

"You're already drunk."

"I'll tell you…" He paused for dramatic effect. "For a beer."

"I'll get you a beer. And then you'll cooperate, or I'll book you on every charge we can come up with."

It startled Maria, the deeper, fuller tone of her cousin's voice. "Wow," she said. "I've never really seen Will on the job before. She's different."

"How long's she been a deputy?" Harry asked.

"Couple of months. Ever since Uncle Garrett decided he plans to retire next year. He's been sheriff since before I was born. My dad's been chief deputy most of that time."

"Huh."

"What?"

"Just… that's a long time for a town to have the same sheriff and chief deputy," Harry said.

She felt herself bristle. "County," she corrected. "And yeah, it is a long time, but it's not like you're thinking."

Next door, Willow left Billy Bob alone in the interrogation room, allegedly to get him a beer. Maria did not think for one minute her cousin was going to serve alcohol to a suspect and wondered what she was up to.

"I wasn't thinking anything," Harry said.

"Sure you were. You're an East Coast scientist."

"You say that like an insult," he said.

"Not an insult at all. It's like telling a Martian newly arrived from Mars that he doesn't yet understand Earth. I'm telling a newly arrived New Yorker that he doesn't yet understand Texas. No insult intended. But you need to know that my dad and uncle are the most trusted men in Quinn County. Every election was fair, and to be honest, Uncle Garrett's never had to do more than put his name on the ballot—"

The interrogation room door opened, and closed hard, making them both come to attention. "Oh, shoot," Maria muttered, because her dad had entered the room.

"I understand you tracked my daughter illegally," he said to Billy Bob.

Her dad's tone was as foreign to Maria as Willow's had seemed, but in a different way. It wasn't even the angry-dad tone he'd used when she'd messed up as a kid. This was something bigger. Something quieter and somehow more menacing. "You assaulted a young woman at your bachelor party."

"Aw, c'mon, you know I wouldn't—"

"One of your friends shot a video, Billy Bob. I've seen it. It's bad."

The jilted groom swore a blue streak. Then he fell silent. At length he said, "Is the bimbo pressing charges?"

Maria clenched her fists and strode out of the small observation room, then through the next door into the interrogation room beside it. "You bet your backside she's pressin' charges," she shouted. "She decided right after I told her I'd carry her to and from every day of your trial on my back, if that's what it takes, you lowlife son of a— I can't believe I almost married you."

"Aw, come on now, Maria Michele, you know it din't mean nuthin'."

"What *din't mean nuthin'?*" She asked, mocking his lazy grammar. "Tryin' to force my friend's head into your lap or punchin' her in the face when she fought back? Is that what *din't mean nuthin'*? Or was it beatin' the hell out of a decent, brilliant man who's tryin' to save the whole goldern world, and tried to keep you off me after you shoved me so hard I took out a whole table full of tacos? Is that what *din't mean nuthin'* Billy Bob?"

"He put his hands on you?" her father asked.

"I barely touched her! I barely touched you before your nerd boyfriend came at me like a maniac." Billy Bob was scared. Finally. He was looking from Lash to Maria again, and then to Harry, who had come in behind her.

"Tell him," Billy Bob shouted at Harry. "You were there."

Her father looked at Harry.

Harry answered with calm, precise recall. "He came at me, she stepped in front of me. He grabbed her, jerked her around and she hit the table. She probably has a bruise on her ribcage. Right side. I shoved him back away from her, and then he decked me."

Maria frowned and ran her hand over her right side, applied a little pressure, and winced. Then she lifted her blouse enough to reveal a pink and purple bruise on her rib cage. "I didn't even notice that last night." She met Harry's eyes, but they were on her bruised skin.

Her father's expression had gone blank and still. Maria knew him well enough to be worried.

"We're gon' need you to tell us where that car is," he said, speaking real slow. "After that, you're free to go. My brothers-in-law might want a word with you, but I really got no say in that."

Billy Bob got out of his chair and took two steps back from the table. "They're fixin' to kill me?" Then he looked at Maria. "They're fixin' to kill me, Maria Michele!"

She saw the alarm in Harry's eyes and tried to send him reassurance without giving up the game. There was no way her dad would let Billy Bob go.

Everyone who really knew her family knew they were good, decent people. But they also knew you didn't mess with a Brand without incurring the wrath of the whole clan. It just wasn't done. Not in Quinn, it wasn't.

"You want me to stop 'em?" she asked. "Tell me what you did with Harry's car."

"I didn't take the goldern car! I walked into the bar, had the fight—"

"Assaulted two people, trashed the place," she said.

"He hit me first!" Billy Bob argued. "Then I walked outside, got in my truck, and left! That's it."

Willow returned. She didn't have any beer, and Maria realized she'd left to give her dad a shot at Billy Bob.

"You can take him back to his cell, Deputy, then come right back," Lash said. And Maria found it odd to hear her father refer to her cousin that way. If it was strange to her, she wondered how weird it must feel to Willow.

Will gave a respectful nod and took Billy Bob by the arm while the suspect tried to talk his way to redemption. She returned seconds later, sans prisoner.

"What did the parking lot cam show?" Lash asked.

Willow looked blank, then alarmed. "Manny's place has security cameras?" She pressed a palm to her forehead. "I didn't even think to ask."

Lash nodded slowly. "That's okay. But you need to get over there and see to it. The system's old enough that it only saves a day or two at a time, as I recall from the last bar brawl Garrett and I had to sort out over there. And if you want to see the footage, you'll have to do it in person."

"That's pretty old," she said.

"Part of it's the user," Lash said.

Willow had lowered her head. "I messed up."

"You're doin' a good job, Willow." Maria appreciated her dad's reassuring tones to her rookie cousin. He wasn't being her superior at that point; he was being her uncle.

"I want to be doin' a *great* job," she replied, lifting her chin and looking him in the eye.

"Well, that only comes with experience, which takes time. You're puttin' in the time, so... *great* is inevitable."

"Thanks, Uncle Lash," she said.

He left them. Willow turned to Maria and Harry, and Maria saw her notice how close they were standing. She hadn't really noticed herself until that moment.

That wasn't true. She'd actually been wondering if she could inch a little closer without drawing undue attention. What in tarnation was wrong with her? She'd just dumped a man yesterday!

Willow said, "We need that footage. I can't believe I didn't think to ask."

"To be fair," Harry said, "I'd have never guessed there were security cameras in that bar." His tone was as kind as Maria's father's had been a moment ago.

"Yeah, well, you're not a cop. But you *are* a genius, so thank you for that. You guys want to ride along?"

Maria said, "Sure, if it means more of Manny's tacos." She grinned up at Harry.

He smiled into her eyes. "You *were* right about those tacos," he said. "Best I've ever had."

"Well, you *are* from New York." Then with a sassy wink, she added, "That was not an insult. Except to whatever passes for tacos up there."

"Hey, my favorite customer's back," Manny said, smiling at Maria when they all entered the cantina. Then he looked at Harrison. "You look a lot better already."

"Thanks for helping me out yesterday."

"I don't know you from Adam, mister, but any friend of the Brands is a friend of mine," Manny said. "Besides, Maria'd do the same for me."

Harrison glanced at Maria as she murmured, "Damn straight."

Willow went on, "Is your parking lot camera working, Manny?"

"Workin' fine." He blinked then got it. "You need the footage from yesterday!"

"Yep," she said. "Billy Bob's denying he stole Harry's car."

Harrison almost said, "Harrison," but bit it back. It was no use. He would forevermore be Harry in the state of Texas.

"Come on back, then." Manny flipped up part of the bar to let them in and left it that way. With a quick glance at the patrons. The silent guy in the sombrero was there, and Harrison wondered if he'd been there all night, or had left and come back.

Manny went into his tiny office, but he left the door open, giving him a clear view of the cash register.

The room was the size of a closet with a desk and rolling chair, which Manny took immediately. He clicked computer keys as the three of them formed a tight half circle behind him. They all leaned in as Manny rewound the recording to the moment Billy Bob's big black pickup had roared to a stop in the parking lot. Harrison leaned closer. Billy Bob got out, red-faced, slammed the door hard and stomped toward the entrance, vanishing from the camera's eye.

Then there was quiet for a while. A semi passed, pulling a dust cloud behind it. And then a large black SUV pulled into the parking lot, but not directly in. Sideways, as if the driver planned to keep right on going. And that was what they did as soon as a man got out of the passenger side, walked over to Harrison's little blue Volvo, got in, and after a moment, started it up.

"I must've left the keys in it."

"No, no," Manny said. "I found them under a table after you left." He opened a desk drawer and pulled out a keyring, passed it to Harrison. Sure enough, his keys. "Must've hot-wired it," Manny said.

As the car backed around sideways, Harrison said, "Stop it right there," and when Manuel did so, "Can you zoom in on his face?"

"I'm not the FBI, son."

"Can you send the footage to my phone?" Willow asked.

"Um..." Manny picked up a pen to write down the phone number she recited. Not a great sign.

"Doesn't matter," Maria said. "Harry knows who that is."

"I don't," Harrison said. "He's wearing a baseball hat and keeping his head down."

"But there's his shape, his stance, his walk. You recognized him, Harry. I saw it in your eyes when he first got out of the car. That's why you asked Manny to zoom."

Harrison blinked and realized she was right, but it couldn't be. "At first, I thought it was Robert. Robert Phillipson, one of my research partners. But there's no reason for him to do something like that."

"It couldn't be a prank, could it?" Maria asked.

"We're scientists. We don't pull pranks."

Willow said, "Are you sure he'd have nothing to gain by stealing your… prototype? He couldn't claim it as his own or sell the design or—?"

"I don't… I mean, I don't think so. It's patented in all our names."

"Maybe you'd best tell me those names." Willow was taking notes on her phone.

"Besides Robert and me, there's Solomon Hadid and Carrie Sayre. I texted Carrie this morning, asked her to get the backup prototype and bring it with her to Silver Springs."

"And they're all supposed to be there?" Willow asked. "At the demo in Silver Springs on Wednesday?"

"Yes."

"I don't know much about patent law," Willow said. "But it seems to me, gettin' your stake back if someone tried to claim it would probably take some time. A lawsuit, maybe. An investigation. Those things can take years."

"Meanwhile," Maria said, "Robert takes the solar tile, sells it himself, and flies off to someplace without extradition."

Harrison couldn't stop shaking his head. "I really don't think that was Robert."

Maria looked at him then shook her head. "I think you do. You just don't want to think it."

"I really don't want to think it," he agreed.

"I want another look at the drop-off," Willow said. "Back it up and play it again, Manny?"

Manny backed up the video and played it again, his hand remaining on the mouse for rapid pausing.

"Stop it there." Willow leaned in. Harrison thought the license plate was too small to read, though. Then Willow said, "Manny, do you care if I send my cousin Orrin over here to take a look at this footage?"

"He old enough to be inside a saloon?" Manuel asked with a smile.

"Twenty-four and gifted with tech. He can send me the pertinent section of video, if it's okay with you."

"Sure it is. Send him on over. I'll make sure it doesn't get recorded over. That much I know how to do." He moved the mouse, saying aloud as he clicked, "File. Save. Done. Anything else I can do to help?"

"Well, since we're here anyway..." Maria glanced at Manny and fluttered her lashes.

"I already have a batch-to-go for you, *chica*. I told Junior to start 'em up soon as I saw that wild red hair through the front winder."

Harrison sat in the passenger seat, Willow drove, and Maria was crammed in between them in the middle. Harrison didn't mind her pressed up beside him. He didn't consider himself knowledgeable in the ways of flirtation, but he'd realized over the course of the day spent almost entirely by her side, that he was mightily attracted to Maria Michele Brand Monroe. He thought any heterosexual man would feel the same. It probably wasn't abnormal. It was just abnormal for him.

He didn't pay much attention to women. He hadn't had time. And it was completely illogical to feel attracted to this one. It couldn't go anywhere. He certainly wasn't moving to Texas and she had her whole life planned out.

And there was no room in his life for a fling. His prototype was missing, his family was breaking up, his father was sick, and his deathbed promise to his dying mother was teetering on the edge of failure.

Harrison's phone pinged. He frowned as he looked at the screen. "It's Carrie's landline," he said, surprised.

"Your research partner?" Maria asked.

He nodded and took the call. "Hey Carrie. Everything okay?"

"Hey, Harrison," said a man's voice. Not Carrie's.

"John?" Both women in the truck looked at him.

Carrie's husband said, "Yeah. I'm calling everyone in Carrie's contacts. They're on desktop, you know. She's uh… she's… I don't know where she is. I'm worried. Have you seen her? You spoke to her this morning, didn't you? What did she say?"

Icy alarm chilled Harrison's spine. He tapped his phone's speaker icon so the others could hear. "We texted this morning," he said. "She was going to the lab to get the backup prototype to bring with her to Silver City this coming Wednesday for the demo."

John sighed heavily into the phone. "That much I knew. She left for Cornell, and I haven't heard from her since. She's not answering texts. Calls go to voicemail."

"Did you call the university? See if she made it there to pick up the prototype?"

"Yes," he said. "She did pick it up, apparently. Your department head checked the safe, and the prototype is gone. But Carrie's car's still in the parking lot."

That was weird. What the hell was going on? "All right, okay, John, listen. I'm gonna have some people look into this, okay? I don't want you to worry."

"Okay."

"I'll call you later to check in. And please call me if you hear anything, all right?"

"Yes. Okay. Thanks, Harrison. Thank God you answered the phone. None of the others did."

Harrison blinked. "You called Robert and Solomon?"

"Yeah. Glad I finally got through to one of you. Let me know if you hear from her, okay?"

"Of course I will. Please do the same." He didn't know if John Sayre had heard him before the call had ended. Harrison stared at the phone, blinking.

"What are you thinkin'?" Maria asked.

Harrison said, "Well, John can get... confused sometimes. I don't think we need to panic."

"I thought he sounded a little off. Dementia?"

He nodded. "Early onset Alzheimer's. He's only forty-nine." As he spoke, he scrolled to the research group text, with just the four of them on it, and sent a message.

Harrison: REPLY. URGENT.

"Forty-nine," Maria said. "That's terrible."

He kept watching the phone, but no one replied. "What

if it *is* somehow connected?" A dark feeling was starting to take root in the base of his brain.

"Call someone else," Maria said. "Someone you absolutely trust who's up there and can go to the University and find out what's really goin' on."

Nodding, he tapped his phone, pulled up his sister's number, and hesitated.

Shamelessly, Maria leaned over and looked at the screen. "She's pretty. Girlfriend?" He glanced at her in surprise. There was disappointment in her eyes, but she hid it quickly. "That silver-blond hair is stunning. Like your mom's, isn't it."

"Just like my mom's," he said. "That's my sister, Lily. But I'm feeling like I don't want to get her involved in this."

"I agree with that assessment," Maria said. "Least not 'til we know what's really goin' on."

"I'll call the university directly." He dialed a number, and when someone answered he said, "I need the maintenance department, please."

He was connected and the phone rang multiple times before someone picked it up with an irritated and gravelly-voiced, "Yeah?"

"Bruce! Glad you picked up. This is Harrison Hyde. I'm working on the—"

"I know who y'are, Professor Hyde."

"I'm not a professor I— it doesn't matter. My car was stolen, and the prototype for the project I was working on was inside."

"Stolen?"

"Yeah, and I—"

"Well, you got the wrong department, then. You should call the dean. And the police."

"The police are working on it. But right now, I need you to do me a favor."

"Sure, if I can help."

"Can you run up to the lab and check the safe? I had a backup prototype in there. I asked one of my partners to pick it up, but I don't know if she left with it yet. And I can't reach her."

"Sure, I can check that out. Give me a few minutes I'll get right back to you. This number good?"

Harrison said it was and disconnected. Three minutes later, his phone chimed, and he read the text aloud. "'The safe in your research lab is open and empty. Sending photo.'"

The photo appeared. It showed the open safe in the wall of the inner lab. Then he frowned and looked closer. "What's that on the door, near the keypad?" You could only glimpse the red smudge from a sharp angle.

Maria leaned in as Harrison expanded the image on his screen. Then he shook his head in frustration and quickly tapped-out another message.

> Harrison: Show me the front of the safe door, please.

Ellipses appeared immediately. Seconds later, a new photo popped up. It was a clear shot of the safe's ten-button keypad, with a smear of something red across its face.

"Holy Moses," Maria whispered. "That looks like blood."

Willow offered to drive them back to the ranch, but Maria said her van was parked at her mom's and they could just walk over and get it. So she and Harry were walking side by side through downtown Quinn, and Maria was trying to see it through his eyes, as if it were the first time she'd been there.

The buildings were one- and two-story structures of brick and adobe. The lampposts were evenly spaced. Their green metal bases supported curlicue arms from which the lamps were suspended. The sidewalks bordering Main Street were cracked but functional. They strolled past the diner, the bakery, the jewelry store, the bank. There was only one of each.

"No Dunkin', or Starbucks, or Burger King here, huh?"

"Not a one," Maria said. "We don't let 'em into town. Quinn Chamber of Commerce has some muscle, and Quinn County backs 'em up. Every business in town limits is privately owned. No chains allowed."

"I like it."

"I love it here. I never want to leave."

They reached the end of the sidewalk and crossed a side street. The house where she'd grown up was a red adobe cottage with a matching building beside it, bigger than the house itself. They sat side by side amid lush green lawns. There was one vehicle in the driveway, her white Ford Transit Van. "Brand Monroe Veterinary Clinic" was painted on the side, the words forming a circle around the X logo of the Texas Brand, also featured on the arch over the ranch's driveway.

She pointed and said, "Mom and Dad live right there, in the house. The clinic used to be next door, but Dad's been slowly converting it back into a garage ever since mom bought a bigger space out on Bluebonnet Lane—another reason I want to live there. I'll be able to walk to work."

"In spite of all this insanity," he said, "I'm kind of dying to see the place."

"The clinic?"

"Bluebonnet Lane," he said. "I noticed the book you were reading with the same name."

She laughed. "How could I resist that title?"

"You couldn't," he said.

She liked the way he smiled down at her when he talked to her. Something stirred in her belly. Billy Bob's smile had never stirred anything in her belly.

"Did the story live up to the title?" Harry asked.

"So far, so good," she said. And she wasn't talking about the book. There was something going on here. At least she thought there was.

"Romance, huh?"

She jumped a little, like he'd asked the question because he was reading her mind. But then she remembered they'd been talking about a book, so she nodded. "My favorite genre. In the best ones, there's always big trouble, but a plucky female lead finds her way through it, falls in love in the process, then triumphs over every challenge and winds up with the sexy male lead pledgin' his devotion. They're upliftin'."

"That explains their popularity."

"I think so. What do you like to read?"

"Non-fiction. Mostly articles and papers by others working in renewable energy research." He took a breath, and said, "I'm restless. I feel like I should be doing something, but there's nothing I can do. It's frustrating."

She put a hand on his shoulder. He must not spend *all* his time doing science. Not with such nice shoulders. "You're doin' everything right, Harry." She unlocked the van and opened the passenger door for him, waved her arm and said, "Care for a ride, kind sir?"

He smiled, though his heart wasn't in it. "I would, thank you." He got in.

Maria went around and got behind the wheel, while her passenger checked out the interior. The back of the van held medical supplies and equipment, a lot of it mounted to the walls in customized holders, shelves, and brackets. She felt her chin lift in pride as he perused it. "Nice van."

"Thanks. It was a gift from my aunts and uncles when I got my degree."

"That's some gift."

"They bought me the van. All the customizations were on me and my cousins, DIY style." The key fob was attached to the strap of her handbag. She started the van and pulled to the edge of the road. Then she stopped the vehicle, looked at him, and said, "How about a little side journey?"

"To Bluebonnet Lane?" he asked.

She hoped she didn't look too eager when she nodded.

CHAPTER FIVE

"*H*ere we are."

Harrison undid his seatbelt as Maria pulled into the driveway of a white, two-story farmhouse with black shutters. "This is gon' be my house," Maria said.

He glanced at the house briefly, before looking at her. She gazed at the place with love in her eyes. "It needs paint." And indeed, the paint on the clapboards was peeling. "And window boxes full of flowers. And I'm for sure changin' out those black shutters."

"The sign says a sale's pending."

"That's 'cause I told the realtor we were fixin' to buy it right after the weddin'. Billy Bob could well afford it." She looked down at the ground. "He said it would be an investment; he'd sell it for a profit once he'd convinced me to move."

"Where to?" Harrison asked.

"Dallas. He has a place there. I told him I'd never leave Quinn. He said I'd change my mind, in time."

He opened his mouth, closed it again.

"What?"

He shrugged and said, "That was never going to work. You know that now, right?"

"Well, yeah. I think I had an inklin' before. The notion to call off the weddin's been naggin' at me for the past month. Maybe longer."

She led him around to the back door, which was painted a deep woodsy green. "This door should be stained wood, I think. With pretty glass insets. And the shutters... I don't know yet, but I'm thinkin' a lighter color, maybe with cutouts."

"Maybe match them to the green on the little hillside behind it."

There was a padlock with a keypad on the door. She entered the code and opened it.

"I um... it's not yours, yet, is it?"

"I've made Cat Shaw show it to me enough times that I know the code by heart. And she wouldn't mind." She nodded at the sign and the curly-haired blonde with a winning smile beside the words CAT SHAW REALTY. "I'm fixin' to apply for the mortgage myself— no help from my family— soon as we get you back on track."

She'd pulled her curls into a band, around one side. The only place they stayed put was where the hair band was. He had the dumbest urge to run his fingers through it. "Come on in."

He followed her, trying not to stare at her denim-encased backside and staring at it anyway, into a light-yellow kitchen. There was fresh stain on the cupboards.

Each cabinet and drawer had a white ceramic knob with tiny yellow roses. They looked new compared to the white-with-gold-swirls Formica countertop. "Someone redid the cabinets?" he said.

"Realtor suggested it to the owner, that and the fresh paint on the walls." She caught him looking at her. They locked eyes and his throat went dry.

"It's a beautiful place. It'll look like it came right out of a storybook, when you finish up. You... kind of fit here." His gaze held hers, and there was a current that ran between them. He felt it tingling in the pit of his stomach.

"I feel like that, too."

Everything in him was urging him to move closer. What was he thinking? There could *not* be a relationship here. This state, this town was not where he lived. His *life* was in New York.

Maria opened the fridge, but it was barren other than a six pack of pop. She took out two cans and handed one to him. "Cat keeps a few things around for potential buyers. I'll restock for her, if I don't get the loan."

She opened a cabinet and grabbed down a bag of potato chips. "Livin' here was the only part of my plan Billy Bob argued with me about. But it was a deal-breaker for me."

See, he thought. Deal-breaker.

She led him through an empty dining room still bearing wallpaper from the previous resident. It was ivory with vertical stripes made of pale blue flowers. Oh, wait...

"Are those bluebonnets? On the wallpaper?"

"Yes! That's why I don't want to strip it."

"You can't strip it. It's perfect."

"I know." She grabbed his hand and pulled him toward the wall, then pressed his palm to the wallpaper. Her hand covered his, to move it slowly up the wall. "Feel that?"

"Yeah." He knew she was referring to the satiny texture of every flower. He was not. She lingered a moment, and he almost turned around, knowing if he did, he was going to kiss her. And that would just be heartless. Why start anything with her? She was an amazing person; she didn't deserve to get her heart broken. Again.

She sighed behind him and moved away, leading him into a fully furnished living room with overstuffed brown furniture, pale-blue walls, and sheer white curtains in its tall windows. "Furniture's all new and comes with the place, if I want it. Cat thinks staging is most important in the living room. I'd say kitchen, but I'm no expert."

He looked at her for a long moment. She looked back. "I want to ask you something personal," he said. "If it's okay."

She nodded.

"Why'd you ever say yes to that guy? Your plan, I know, but... *that* guy?"

Sighing, she sank onto the sofa, but only on its edge. She opened the bag and handed it to him. He took out a few chips and handed it back.

Maria ate some potato chips and thought about her answer, but mostly she was still wondering if Harry had felt the way she had when their hands had been pressed together and their bodies so close a minute ago. Her heart hadn't yet resumed its normal rate. But he'd asked a question, and she wanted to give him a real answer. For some reason it felt important to be real with him.

"Like I said, I've been asking myself that for a while now. There are expectations out here, you know? I got my license to practice. My career is set, the business is great, and it's part of the fabric of Quinn. People depend on the clinic. Our patients are like family."

"I've lost the thread," he said, but he was paying attention. He looked at her when she spoke, with keen interest in his blue, blue eyes. *Gosh*, they were blue.

"Expectations," she reminded him and herself. "So like I told you, my next steps were to choose a husband, marry him, and have a couple of kids. That's what you do out here. That's what's expected. And the clock's tickin'. I spent years on my education."

He rolled his eyes. "You're what, twenty-five?"

"Good guess. I want a husband and two kids within the next five years."

"Five years?"

She could see he was doing math in his head.

"So including nine months for each pregnancy you'll need to get the husband within three-and-a-half years."

"Two-and-a-half. I'll wait six months between baby one and baby two. And you don't always get pregnant right away, so you have to allow a couple month's worth of tryin'. So now we're down to two years, give or take. And honestly, don't you think there should be a honeymoon period for a couple before they reproduce? What if you aren't compatible?"

"So that means—"

"That means, the clock inside my head was tickin' loud and messin' with my common sense, I think. Billy Bob was more or less local. Grew up nearby. I'd never heard anything bad about him. We dated for a couple of months and seemed to get along okay. He's gainfully employed, and agreeable to my plan, and, well, he asked."

Harrison shook his head. "And yet you're so smart about so many things."

"Ouch."

He held out his hand, and she tipped the bag his way. He took a handful this time.

"How are you holdin' up with all this?" she asked.

"Ah, nice change of subject."

"I thought so."

He laughed and she liked the sound. And she liked how *her* house felt with him in it. With them in it, together.

"Thanks for asking," he said at length. "I'm… I kinda feel like the ground just fell out from under me, too. I admire how you have your life all figured out, know exactly what you want. I feel like I'm in free-fall with no idea where I'll land."

"You hide it well," she said, looking more closely at his face. "But no wonder you feel that way. It was your life's work."

"There are notes and plans. I can build it again, but if someone beats me to it somehow, despite the patent, there wouldn't be much point. Either way, this has made me realize that I have no idea what I want my life to look like, long term."

"No?"

He shook his head. "On her deathbed, my mother made me promise to keep the family together, and I'm failing. But I don't think I can even process any of that until we find Carrie."

"Oh." She blinked. "Were you two—?"

He looked surprised. "No. She's devoted to her husband." He pulled out his phone and turned it her way to show a photo of a plump-cheeked, fifty-something-scientist, in the arms of a smiling man. "That's Carrie and John right after their late-in-life marriage. I was a groomsman."

Maria looked at the photo and felt a surge of relief. He'd only ever mentioned three women, and none of them were a girlfriend. She handed the phone back to him, even though her thumb had been itching to scroll a little. How could he not have a girlfriend, a guy like him?

"I hope she's all right," she said. Then she blinked as the pink cloud cleared from her smitten brain and let in some sunlight. "Wait a minute. Wait just a minute. Yesterday in the afternoon, somebody stole your car. This mornin', somebody broke into that safe. I mean, did they?"

"Well, yeah, you know they did."

"No, I mean, did they *break* into the safe? Or did they open it?"

"I don't know."

"You should find out. But either way, it's gotta be, what, a twenty-four-hour drive?"

"Thirty-three. But they could've flown."

"Mmm, either that, or it's more than one person. And, PS, Harry, how did they track us down at Manny's Cantina? Seems like maybe they've been behind you since you left Florida."

Harry nodded. "Or tracking me electronically. Hell."

"How would you know?"

He pulled out his phone, checked its settings while Maria drove. "It's not the phone. But it might be the car they're tracking, or even the solar tile itself."

Maria's phone pinged. "It's Willow," she said, and answered on speaker. "Hey Will. What have you got?"

"Harry still with you?"

"Yep."

"Tell him we've located his car out at Slap-Jack-Jimmy's."

Harrison looked at Maria for clarification. "It's a junk-yard," she said.

"I'm heading out there now," Willow went on.

"So are we." Maria ended the call and surged off the sofa, rolling up the chip bag on the way to the kitchen. "I'll have to show you the second floor another time."

Maria pulled her van off the road near the junkyard, got out, and stood with her hands on her hips, surveying the view from the edge of a drop-off. Harry got out and went to stand beside her. It was hot, dry, and dusty. When the wind blew, you could feel the little bits of earth it carried. Everything was cast in red.

The junkyard was located in a vast, played-out gravel bed. Razed earth and rock walls formed the boundaries of a wide, flat area about twenty-five feet lower than road-level where they stood. It was acres in size and had an earthen driveway that curved down into it. Hundreds of cars in various states of rust formed crooked rows that made no sense to the unenlightened eye. On the far right, a blue and yellow car-crusher waited with its mouth open. A yellow forklift was parked nearby.

"No gate?" Harry asked.

"No need. Slap-Jack Jimmy and his cronies watch over it all day, and three Rottweilers guard it all night."

"Slap-Jack Jimmy," he said, monotone.

"Right."

He nodded. "So, you just drive right in?"

"Not if you like your car," she said. She watched him look at the downward sloping, curved driveway, and see what she saw, the crumbling edges, the steep drop on the open side, the broken bits of glass winking in the overripe Texas sun.

He nodded. "So, where's the uh… office?"

Maria pointed at a cinderblock shack out past a pancake stack of flattened cars. "Shall we?"

"We shall."

She liked that answer a lot but slapped his elbow away, laughing when he offered it. "You're feeling better," she said as they walked down the driveway.

"If the car's here, the tile is here. I have hope."

"Not if the tile is what the car-thief was after," she said. "And it's looking like it was."

"He'd never find it. Not where you hid it."

Maria bit her lip.

Harry said, "What?"

"I wasn't tryin' to hide it, or I'd've picked a better spot. I'm thinkin' a tackle box sticks out like a sore thumb in the desert."

"We're only near the desert," he said.

"Either way, let's not jump to conclusions until we talk to Jimmy."

They traversed a path between two rows of cars to the square, cinderblock building. Its door stood wide open. Two male Rottweilers and one female lay snoring side by side, in front of an electric fan, but there was no sign of Jimmy. "Guess he's out," Maria said, turning to Harry.

He was holding a finger to his lips going, "Shhh." His eyes were on the dogs, and they were wide. The snoring had stopped.

Maria turned again, as the huge beasts spotted her, surged to their feet, and lunged.

"Maria, look out!" The next thing she knew Harry was pulling her behind him, and standing between her and the rotties, who had stopped in their tracks to stare at him.

"It's okay." Maria peeked around Harry's shoulder. "Hey, Hoss, good boy. Hello, Little Joe. You're a good dog, yes, you are. Hey, Lorretta. What a pretty girl."

The dogs wiggled their stump-tailed butts and smiled, dripping drool as Harry finally lowered his arms, which he'd been holding behind him to either side of Maria.

She came around him and crouched to greet the dogs.

"You know them," Harry said. "Of course you know them, you're the town vet."

The words were like warm honey. "Town vet," she repeated. "That's the first time anyone's called me that. My mom's been the town vet forever."

A sharp whistle from off to the right sent the dogs running to where their human was making his way toward them. Jimmy wore his trademark bib overalls, no shirt, and a stained brown bowler hat. Maria waved, and Jimmy waved back, moving toward them slowly. He had a pronounced limp and swung his arms when he walked, to help himself along. It would take him a minute.

Maria brushed her hands together, releasing a dog-hair cloud, then she turned to face Harry full on and looked him dead in the eye. "You just got between me and five-hundred pounds of junkyard dog."

"They're like puppies with you."

"You didn't know that. For all you knew, you were about to be mauled." She laid her palm on his chest, right over his heart. She didn't know why she did that, but it felt right. "Color me impressed to heck and gone. Thank you."

He looked away, and his heart beat faster against her hand, but she leaned around and caught his eyes with hers and held on. "Seriously, thank you."

"*De nada.* Maybe mention it to your father. He got a funny look on his face when I told him *you* stepped in front of *me* at the Cantina that day."

She raised her brows. "What do you care what my dad thinks about you?" And then it occurred to her why he might care what her dad thought about him. Maybe he was feeling a rising tide of something for her, like she was for him. The notion startled her so much she stumbled backward, pulling her hand off his chest, but she tripped over a stray carburetor. Harry grabbed her by both arms. "Whoa, easy there."

She got her balance. "Th-thanks." Then she looked at him. She'd been doing a lot of that. She liked his face. She could spend a lot of time looking at that face.

Harry seemed to realize he still had his hands on her outer arms, and that they were standing pretty close to each other. Like they were about to kiss or something.

She really wanted to kiss him.

He let go, took a step back and the moment ended, but her head was spinning. Gosh, she'd only just jilted Billy Bob yesterday, and all of a sudden all she wanted to do was make out with Harry.

"Y'all're here 'bout the Volvo, yeah?" Jimmy asked. He'd finally made his way to where they stood. The dogs were wandering on their own.

"Yes," Harry said. "It's blue, ten years old, and—"

Jimmy turned and pointed. They both looked.

Harry's little blue car was nose-down, at the bottom of a steep drop from the road, pretty close to where they'd been standing, surveying the place minutes ago.

"My car," Harry said. "Oh, man, Ol' Blue."

"Really?" Maria asked, secretly delighted. "My mamma had a dog called Ol' Blue when she was growing up. Blue Boy, at the ranch, is his great grandson." She smiled into his eyes, and felt something there, for sure.

"Deputy Willa's fixin' to meet y'all here," Jimmy said. "She said not to put a finger on it 'til she does."

"How did it get there like that?" Maria asked. "It looks like somebody pushed it right over the edge."

"That's just what somebody did," Jimmy said.

That seemed to snap Harry out of his stunned stare. "How do you know?"

"Tire tracks up top tell the story, plain as day. I figured that's what y'all were lookin' at up there."

"Ah, hell." Harry stared at the car for a full minute, and just when Maria was about to ask if he was okay, he shook his head like a wet dog and said, "It might still be inside." He headed through the car maze, toward his gravity-defying hatchback.

"How is it staying up on end like that?" Maria asked.

"There's a stack behind it," Jimmy said. "G'on, you best git after him. Deputy Willa'll be along."

Harrison stood beside his car, trying to figure the best way to get inside. It stood nose-down, tilted slightly, leaning against a flattened stack of vehicles. The rear tires rested against the stack, but the whole situation was unstable. One wrong move could send it crashing down. But he had to know.

The impact had been so hard the rear hatch had popped open. Or maybe it had been open already before the car was pushed. Maybe it had been opened because the car-thief had opened it, and reached in, and stolen the tackle box and his entire life's work.

He had to decide something soon. Maria would be along any minute, and so would her cousin the deputy, who'd left explicit instructions not to touch the car. He decided he could get the best view inside the car from the top of that multi-colored flattened vehicle pancake stack. He went to it, shoved it with his hands to see how wobbly it was. Not wobbly at all, but warm to the touch in the hot sun. He gripped a rusted yellow edge and started to climb.

When he reached the top of the stack, he looked down at his car. Its nose was on the ground, and its back-end was held up by the stack of flattened cars he had climbed. From the top, he could look right down into the open hatch.

Maria cried, "Jeeze, Harry, what're you doin' up there?"

"It's fine, I'm not touching anything. See?" He held up his hands, turned them back and front. "I can see my duffel in there. Everything I packed for this trip."

"Mine's on the ground over yonder," she said pointing. "Must've flown out. Can you see the tackle box?"

"No, but it might have flown into the front seat. Or it might be under the duffel."

"Hold on," she said from closer, and then the stack he was standing on wobbled, and he realized she was spider-climbing up the side after him.

"Holy— here, here." He reached down, they clasped forearms, and he hauled her the rest of the way up. She turned to look into the back of the car, just as he had. It would be so easy, he thought, to climb inside and take a careful look around.

Maria heaved a sigh and said, "How can we not look?"

"That's what I'm saying."

She nodded. "Go on, just try not to touch more than you have to."

Harrison pulled his sleeves over his hands to grip either side of the open hatch, then eased himself in, feet-first, his back sliding along the carpeted cargo hold, or what he and his sister as kids would have called "the back back."

He stayed right in the center and slid lower, toward the front seats, bracing his feet on the back of them to stop his progress. He almost groaned out loud when he saw his demolished laptop, bent in the middle, ruined. Then he grabbed the duffel and picked it up to see underneath and behind it.

"You see it?"

"Not yet. But I'll be glad to have my own clothes again." He hefted the duffel up toward her, felt when she clasped it, and then the car took a sudden leftward jog that threw him sideways, and pulled Maria right inside, head-first. She landed with her head between his knees, and his face between hers.

"What the hell are you two doin' in there?" Willow's shout was muffled because she was standing outside the car. Maria lifted her head, looked at her cousin through the side window, and gave a little wave. Harrison had to bite his lip not to burst out laughing and maybe tip the car over.

"Come on out of there," Willow said. "You're contaminatin' evidence." She pointed to the car's front passenger side door. Harrison rolled his eyes. They'd approached from the driver's side and hadn't seen it standing wide open.

Maria, being on top, so to speak, went first, crawling lower, head first over the back seat into the front, rubbing every inch of her body over his on the way. He thought his eyes would pop.

Something had shifted between them. And it was dumb, because they wanted very different things in very different places.

"The tackle box!" Maria's exclamation came from the front seat. "On the floor, driver's side all tangled in my ruined weddin' dress." She whispered that part, probably so Willow wouldn't forbid him touching it.

He dropped the duffel bag into the front seat, then turned himself around so he could go headfirst like Maria had. When he made it into the front, he tossed the duffel out the open door, then he used a fast-food napkin from the console to untangle the tackle box from the dress. "You want the gown?" he asked.

Maria shook her head. "Not in the least."

He was unreasonably glad to hear that, and just as glad to see the tackle box. His dad would've been heartbroken if it had been lost. He climbed out of the car with his treasure.

"What part of 'don't touch anythin' did you two not understand?"

"We *barely* touched anythin'," Maria said. "Besides, he has to see whether the solar tile's been stolen."

Willow sent her a dubious look, and Maria shrugged, picked up Harrison's duffel and moved it beside her feet.

"This is going to the ranch, not the evidence closet. And so's my bag, which is right over there." She nodded at her bag, lying up against a rusty muffler nearby.

"You're fixin' to get me fired before my first two months are up," Willow said.

Harrison appreciated Maria looking out for him, but he was more interested in opening the tackle box. He set it on the ground and looked up at Willow. "Can I open it?"

The newest deputy nodded. "Carefully. Yes, like that."

Using his shirt sleeves, Harrison flipped the latches, touching only the very edges, and opened the lid. He expanded it fully, again touching only an edge with his sleeves, exposing all the interior trays and compartments filled with hooks, sinkers, rubber worms, and an array of lures. But there was no black box. He looked in the little compartments amid the tackle, in case the tile was loose among the tackle. He searched in between the trays in the bottom, where he moved items by tipping the box one way, and another.

"It's gone," he said. The words were heavy. It hurt to say them.

"Could it have fallen free?" Willow asked.

He glanced back into the car. "The tackle box was latched."

"We'll get it back." Maria squeezed his upper arm. "We will, Harry. You don't know my family. We can fix this. We can help."

He looked into her eyes and knew she meant it.

"At least this tells us something. A lot, actually," Willow said. "For one thing, to my mind, it clears Billy Bob. Not for the assault, but for the theft. This was somebody who knew exactly what they were lookin' for."

Harrison backed away and pushed a hand through his hair as Willow went on. "I've been in touch with the campus cops at Cornell about Carrie Sayre. Her husband had already called the Ithaca City Police so I contacted them. They told me who to contact at the FBI."

Harrison came to attention. "The FBI?"

"State lines were crossed," Willow said. "And I get the feeling they're treatin' this as a very big deal. Environmental Espionage, was the term they used."

"They *ought* to take it seriously," Maria said. "Harry's invention will change the world."

But Harrison wasn't so sure. He paced, rubbed the back of his neck, and tried to put pieces together in his mind, but they didn't fit. "This doesn't make sense. There's no way anyone could get away with this. We patented the device."

"Who, specifically, filed that paperwork, Harry?" Willow asked. "Was it you?"

He looked up slowly. "No. Carrie took care of it."

"Carrie," Willow repeated, "who went to pick up the prototype from the University, vanished without her car, and stopped answering her phone."

"Yes," he said. Then he snapped his fingers. "There's surveillance on campus. Some of it must have caught Carrie leaving."

"No," Willow said. "None of it did. Either she deliberately avoided the cameras or someone else made her."

"My God," he said. Then, "I haven't had any luck reaching Solomon or Robert, either."

"Neither have the cops up there." Willow frowned, then looked around the junkyard, and suddenly Harrison felt exposed.

"I'll stay here and see if I can get any prints from the car before we move it to the impound," Willow said. "I think the best thing for you two is to head back to the ranch. We don't know where this person is, the one who did this. What we do know is that they want your gadget, and that your other three partners are unaccounted for."

Maria's hand clamped onto Harrison's forearm like a vise. "Willow, do you think Harry's in danger?"

"I don't know yet. But better safe than sorry, right? Best place for both of you is at the ranch. Lots of people around, just in case."

Maria looked at Harry. "Are you okay with that?"

He didn't think he had any other option. "Yes. Yeah. Thank you."

"You take care with that tackle box, okay Will? It's special to him."

"I will."

Maria nodded. "Come on, Harry." She went and picked up her duffel, slung its strap over her shoulder and took his hand to start the trek back up out of the junkyard. He grabbed his own bag, then took hers as well.

When they'd gone a few steps, she leaned up and whispered, "We won't sit around twiddlin' our thumbs. We're gon' do some investigatin' of our own."

"From the ranch?"

"Trust me," she said. "I've got *resources*."

CHAPTER SIX

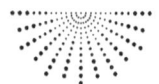

*S*he drove. Of course she drove. Harrison didn't have a car anymore. Willow had imported a forensics team from somewhere to go over what was left of it. They would be there in the morning.

He sat in the passenger seat, pretending to look out the window at the passing terrain, but he was actually looking inward, at his life. Or lack of one. He'd had work. He'd had nothing but work, with brief side journeys to visit his sister in her life and their dad in his life. He should've seen them far more often.

"We'll get it back." Maria had said it multiple times.

"I don't know."

She was quiet for a minute. Then she said, "What if you don't?"

He swung his head around to look at her. "What if I don't get it back?"

"My mamma says when you're worried or in a state of dread, think of the worst thing that can happen, and figure out how you'd get through it. Because you know you will. You got no choice. She says it takes away the dread. So, what if you don't get the prototype back?"

"I guess… I can make another. Unless the person who took it takes my rights to it, as well."

"You can make another. You have all the notes and things?"

"Backed up to cloud storage. Yeah."

"So, if this person tries to take your rights, all that's proof it was yours. You could take them to court, if you had to."

"That's true."

"And you'd most likely win. You're in the right."

"I probably would win, if it came to that."

"See? Better, right?"

He looked at her. She was always so upbeat, with the possible exception of a breakdown in the restroom at Manny's just before her ex had shown up. It was kind of amazing. "Better," he said. Not much, but she was right. He could build another prototype. He could prove he'd worked on the original design. And there was the patent, too.

She drove under the Texas Brand arch, along the winding driveway, and pulled along in front of the inviting front porch.

An hour later, Harrison was enjoying an unnecessarily huge dinner with Maria's Aunt Chelsea, Uncle Garrett, Bubba, and Blue Boy. The droopy bloodhound laid under the table, watching for scraps. He only took those that fell within reach of his tongue, with minimal physical motion required.

He'd been fielding questions about his life in New York, his research, and his mom, once he'd mentioned her.

"I'm sorry you lost her," Chelsea said. "If you ever want to talk, it's what I do."

"Thanks," he said. "That's kind. This place..." He set his fork down. "It's special. I appreciate your hospitality."

"Any time," Garrett said, and the others echoed the sentiment.

Harrison didn't think he'd ever felt more welcome, other than in his own home. This family was like a bigger version of his own. Oh, their surroundings were different. Their customs. But the love, the core that held the rest together, that was alive and well in the Brands. It was too familiar to doubt, and too warm to resist.

After dinner, his offers to help clean up firmly refused, he'd headed up to his room. First, he took a long hot shower, and then, from the rocking chair by the window, placed a video call to his dad and sister. They both answered.

"Harrison!" his father said, beaming. "Oh, it's good to see your face, son. How is the car trouble?"

He hadn't told his dad the whole story and neither had Lily, as far as he knew. He'd asked her not to. "Well, the truth is, Dad, my car was stolen. They were after the proto-type and they got it."

"*What?*"

"What about the backup?" Lily asked.

"We don't know. Carrie went to pick it up, and then she

went missing. Her car's at the school. The safe was open, the backup's gone. She's not answering calls or texts, and her phone's off line."

"Oh my God." Lily pushed her silvery blond hair off her forehead, gathered it into her fist atop her head, then shook it before letting it go. Their mother used to do the exact same thing when frustrated.

"What are you going to do, son?"

"I don't know. I'm here, for now. Safe and sound. And the FBI's involved, so—"

"The FBI?" They said it in unison. There was a tap on his bedroom door, and he called, "Come in."

Maria came in, dessert plate in hand. Chocolate cake. God help him. "You missed dessert."

"Who's that?" his sister asked, while his dad looked at every corner of his computer screen. He only did video calls on the computer.

"Oh, I'm sorry," Maria said. "I didn't mean to interrupt."

"It's okay." He got out of his rocker, taking his phone with him to stand beside Maria. "Dad, sis, this is Maria. She's part of the family who... uh, took me in."

"Oh, *that's* Maria." That was Lily, and her voice carried both a lilt and a question.

"Maria, this is my sister Lily and my father, Hyram Hyde."

Maria smiled fully. "Well, hello, folks. It's so nice to meet you. My goodness, Lily, you are stunning. And Hyram, it's a pleasure. You've raised an amazing son. I want you to know, we're taking good care of him."

"I can see that," Hyram said with a nod, probably at the cake she held.

She laughed. "So is the H a thing?" she asked.

"The H?" Harrison asked.

"Harrison Hyde, Hyram Hyde."

"Oh, yes," Hyram said. "My wife and I decided we'd name our daughter after her, and our son after me, but I didn't want to saddle my boy with *Hyram*, so I just went with another H name."

"And Lily, that was your mother's name?" she asked his sister.

"Yeah. Lilly Marie. I'm Lily Ellen. But I don't think I'll ever live up to it."

"Oh, I don't know about that." Maria looked up at Harrison. "I'll go, let you have your family time." She set the cake on a stand, and leaning into frame once more, said, "It was so nice to meet you both."

"You, too," they called. Maria backed out and closed the door.

And then Lily said, "That girl is at least halfway in love with you, big brother. You realize that, right?"

"More than halfway," his father said.

And that pretty much ruined any hope Harrison had of sleeping that night.

The next day, after breakfast, Maria said, "We're gonna

distract you for a couple of hours. You're gonna want to wear shorts. You bring any shorts?"

"I did, as a matter of fact." Harrison headed up to the guest room and rummaged around in his duffel for a pair of shorts. He hadn't unpacked. Didn't expect to be around that long.

When he went downstairs, Maria met him at the bottom, then headed for the front door. Blue Boy lifted his head from the braided carpet in front of the fireplace, sighed heavily, and lowered it again. Outside, there were motors rumbling.

Four ATVs were lined up in front of the porch. Two of the ATVs had people on them. He couldn't see their faces behind their visored helmets but he presumed they were cousins.

"Have you ever ridden one?" Maria asked, leaning close so he could hear her.

"Nope."

"C'mere." She took his hand and pulled him to a small, red four-wheeled vehicle. "This makes it go," she said, demonstrating the throttle. "And this makes it stop. Ever drive a stick?"

"Learned on one."

"Good, this here's your shift. No clutch necessary. Only four speeds, see the diagram?"

"Yes."

She took the helmet that was dangling by its strap from the handlebar and handed it to him. "It's easy."

It was. Harrison followed Maria with the two masked

bandits bringing up the rear, and he knew she was taking it easy on purpose.

The Texas Brand was something to see, though. Vertically challenged woods, with paths created by cattle, rolling pastureland, with the desert nipping at its edges in some places, and a wide, blue sky. There were large, slow-moving cows, lazing in the shady woods, or grazing in the grassy places. They ranged from mostly white with red blotches and freckles, to mostly red with white patches. But their most distinct feature was their long, nearly horizontal horns. It was hypnotic watching them move, because the horns gave them a slow-motion quality.

Beautiful creatures.

No horses out there, he noticed. The horses grazed closer to the main house.

At length, they left the trail and meandered through trees that gave way to a small pond with water so clear you could see straight to the bottom. He recognized the swimming hole from his recent horseback tour. There was a tire hanging by a rope from a tree limb that extended out over the water.

Maria stopped her machine and took off her helmet, shaking her curls free. Harrison pulled up alongside and removed his own. When he got off, his legs felt a little stiff. Partly from his trail ride yesterday. The other two pulled up in the same way, got off and removed their helmets. The two blond cousins, the siblings. He thought they were the youngest and tried to recall their names until Maria saved him. "You met these two earlier, my cousins Orrin and Drew."

"We heard about your car," Drew said. "That stinks. I'm really sorry." The sparkle of youth infected her eyes and her sympathetic smile. She was young, twenty-one or two he guessed.

"Thanks. It's just a car, and it's insured."

"I think your project being stolen stinks more," Orrin said. He was probably a little bit older than Drew. Same coloring, same lithe build, but in a sturdier version. The exuberance was missing from the brother. He had a sullen look to him. In that way, he might be his kid sister's opposite. "Maria told us you'd been working on it for seven years."

"That's why we're gonna help you get it back," his sister said.

"You are?" Harrison glanced at Maria, knowing she'd be ready with an explanation.

She didn't disappoint. "Know how Drew got her name?" Then she grinned and nodded at Drew. "Tell him."

Drew, nodding, said, "Mom's a P.I. Penny Brand Investigations. And it's got a penny on the logo, so you don't really know if it's the brand name or her name, but it's really both."

"Because her first name is Penny," Harrison interpreted. "That's pretty clever."

"I know!" She kept talking while Maria unstrapped a giant picnic cooler from the back of her ATV. It was so heavy it seemed to stretch her arms. He hurried to take it from her, but she dodged him and said, "I got it."

Drew hadn't missed a beat. "Anyway, when my mom was a kid, she was nuts about Nancy Drew. The books were old, even for her generation. But she loved them. The stories inspired two of her life goals; become a P.I. and, if she ever had a daughter, name her Nancy."

He was still trying to figure out how this connected to her helping him get his prototype back, but he had to admit, he was into the story at this point, so he paid attention. Orrin spread out a big blanket. Maria started taking food out of her cooler and laying it out with a stack of hard plastic plates and real silverware.

"But when she held me for the first time, and started calling me Nancy, Mamma said I howled. Every time she said that name, I would just wail. And then my dad—"

"My Uncle Ben," Maria said in a quiet aside as she took two covered dishes from the cooler and whipped off the lids. Leftover chocolate cake and a full-sized pie. Apple, maybe. His stomach growled.

"Well, my dad took one look at me and said, "Drew. Not Nancy, but Drew." Well, I stopped bawlin' and looked him right in the eye."

She was beaming. What a happy young woman she was. Harrison smiled and caught Maria smiling too. They shared that for a second, smiling for the same reason at the same time like a shared secret.

He looked at Drew's brother. "How about you, Orrin? Your name's not very common."

Orrin said, "I'm named after our grandfather, Orrin Brand. No magical story behind it."

"Don't be a pissant," Drew said.

He didn't reply.

Maria sat down, took a plate, and everyone else followed her lead. And for a while, they were too busy pretending to weigh the options before deciding on a piece of each. And then they were too busy eating to talk. They poured themselves long, tall glasses of sweet tea from a cooler Orrin had brought, and sat in a shady spot underneath a low, broadlimbed tree. The tree reached right out over the pond, some of its tendrils touching the water, like it was taking a sip.

"I can't recall ever being in a more peaceful place," Harrison said at length. "You're so lucky to have all this."

"Yeah?" Maria said. "I thought you planned to live in some University-owned mansion for elite professors who saved the world."

"I don't think I put it quite like that."

"She reads into things," Drew said. But she was looking from one of them to the other with curious eyes. Then she shook herself visibly, and said, "So the reason we're here— our mom has resources we can... use. And we know the ropes."

Orrin nodded. "We've been learnin' *the ropes* since birth."

"We were either with her at her office or with Dad at his dojo our whole lives," Drew went on. "So we can do two things really well. We can sleuth, and we can fight."

"Fight?" Harrison couldn't stop himself from blurting the question. She was five two and so slightly built he thought a strong wind could carry her away.

"We have three black belts each," Drew said with a little bit of pride.

"We know our stuff," Orrin agreed, nodding. "We can help."

"So, what's your theory, Harry?" Drew asked. "What do *you* think happened?"

"I don't know." He took a sip of the tea and realized nobody had spoken, and everyone was looking at him, waiting for a better answer. Okay, what did he think? "I think someone stole both the prototypes of my solar tile. I think they're probably planning to sell the technology. I just don't know how they think they can get away with it. It's patented in all four of our names."

"You and your research team," Drew said.

"Yeah."

"Names?" She moved her phone a little when she asked, and he realized she was recording, rather than taking notes.

"Carrie Sayre, S-A-Y-R-E. Robert Philipson, one L, and Solomon Hadik, all Os, H-A-D-I-K."

She smiled so widely he was confused. And then she said, "Thanks for takin' me seriously."

"Like I'm gonna doubt the daughter of a P.I. named after Nancy Drew who has three black belts?"

Drew laughed and blushed. She reminded him of his sister, before they'd lost their mom. Since then, Lily had been… muted, her light, dimmed.

"So, it's patented, you said," Drew went on. "Have you seen the patent documents yourself?"

"No. Carrie took charge of all that."

"And she's missin'?" she asked.

"I've been getting updates from her husband, my sister,

and the head of my department. Willow's in touch with the FBI. There's still no sign of Carrie, though. Her credit cards haven't been used. Her phone is either dead or turned off, I guess."

"Would you send me their photos?" As Drew asked it, she tapped his phone with hers and her number popped up on his screen as a new contact. He saved it, then scrolled to his photos, tapped three of them, and sent them to her. Then as an afterthought, he opened his contacts and shared Carrie, Robert, and Solomon's info with Drew as well.

"I'm sendin' you a link," Drew said, simultaneously with the whoosh sound effect and another notification. "That's where you can search patents. Find yours. But later, the signal's weak out here and it'll take all day, and that water's waitin'."

"And we waited fifteen minutes after the meal, despite that it's a myth with no science behind it," Maria said. "Last one in's a rotten egg." She peeled off her shirt on the way to the tire swing. She had a bikini top underneath, baby blue. She hit the tire, one foot on the inner edge, one hand on the rope that held it, leaning back like Tarzan's Jane to make it swing, then wider, and then she hooted as she let go and plunged into the water.

The other two followed her, so Harrison guessed he was the rotten egg.

He was only a few years older than Maria. But he hadn't acted like that since high school. No, maybe even middle school. He peeled off his shirt, kicked off his shoes, ran to the tire, and just went for it, swinging way out and letting go. He splashed down into cold water, sank deep, then thrust out his legs and paddled up again. When he surfaced, the three cousins were hooting and raising their hands for high fives.

Harrison looked at their grinning faces and then past them at the serenity around him. It was sinking into him, this place, soothing him, making him believe everything could still work out okay.

Maria splashed him, and he dove and swam away. They played like a bunch of kids and eventually slogged to the shore. Drew had towels in her ATV's storage compartment and as she handed them around, hoofbeats approached. Fast ones.

He toweled off fast, every alarm bell in his body going off at once as he pulled his shirt on. Willow came riding in on her thoroughbred, Sundance. She slid to the ground, walked purposefully to him, put her hands on his shoulders, and opened her mouth. Then she closed it again.

"What?" A hole opened in his stomach.

Willow lowered her head. "Your research partner, Solomon Hadik... he's dead, Harry. I'm so sorry."

The word *dead* slammed him in the chest, knocking him a few steps backward. "Solomon's dead?" He had to repeat the words to make sense of them. "Solomon's *dead*?" And then questions came. "When? How? What in the name of God— he was a vegan for cry—"

"We don't know the cause of death yet," Willow said. "There was a break-in at his apartment, signs of a struggle, but no obvious injuries severe enough to have killed him. We'll know more after the autopsy. The FBI wanted to put you into protective custody. But Uncle Garrett and I convinced them you'd be just as safe at the ranch with a sheriff and deputy. I'd like you stay, for the time being."

"But—"

Drew said, "I think that's smart. Cause how's anyone gon' get away with takin' credit for, much less sellin' rights to something that four scientists can prove they invented unless—"

"Unless they get rid of the four scientists," Orrin said, finishing his sister's sentence. "Dang."

"Shoot," Drew whispered.

Ice crept up Harrison's spine. "My God, what about Carrie?" He paced a few steps away, then back. "What if they killed her, too? What will her poor husband do? He needs her."

"If your friend Carrie can be found, the FBI will find her," Willow promised. "Multiple agencies are coordinating on this from Ithaca, and they're sending a team here, to work the case from our end. My part, for right now, is to keep you alive. This just got a lot more serious, Harry. And a lot more dangerous."

He swallowed hard.

Maria slipped up beside him, clasped his hand and said, "Nobody's gettin' anywhere near him on my watch."

"We got your back, Harry," Orrin said, stepping up to clap a hand on his shoulder.

"Pack up and let's head back to the house," Willow said. "I'll ride with you to keep watch."

And she did just that, riding alongside their ATV caravan. Harrison had never felt more exposed. His nape and the small of his back, tingled as if they could feel crosshairs trained on them. He wished Maria would cut loose and go faster but yelling that at her would make him look cowardly, and he'd rather brave the fires of hell than look bad in her eyes.

He'd never felt bigger than when she'd thanked him for standing between her and the Rottweilers. The way she'd looked at him had been— wow.

The attraction between them was intensifying, no question about it. He needed to spend time figuring out what to do about that. But he couldn't even begin to give it the thought it deserved, not when Solomon, a man he'd worked with for seven years, was dead. Maybe murdered. And Carrie, missing. Maybe dead, as well. And Robert...

Harrison had worked with Robert Philipson for seven years. He just couldn't believe his friend could be behind this.

There was a plethora of vehicles out front when they got back to the ranch. They pulled their machines to a halt and shut off the engines. Maria took off her helmet and said, "Guess the call's gone out."

"What call?" Harry asked.

"The call that a Brand's in trouble," she said, noting Uncle Wes's truck, Uncle Elliot's truck, Uncle Ben's truck, her mom's van, and Uncle Adam's big tan SUV.

When they went inside, the house was packed.

Everyone was talking at once, they'd all brought food... and shotguns, none loaded. "You don't go indoors with your hat on or your gun loaded," was one of her favorite "Uncle Garrettisms."

Maria glanced up at Harry. He was looking around with wide eyes, so she cut a whistle to shut them all up. "Everyone, this is Harry—"

"Harrison."

"— Hyde." She looked Harry right in the eye. "And whether some thief steals credit for his solar tile or not, everyone here should know he's the one who created it. He's the one who helped save the world. Assumin' we do."

"Hot damn!" Uncle Wes said. Everyone joined in, shouting *hell, yeah* or its equivalent. Harry's cheeks turned red. He muttered "thanks" several times as her relatives applauded him. The ones close enough clapped his back or shoulder.

"Not just me," he said, softly, which had the effect of silencing everyone in the room.

Uncle Garrett and Bubba stood side by side. Bubba had grown as tall and broad as his adopted dad, but he had the swarthy complexion of his birth father. His mother had been Chelsea's sister. He'd always called them Aunt Chelsea and Uncle Garrett, even though they were legally his parents.

Uncles Elliot, Adam, and Wes stood together. Aunt Chelsea was offering sandwiches from a platter she'd manifested from thin air, and the other aunts, Esmeralda, Taylor, and Kristen were sending speculative looks between her and Harry.

"I had a team," Harry went on. "Solomon was brilliant. There wasn't a problem he couldn't think his way around. He was socially awkward, and painfully shy, and too old to be single, as his mother told him a hundred times." He paused and swallowed. "He was her only son."

Heads lowered around the room.

"And Carrie..." He had to stop for a breath. Maria saw him swallow. "She's a middle-aged woman with a genius IQ and a husband who needs her. He has early onset Alzheimer's and no one else to rely on."

"Hold onto hope," Aunt Chelsea said. And everyone murmured in agreement.

Baxter, Maria's oldest cousin emerged from the throng. He had shaggy blond hair and black-framed glasses. He handed Harry a white box with an apple on its lid. "Figured you'd need a laptop. We heard yours was ruined in the car."

"Holy... Baxter, that's too much."

"We went in together, we cousins," Baxter said. "We want you to have it."

"This is..." Harry clutched the box in one hand. "That's an amazing thing to do. Thank you. I can log into the cloud, download my backup designs, my notes." He wove straight through the fam to the stairway, talking more to himself than anyone else, and took the stairs two at a time. "I can search for the patent, check Carrie's social, and Robert's too, and..." He was still talking all the way out of earshot.

Maria shook her head, then looked at the amused faces of her relatives. And one by one, they looked back at her, their eyes full of questions.

Oh, heck, no. She wasn't ready for that. "I'm gon' um…" She searched her mind for a reason to go upstairs after Harry. "He's gon' need the Wi-Fi password!" She headed for the stairs herself.

"If the whole gang's stayin', we're gon' need to make use of the bunkhouse," Uncle Garrett called. "This family's outgrown the ranch house."

"I call the bunkhouse for the cousins," Trevor shouted, and her other cousins agreed loudly as Maria climbed the stairs.

CHAPTER SEVEN

*H*arry had changed into dry clothes— jeans and a T-shirt. There was a knock on his door before the new laptop had even booted up. He said "come in" without thinking or getting off the bed where he sat, back-to-headboard, tapping keys.

Maria came in with two foamy mugs and an iPad under her arm. She'd taken time to change, as well. She was wearing denim shorts, and a T-shirt that said, "too busy dancin' to get knocked off my feet" over an image of sparkling shoes. "I was afraid you were bringing more food," he said, jumping up to take one of the mugs. It was ice cold and foamy. He sniffed. "Root beer?" Then he took a sip.

"Homemade root beer. And yes, food *is* a thing here. Anytime I stay, I have to diet for a month to make up for it."

"That's right, you don't live here, normally," he said.

"I was livin' with my folks when I wasn't at school. But

now, everything I own is packed up, for my planned move to Bluebonnet Lane. Everything, that is, except the stuff I brought here, where I spent the whole week before the weddin'."

"Right, you and your cousins were staying here, you said."

"Yep. We wanted to spend the week together. So rare that Bubba gets home these days. We were here a lot as kids, every break from school, and most all summer. It's the Brand family hub, I guess."

"I get it." He set his root beer down, then returned to his spot on the bed, pulling the laptop onto his outstretched legs. "I feel that way about Ithaca. Not with the generations of family in the same place, like you, but my family is there. I spent my whole childhood there. Every family event was held on the shore of Cayuga Lake. And those autumn trail rides... I can't imagine fall without color."

"I've never seen that, except in pictures. They don't look real."

"They're real, but you can't capture it in a photograph. The colors are more vivid, in motion with every breeze. You can feel autumn in New York. You can *taste* it."

She was studying his face. "I want to see it someday."

He would love to show it to her, he thought.

Maria cleared her throat, lowered her eyes from his, and pulled a scrap of paper from her jeans pocket. "Wi-Fi password," she said, handing it to him.

"Right. I'll input that right now."

"I thought I could help. Brought my iPad." She held it

up. Then she pulled the rocking chair closer to the night-stand where her root beer awaited.

Harrison keyed in the password, hit enter, and watched the computer connect. Then he logged into the cloud to set the machine up from his stored backup. "There. It'll take a while, but it's underway." He looked over at Maria, in the rocking chair with her tablet, and found her eyes on him. They were almost always on him. There was something warm about the way she looked at him. It made him feel ten feet tall. "That was amazing of your cousins, going in on a laptop for me."

"I agree. I had no idea they were doin' it."

He looked toward the door. "I kind of took it and ran, didn't I?"

"You thanked them," she said.

"I need to do something nice for them. For all of you."

She lowered her eyes. "Not me. You wouldn't be in this mess if not for me."

"That would only be true if your good ol' boy Billy Bob had been behind it. But I don't think he stole the solar tile."

"Billy Bob wouldn't know it was worth stealin'." She tapped her iPad screen to bring it to life. "What can I do?"

"It's gonna take some time to download my backup from the cloud," he said. And he set the laptop aside. "We could use your tablet to run the patent search."

"Okay." She took another drink of her root beer, then hopped out of her chair. "Shove over."

He did. She sat on the bed beside him, her back against the headboard, knees bent, tablet resting against the slant of her thighs. He reached across to tap in the URL. His forearm rested on her bare thigh for a moment, and he went still, then said, "Why don't I just…" while she said, "You take it."

He took the tablet, but his eyes stayed on her thighs for a few seconds longer than the tablet did. Then he took it and swiped and tapped, and soon he was typing terms into the search bar. But he was too broad, and hundreds of results popped up.

"Try under your names, you and your team," Maria suggested.

He keyed in Solomon Hadik and a handful of patents popped up. So did the recurring lump in Harrison's throat.

Maria's warm hand slid over his, like you'd pet a cat. "I'm sorry," she said.

"I know." He scrolled the list of Solomon's patents.

"What are they?" Maria asked.

He glanced at her, reminded himself she was a scientist, too. Hard to remember when she was so damn cute all the time. Neanderthal remnants in his brain didn't automatically connect cute and sexy with smart professional.

Wait, *sexy?*

Yes. Sexy as sin.

She moved on the bed, leaning away from him to get her mug. When she leaned back again, she was touching him from shoulder to hip to thigh, to knee. Her shorts left her legs bare and made him wish his were, too…

Whoa, now! Not good, not good, not good.

"Um, right, Solomon's patents. They make fuel burn more efficiently in different types of combustible engines, small and large. He has a separate patent for each type."

She nodded, then said, "Try searching under Robert. Of them all, he's the only one who resembles the guy that took your car."

Nodding, he entered Robert's full name, hit enter, and thought he'd made a mistake when nothing happened. He tried again. No results. Zero. Robert had never patented a thing.

"Trying Carrie," he said, tapping the screen. "Just her two patents. She came up with this foam you used to insulate mugs that can keep their contents hot for hours. Licensed the rights, but kept the patent. She's always been ingenious about things like that, maximizing profit from her work. The second one of hers was the same, but in thermal canisters."

"I didn't know how any of this worked before."

Her "I" always sounded like "Ah" and it made his spine tingle every time she said it. Silence stretched out and he realized he was staring at her thighs again, and she was staring at him staring at her thighs. He looked at her face instead, but that brought his lips awfully close to hers, and her gaze grabbed his and held on.

He was going to kiss her. Yes, he was going to do it. He tilted his head ever so slightly. Her brown eyes widened, but she didn't turn away, and then he pressed his lips to hers even while his brain was telling him it was a terrible idea. He kissed her.

She slipped her hands around his nape, fingers sliding up into his hair, and she kissed him back. And then their lips parted. He started to lean in again, and the next thing he knew, she was shoving a frosty root beer mug in between them.

"Uncle Garrett's homemade root beer's good, isn't it?" she asked, nodding with her eyebrows arched high.

He took a sip, having no choice as she put the mug to his lips. It was sweet, but not as sweet as that kiss. "It's amazing."

"Told you." She sat back on the bed and resumed sipping from her mug as if nothing had happened, so he tried to rein in his feelings of desire, arousal, yearning, confusion, and then desire again.

He distracted himself by resuming his search for the patent.

By the time the root beer mug was empty, he'd determined that no patent had been filed for the solar tile. He didn't know why Carrie hadn't done it, but she hadn't.

"What's stopping you from filing it right now?" Maria asked.

"I'd need a prototype."

"Can you build a new one?"

"I'd need my lab. My equipment."

She pursed her lips, which made him look at them, which made him think about kissing her. Then she said, "How long would that take?"

He shook his head, doing internal calculations. "Weeks."

"Do you think it would be too late?"

"I do."

She grinned and it felt like sunshine. "You did it again."

"Did what again," he asked, a little bit lost in her light.

"Said 'I do' to a runaway bride. You'd best stop teasin' me, or I might start to think you mean it." She slid off the bed. "Imma take the glasses downstairs," she said. "I'll be back."

He nodded and watched her go. When she closed the door, he closed his eyes and blew every bit of air out of his lungs. Instead of passing, his attraction to her was getting bigger every minute he spent in her presence. And she knew it. He'd revealed it all with that kiss.

He'd wanted more. To keep on kissing. To do more than kissing. So, now what?

His text-alert chimed, saving him from having to think too hard about that question just then. When he saw that the text was from his research partner Carrie's husband, his heart tripped over its own beat.

John Sayre: The blood on the safe was hers. It was Carrie's

Harrison: Oh no. I'm sorry. What can I do, John? What do you need? Are you with someone?

John Sayre: There is no one.

Maria exited Harry's room, leaned back against the door, and pressed her free hand to her heart, which was racing.

He *did* want her, too! He *did* feel all the same things she did. He'd told her every bit of it with that kiss.

"Ohmygoshohmygoshohmygosh," she whispered. She wanted him so much, and yet she was scared to trust her own judgment, after barely avoiding the disaster of marrying Billy Bob.

She should've kept on kissing him. She shouldn't have freaked out. Maybe now he wouldn't try again.

She leaned off the door and headed for the stairs, but she hadn't got very far when Harry called her name. She turned, saw his face as he leaned out the open bedroom door, and knew something was wrong. She set the root beer mugs on a nearby stand and started back as he came toward her. They met halfway in the hall, and he showed her his phone screen.

Shock rippled through her, and it must have been far worse for him. The blood on the safe door was Carrie's. She put a hand on his shoulder. "It was only a little bit, though," she said. "She might still be okay."

"Solomon wasn't," he said softly.

Willow came up the stairs and joined their huddle. "DNA results on that blood from the safe are in."

"I know," Harry said. "Carrie's husband texted me. He's terrified. I don't think he'd heard about Solomon yet, and I didn't think it would do any good to tell him."

"If Carrie Sayre is alive, we'll find her," Willow promised.

"What if they're looking in the wrong place, though?" Harry asked. "Whoever did this… was *here*."

"Looking for you," Maria said, and the notion sent a shiver up her spine.

"Or for the prototype, which they got," Harry said.

"Or for both," Maria argued. "They'd have grabbed you, too, if you hadn't been busy gettin' your face punched in at the time.

He rubbed his jaw like a reflex. "Maybe I should thank Billy Bob, huh?"

"I hope you're kiddin'," Willow said.

"He's kiddin'." Maria sighed. "Willow, has there been any sign of the fourth partner? Robert Philipson?"

"No sign of him," Willow said. "He'd booked a flight into Silver City but never used the ticket. His car is in his driveway. The last transaction on any of his bank accounts or debit cards was two days ago."

"Maybe they got him, too," Harry said.

"Or he's the bad guy." Maria was sure of it.

"It wouldn't make any sense." Harry was looking at the floor, but not really. Maria suspected he was deep in thought.

"Tell me why not," Willow said. "What are you thinkin'?"

Harry looked up and said, "Robert's a decent guy. I've worked with him for seven years. I just don't think he'd do this." He paced a few steps away, stopped and turned to face them, snapping his fingers. "And he wouldn't have needed to wait for Carrie to open the safe. We all have the combination."

"That's a good point," Willow said. "Although he could've just been there first, or come in while she was openin' it. Just because he was there when she was, doesn't mean it was planned that way."

"There's the surveillance footage from Manny's that resembles him," Maria said. "Then again, it was just height and body type. Couldn't see his face. He wore a hat."

"I've never seen Robert wear a hat," Harry said softly.

He was clearly fond of his co-workers, grieving for Solomon, terrified for Carrie, and defending Robert. "Besides," he went on, "even if one of us decided to kill the other three and try to claim full credit for the invention, how would they expect to get away with it?"

Maria said, "Only a scientist would think taking credit for the invention would be the goal."

"Well, what else would it be?"

"What it always is. Money. Who cares who invented it?" Maria asked. "It's the guy who has it in his greedy, thievin', no-good hands at the time of the sale who's gon' take the money and run."

"But why?" Harry asked. "We stood to make good money from the tile. All four of us."

"Sure," Maria said. "And if there were just one, they'd have made four times as much."

"We should be talking to the potential investors, too," Willow said. "They know about the solar tile, and they also know who you all are, yeah?"

"Yes," Harrison said. "We've had several meetings with them. They flew to us."

He turned and walked away from them, into the guest room. When he came out, he had his phone in hand. While scrolling it, he said, "I have all the investors' contact info."

He paused there. "I wonder if anyone's called them to cancel the demo on Wednesday."

"Hold up," Willow said. "How about if I call 'em? Since it's part of an official investigation."

From below, Drew said, "Hey!" Then she came upstairs and headed their way, all denim and lace in jeans and a pretty blue blouse. Her blond ponytail bounced when she walked. "The cousins have opted for the bunkhouse tonight," she informed them. "You're with us, Harry. We're all clearin' our stuff out of here to make room for the elder-Brands."

"Oh," he said, looking at Maria as if for affirmation.

She said, "It'll be way more fun out there."

"Yeah," Drew put in, "and you won't have to hide in a hallway for a secret meetin' to which I was not invited."

Hands on her hips, Willow said, "I'm a deputy and you're a twenty-year-old amateur."

"Twenty-two!" the little blonde retorted. But then she shifted her gaze to Harry. "The guy who stole your car isn't stayin' anywhere local between here and Manny's. Any stranger in town would've been noticed."

"I wasn't noticed," Harry said.

To which all three women replied without a word. One snorted, one laughed, and one rolled her eyes.

"Oh, you been noticed," Drew said. "The rumors are *juicy.*"

Maria shook her head. "Drew, don't—"

But she kept on talking. "Folks are sayin' Harry's the reason you dumped Billy Bob at the altar. That you'd had a secret tryst, and he couldn't bear the thought of you marryin' someone else." She put a lot of drama into her words. Hands to her heart, she went on. "So he came to the church on your weddin' day and stole you right out the back door."

"Who? Me?" Harry asked, and he looked from one of them to the next. When their eyes met, Maria couldn't look away. Her cheeks felt warm, and his were a little bit pink, too.

Willow cleared her throat, and they broke eye contact. Maria turned a little bit and lowered her head, so nobody would notice her trying not to smile. It got Harry's attention, though, and he said, "This feels like it's getting dangerous. For you, all of you, the whole… clan."

"Not as dangerous as it might be for you, out there on your own," Maria said. "There's strength in numbers. You just hold on with us, Harry. Things are fixin' to improve. I just know they are."

CHAPTER EIGHT

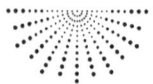

*H*arrison and Maria were standing in a clothing shop in downtown Quinn. She wore jeans, a light blue tank top with a lightweight plaid button-down over it, unbuttoned, and a straw cowboy hat. Her coppery hair hung in a thick braid on one side.

An hour ago, Harrison had received a text from Carrie's phone.

> Carrie: Meet me at the corner of Main and Austin, 7 pm. I have the prototype.

It was only six fifteen, but this shop had a clear view of the vacant brick building on the corner of Main and Austin. There was a *For Sale or Lease* sign on its lawn.

"It's a hot one, even for Quinn," Maria said. "You'll be swelterin' when we go back outside. I think we came to the right place."

He looked around the blissfully cool shop. There were racks of cowboy boots on one wall, clothing on the other.

Somewhere outside, Willow surveilled both them and the meet site along with Maria's father and uncle. Quinn's finest. Harrison and Maria had been told to kill time in the shop until five minutes before nine and then head across the street to the meeting site.

"You're not gonna *Pretty Woman* me, are you?" he asked.

She grinned at him. "You've seen *Pretty Woman*?"

"My sister made me."

"I thought she was younger."

"Meaner, though."

Something changed in her face. It softened. "You're close to your sister. I can tell."

"After Mom died, we pulled together, the three of us. It got us through the loss, you know?"

She nodded.

"We're a lot like your family, only smaller," he said. "Are they that way all the time? Protective? Close?"

"Oh, yeah," she said. "And more. Always up in each other's business. Always meddlin'. Nosy as all get out. Everybody thinks they know best." She rolled her eyes. "Like I should complain. In my case, they were right."

He let her soft accent soothe him. "After a while, I had to get back to the project, and things have… I don't know… changed. I feel like we're drifting. That's one of the reasons I can't think about—"

She plucked a hat from a shelf, pirouetted, and dropped it onto his head. Then she turned him to face a small mirror. It was a cowboy hat, straw, well made. It had a beaded band he thought was Native.

"The artist is Comanche, a local. She wins art prizes,

gets written up in magazines all the time." She adjusted the hat on his head at an angle.

He looked into the small mirror set near the hat section, while Maria read from the dangling tag. "The green turquoise beads represent mountains. The blue ones above and below are water and sky."

He looked at the price tag that hung from the brim then blinked and looked again. "There are too many digits in this for a hat."

"It's on me. And don't argue."

He blinked and for the first time thought about her family, the ranch, the size of it. "You're wealthy, aren't you?"

"Don't they teach you good manners back east?"

"Sorry. They don't let me out among people much."

"You don't socialize?"

"Been too busy with the project."

"So, then there's no… girlfriend. You never said."

He shook his head left and right, stuck in her eyes until she took the hat off his head and headed up to the counter. A young man flashed her a smile that said he was interested.

"Maria Michele," he said. She probably thought that accent was sexy. "It's so good to see you here. I heard you're still single. Billy Bob must be loco, to let a gal like you get away."

"Nobody *lets* me do anything, Monolito. I do as I please." She plunked the hat onto the counter. "Don't wrap it, he's wearing it out."

He nodded, but the looks he sent Harrison were not friendly. Not hostile exactly, more like he'd cut ahead in the line of men awaiting a shot at Maria Brand. It must be a long, long line, he thought. She was amazing. Maybe it was just hitting him how amazing. Confident. Beautiful. Smart. Comfortable in her skin. Authentic, probably the most authentic person he'd ever met. She knew what she wanted and was going after it— the clinic, her house on Blue-bonnet Lane. She'd have no trouble finding a husband so she could get on with the rest of her plan. All she'd have to do is pick the one she wanted.

She tapped a card, took the hat. They moved toward the front, but didn't leave the shop. It wasn't time for a few more minutes. They pretended to browse near a window that faced the place where they were supposed to meet Carrie— or whoever had her phone.

Maria reached up to push a hand through his hair, sending a tingle all the way to his toes. Then she settled the hat onto his head, adjusted the angle, and said, "There," in a kind of raspy whisper that sounded like sex.

Harrison swallowed hard and didn't say anything.

"So yeah, my family's wealthy," she said, resuming the earlier topic. "A while back, my mom and uncles had to make a decision. To continue to make it in cattle ranching, you either had to go toward a factory feedlot model, or lean all the way into the new regenerative agriculture model. There was no more in-between. My family loves this land. We feel connected to it. A feedlot would've destroyed it. So, they went regenerative. Because they got in early, they made a bundle, invested it wisely, rinse and repeat. Now every last one of their offspring gets a check every month."

"Nice."

"It is." She glanced up. "That hat looks good on you."

"Doesn't go with my shoes," he said, looking down at his casual loafers.

"Maybe you need some boots."

"No, the hat's plenty."

"For now," she said. Then she went quiet, gazing out the window. Every once in a while, the shopkeep looked their way, but he didn't seem worried.

"You know, Maria, you had a narrow escape with Billy Bob."

"You can say that again. Who knew he had a violent streak?"

"No, I mean... you can do better. He's nowhere near good enough for a girl like you."

"Are you flirtin' with me, Harry Hyde?"

"Am I?" he asked, and he hadn't meant to say it aloud.

"Time to go," she said. "Five of."

They stepped out of the shop, and the bell on the door jingled. They had to walk to the corner then cross the street. A group of people was walking toward them, and Harrison used it as an excuse to put his arm around Maria's shoulders. She moved closer, so their hips brushed when they walked, and it felt good.

She pointed out her uncle Ben's dojo, the volunteer fire department, the post office, all within sight. She nodded across the street. "You wouldn't know it to look, but that diner right there has the best barbecue in the county."

"You're gonna have to prove that." He grinned at her, and they pivoted to cross the street.

There wasn't another vehicle in sight, until there was. It came out of nowhere, a truck, careening full-speed. Maria was looking at him, so she didn't see it. He lunged, pulling her with him, dove because he wasn't going to make it in time. He pushed her as hard as he could, launched her off her feet, and then he felt a glancing blow to his shoulder that sent him skidding across the pavement and just barely out of the path of the massive tires.

"Harry!" Maria shrieked, and then she was pulling him up onto his feet on the sidewalk where he'd landed, brushing at his clothes, looking him over. His hat was long gone. "Are you okay? Lord almighty, it looked like he plowed right into you!" As she said it, she looked toward the road, and so did Harrison, but the truck had already sped away.

"I'm okay." She had blood on her forehead.

"You're hurt."

"Hit the lamppost is all. I'm good."

"You're bleeding," he said, and he felt sick to his stomach.

"It's nothin'."

Brands swarmed. "That was deliberate," Willow said, while Lash grabbed his daughter and turned her around to inspect her. "I was too busy looking at the two of you to get a description," he said.

"I'm fine, Dad," Maria said.

Lash released his daughter, then grabbed Harrison without warning, and full-on hugged him, clapping his back multiple times. Every clap sent reverberations of pain through his shoulder. "You took that hit for her. You just saved my little girl's life."

"Anyone see the truck well enough to get a description?" Maria asked. She was holding a red bandana with some ice in it to her forehead. A young woman from the diner had brought it out for her, muttered that the boss had called 911, and retreated inside again. "What did it look like, Harry?"

"Big and fast," Harry replied. "Text your mom. We should..." He turned to look at Bubba, who surprised him by reading the look and nodding.

"I'll get the truck." He hurried away.

"It was a white Chevy," Willow said while tapping her phone. "Not sure about the year, but it was an older model. I got a partial plate."

"I got a photo," Garrett said, holding up his phone.

"You got a *photo*? Dang, you're good," Maria said. "Well, let's see it already."

He tapped his phone and handed it to Maria.

She looked at the photo, and Harrison looked at it, too, because he was standing close to her. Garrett must've snapped it just as the truck had connected with Harry's shoulder, and from the angle of the shot, you'd have thought the rig would have flattened him. It also caught Maria in motion, a blur, as Harry had pushed her so hard.

Harrison had been looking at her, not at the truck. Lash

had his hand out, so Maria passed the phone to her father. He looked at the screen, and then he looked at Harrison again, lips pressed, nodding, respect in his eyes.

Bubba pulled up with his big motor rumbling. "Anybody need a need a ride home?"

"Thanks Bubba," Willow said, then she addressed Maria. "We have to stay here. It's a crime scene. We need to follow up on that truck. You be careful." Then to Bubba again, "Straight back to the ranch, no stops, you hear?"

"Yes, ma'am."

Harrison opened the passenger door and went to help Maria up, but she hopped up on her own without a problem. Then he got in behind her. Before Harrison shut the door, Lash handed up his hat, which had been knocked off in the collision.

"It's a good hat, Harry," he said. "I like it."

Harrison took it and put it back on his head. "Thanks. I like it, too."

"All he needs now's a white horse," Willow said with a wink Maria's way.

Maria rolled her eyes, and Harrison closed the door.

"So, this is the bunkhouse?" Harry asked as Bubba pulled up in front of the one-story clapboard building.

Bubba got out immediately, took his bag from the back of the pickup and headed toward the long narrow building, leaving Harrison and Maria alone in the truck.

"Aren't we putting the ranch hands out?" he asked.

"Oh, other than special occasions, they don't stay on the ranch anymore like back when my dad worked here," Maria said. "They work regular hours, clock in and out. A few have homes and families of their own, but most are single men. They fill every room at the little Quinn Hotel."

"I saw the Quinn Hotel in town. Bar downstairs, rooms upstairs. Like something out of the old west."

"It *is* something out of the old west," she said. "It's two and a half centuries old. But today, the bar kitchen makes a mean pizza."

"We should've picked one up," he said. "Now that the drama is over, and I'm sure you're okay, I'm starved." He reached for the door handle.

She covered his hand with hers. "Now that you're sure I'm okay, you're starved?" she asked. "That requires clarification."

He looked at her, looked away. "I was worried. It made me sick to my stomach."

She swallowed hard. "Made me sick to my stomach, too, when I saw that photo. Cause it looked for all the world like you should've been flattened."

"Looked that way from my angle, too."

She shook her head. "You saved my life, Harry."

"Well, you saved mine. From Billy Bob, I mean."

"Heck, he wouldn't'a killed you." She shrugged a shoulder and said, "I like you."

"I like you, too." It was an automatic reply.

She said, "I mean... you know... I *like* you."

"Oh." He had to think of how to respond to that.

"That's okay," she said. "I thought maybe— you said it made you sick to see me hurt, and then there was that spine-tinglin' kiss, before, so— let's go inside, huh? The gang moved all our stuff for us— hope you don't mind."

He touched her shoulder, so she turned back. And he leaned in and pressed his lips to hers, kissed her like he had before, and then he pulled back enough to talk, and said, "I like you, too. A lot."

She smiled, and it lit her brown eyes.

"It's just that I can't—"

She pressed her finger to his lips. "You fixin' to ruin it?"

He stopped talking. She tugged on the front of his shirt, pulled him in for one more kiss. She burrowed her fingers into his hair, and he wrapped his arms around her waist, and they kissed like teenagers after prom.

Then she let him go and got out of the truck.

He couldn't start anything up with Maria.

He'd already started something up with Maria.

He'd told her he couldn't live in southwest Texas, no matter how much the place kind of took his breath away. His dad and sister lived in Ithaca— for the moment. His job was in Ithaca. His mother was buried in Ithaca. It was illogical to pursue his feelings for Maria.

My God, he had *feelings* for Maria.

"Hey, there you are!" Shaggy, blond Baxter came and

clasped Harrison's hand, went to slap his shoulder, but he dodged it with a kind of graceless swoop.

Baxter was as tall as all the other male Brands, but not as wide. He wore black-framed glasses and sneakers, not boots. "Come on around back. We have pizza and beer."

Then he went back the way he'd come. Maria took Harrison's sleeve, not his arm, not his hand, just his sleeve. It was dark and she knew the terrain. As they moved around outside of the bunkhouse, toward the back, an orange glow suffused the darkness. The source was a campfire, a house-length away for safety. Lawn chairs, fallen logs, and coolers served as seats. Baxter handed Harrison a beer, and then the kid with the dark curls— he searched his mind for the name— Trevor, son of Maria's Uncle Elliot and Aunt Esmeralda— brought over a pizza box, holding it open in front of the two of them. Maria took a big slice, so he followed suit. Maria said, "Here's a spot," and led him to a log covered in dry, brown moss. They sat and it was like a cushion.

Harrison looked at the gathered group and did a mental pop quiz. Orrin and Drew, brother and sister, seemed to stick close when in large groups. Drew seemed protective of Orrin. In addition to Baxter and Trevor, there was Bubba, who'd driven them. And just then, Willow came traipsing around the bunkhouse with a rucksack over her shoulder. "Got room for one more?"

"You bring beer?" Bubba asked, but then he hugged her, and the two of them found food, and places to sit.

They ate pizza. Harrison wasn't a drinker, but the beer he was handed tasted good tonight, so he was taking a swig between bites. Every now and then somebody would say something random about the weather or the cattle. And then finally, Drew, the youngest, piped up with, "We've all seen the video."

"What video?" Harrison asked.

"Yeah, what video?" Maria echoed.

"You don't know about the video?" Drew asked. "They don't know abut the video."

Willow said, "The diner had a camera. Caught the whole hit-and-run. A waitress uploaded it to the internet before we told her not to. And it's getting a lot of views."

"I don't know why nobody's talkin' about it," Drew said.

"We didn't want to make Harrison uncomfortable, Drew," Bubba said.

"What's to be uncomfortable about? He's a hero. You saved her life, Harry."

"Harrison." Maybe now that he was a hero...

"Damn straight, he is," Trevor said. Then he hefted a beer, and Harrison wondered if everyone there was twenty-one. Since Willow was a deputy, he presumed they were. "To Harry—"

"To Harrison!" Bubba, shouted. "For saving one of our own!"

"To Harrison!" Everyone raised a bottle.

His face got so hot he pressed his dewy, brown bottle to his cheeks. He didn't know what to say.

"See? You made him uncomfortable," Willow said. "That said, you, Harry, are a part of our family now. It's not optional." She raised her beer then took another sip.

He realized that beside him, Maria was looking at her

phone. He looked too, then looked away. It was too much. Maria got to the end and lifted her gaze to his. They locked. She didn't say anything. It seemed like she wanted to and then just didn't.

"So, what's your family like?" Drew asked, oblivious to the current zapping between him and Maria.

"Smaller, for sure," he said. "I have one sister, Lily, a few years younger. She just passed the NCLEX, so now she's an RN in search of her first job. My dad is a retired chef and my best friend. He has his own apartment but his health isn't great. Asthma, former smoker. He's lookin' at retirement communities in Florida."

"I used to struggle with asthma when I was a kid," Baxter said.

"How about your mom?" Drew asked.

He lowered his eyes, focused on the fire. He could almost imagine her face in the flames. "She passed a year ago. Cancer."

"Oh, I'm so sorry."

Murmurs of sympathy moved like a wave through those gathered.

"So what do y'all think is happening here?" Baxter asked. "And how can we help?"

So, for a while, Harrison explained everything that was going on, as far as he knew it, with a lot of input from Maria. At one point, she was finishing his thoughts, and he was finishing hers, and everybody else was rapt.

Bubba said, "It's pretty clear they ain't lookin' to just kidnap you, Harrison." He was the only one of the group who called him by his name. "They plumb tried to kill you."

"And they've killed once already," Willow said. "Your partner Solomon."

He lowered his head. "Do you think Robert and Carrie are already... I mean that text obviously wasn't from her. It was from whoever has her phone. Whoever, maybe, has her."

CHAPTER NINE

*M*aria could tell that Harry was hurting, and not just physically. His whole life was inside out, and here he was alone among strangers. And then it hit her so hard she snapped her fingers and blurted it aloud. "Your dad and sister should come down! We can boot out a couple of the relations to clear a room. Baxter's parents' place is within shoutin' distance."

He lifted his head, meeting her eyes while her cousins all shouted hell, yeahs. "You don't think it would put them in danger?"

Bubba said, "This ranch is the safest place on earth right now."

"There's a deputy in your bunkhouse," Willow added, "and a sheriff and his chief deputy in the main house."

Maria said, "And two triple black belts sitting among us."

"But it's your mom they'd have to worry about," Drew

said. "Aunt Jessi doesn't suffer fools." Beside her, Orrin nodded emphatically.

Trevor said, "Remember when that guy in town told my mom to go back where she came from?"

"I was there," Maria said. "We were picking up supplies for Sunday barbecue— you're gonna love Sunday barbecue, Harry. Anyway, it was me, my mom, and Aunt Esmeralda, coming out of the market, and this guy yells at her."

Trevor said, "My mom just froze. She didn't know what to say. And then Aunt Jessi, she turns to Maria and says, 'Hold my groceries, baby girl.' Then to my mom, 'Call 911. This guy just… I don't know, grabbed my ass, I guess. The rest was self-defense.'"

"The guy heard every word of it," Maria said, picking up the story. "He put his thumbs in his waistband and grinned, and he said something like, 'ooh, looks like I'm in trouble now.'"

"He wasn't a local," Trevor put in with a sad shake of his head.

"They never are," Willow added.

"My mom walked up to him," Maria said. "He was still runnin' his mouth about Aunt Esmeralda when Mom kicked him right in the cojones. When he doubled over, she kneed him in the chin. By the time the police car came screaming into the parking lot, he was flat on his back, hands coverin' his face, and my mom was standin' over him ready to do more damage. There was some blood."

Trevor was laughing at this point. "So, the deputy gets out of the car and walks over to the guy. 'You all right, sir?' He helps the guy to his feet, and the dude starts yellin',

'That woman— right there, *that* woman, she assaulted me!' And then he's standin' there, and Aunt Jessi's only a few feet away, and a crowd has gathered, and they're lookin' at him, six-two and cut, and then at her, all petite and pretty. And they start laughin'. And the guy looks around all upset, and the deputy, Uncle Lash, walks over to Aunt Jess and says, 'Hi, hon.' She hugs him and gives him a kiss hello and he asked what happened.

"'Guy grabbed my ass,' Aunt Jessi says. And the guy starts blusterin' that he did *not* grab her ass, and my mom, Esmeralda, in case you're lost, says she saw the whole thing. He grabbed her ass *hard*. And Uncle Lash asks Aunt Jessi if she wants to press charges, and she says not as long as the guy's out of Quinn by sundown."

Harry smiled throughout the tale. Trevor was so good at that, Maria thought. Anyone needed cheering up, he was the go-to guy. Everyone laughed at the tale, even though they'd all heard it a hundred times.

"How about some music, Bubba?" Drew called out.

"Can a guy eat first?" Bubba asked, but his guitar case was leaning against his folding chair.

"Bubba's a country singer," Maria explained. "Had a big hit last year."

Harrison frowned and looked Bubba's way, and the big guy said, "You won't recognize that name. My given name is Garrett Ethan Brand, but I've been Bubba since my mamma left me on that doorstep. Professionally, I go by—"

"Ethan Brand," Harry said. "I *have* heard of you. *Country Kind of Love* must be my sister's favorite song."

"That's nice, she likes my one and only hit. Huh, maybe

she *should* come down for a visit. A fan would boost my ego."

Harry looked around at the others. "What do the rest of you do with your time?"

Drew said, "Youngest first! I just finished college because my parents insisted, but I intend to be a private investigator like Mom."

"Her parents are my uncle Ben and aunt Penny," Maria whispered.

"I take the licensing exam next month," Drew said.

"I could have guessed that for you," Harry said. "Is there a lot of call for that in such a small town?"

"Very little," she said. "So there's some drivin' involved. But you'd be surprised how much of the work is remote. Internet-based. It's all tech these days."

"Makes sense." Harry nodded at Orrin. "You too?"

Orrin lowered his head a little. "I help out, but it's not my forever thing. I haven't found my forever thing yet."

"Who's next youngest?" Harry asked, then he pointed at Trevor, and raised his brows.

"Good guess," Trevor said. "You could work at the fair!"

"And you are... a stand-up comedian?" Harry asked.

Everyone burst out laughing, especially Trevor. He said, "Everyone says I'm funny. You want to see funny, hang out with my dad. But no, I teach English as a second language to immigrant kids in nearby border towns."

"Wow. That's amazing work."

"Thank you."

"Thank *you*," Harry said.

"I'm next," Willow said. "But you already know my gig."

"The newest deputy in town," Bubba said. "And the youngest. It's a record."

All eyes turned to Baxter, and Maria couldn't wait. Baxter's hair was dark blond and shaggy. He wore black-rimmed eyeglasses, and whatever clothes he was most comfortable in. Tonight, that was a pair of dark blue warmup pants with loose legs and deep pockets, and a gray T-shirt.

"I'm the oldest. My mom is Jasmine, adopted dad is Luke, a cousin of the elder Brands. I—"

"Wait. Harry has to guess first." Maria was holding her hands up between them, like she was preventing a fight. Then she looked at Harry and nodded.

She watched Harry look Baxter over. Baxter leaned back in his lawn chair, long legs outstretched, using a basketball sized rock as a footstool, smirking and sipping his beer.

"I don't know what kind, but he's some sort of scientist," Harry said, and Baxter choked on his beer and almost tipped his chair over. Beside him, Bubba clapped his back. "Easy, there, old man."

Harry was looking at everyone. "What? Did I get it?"

Bax wiped his mouth. "Biophysicist. How the heck did you—?"

"Takes one to know one, I guess. What are you working on?"

"Growing food in the desert. You?"

"Making a one-inch-square solar panel that does the work of one sixteen square feet."

"*That's* what they stole?" Baxter asked. "The folks kept

146

saying solar tile, I was thinking much larger, though. But that's… that's a paradigm shift."

Harry nodded. "And it will be, no matter who takes the credit for it," he said. "That's what really matters."

"I keep tellin' you," Maria said, "this isn't about takin' credit. Only a scientist would think that way. And how many scientists do you know, goin' around killin' people?"

Harry frowned and so did Baxter. They exchanged a look and then a shrug. Around them, everyone was nodding in agreement with Maria's theory, which was, she thought, obvious.

"That's too heavy a topic for a campfire, though," Bubba said, sliding his guitar strap over his head. He began strumming. Everyone sat, or stood, rocking or tapping in time, or just relaxing with their beers. Maria could see Harry beginning to relax.

"I'm beat," Harry said after another hour. "Don't let it break up the party. I could listen to you all night, Ethan, but I think I need to turn in." He got up, then added, "Thank you guys. You've been amazing."

"*He's* thankin' *us*," Ethan said with an eye roll. "We owe you, Harrison."

"The guy driving that truck was after me," Harry replied. "That makes it my fault."

"Well, it's my fault you're here in the first place," Maria said, "so…" Then she turned to the others. "I'm gonna get him set up in the bunkhouse."

"Third bunk, bottom," Drew said. "In deference to you bein' beat up twice in a row, second time by a truck." She winked at Maria and said, "You're on top."

They started toward the bunkhouse, which was far enough away to keep it safe from any stray campfire sparks. They were nearly there when Willow said, "Hold up." She'd come after them.

They waited where they were, and she joined them, phone in hand. "Just got a text from Ithaca PD. Preliminary exam shows your friend Solomon died of a heart attack."

"A heart attack," Harry repeated.

She nodded. "It's definite."

"But his place—" he began.

"Was ransacked, yes," Willow said, "and there were signs of a physical struggle, but that's not what killed him. He had a heart defect he probably didn't even know about."

"Okay," Harry said, and then he said it again and met Maria's eyes. "That's good news, right? Whoever did this, didn't kill Solomon."

"Oh yes, he did," Maria said. "Just maybe didn't intend to."

"Maybe he doesn't intend to kill Carrie, either." He closed his eyes. "Thanks, Willow."

"You're welcome." Harry went on inside.

Maria hung back, since Bubba was on his way over. He reached past her, pulled the bunkhouse door closed, and said, real soft, "Seriously, if you want us to clear out of here—"

"What kind of a woman do you think I am? I'm a few days out from my would-be-weddin'. What's the matter with you?"

She shoved her way past him into the bunkhouse, and

right before she slammed the door, heard Drew say, "Whoa. She's got it worse than I thought."

She wondered if Harry had heard it, too, and was almost afraid to look, but then she did. He'd wandered to the back of the bunkhouse where the beds were stacked and had found his bunk.

Maria went to the bedding closet and took two fresh, ribbon-entwined stacks of crisp white bedding, pillow and all, and set them both on the top bunk. Then she took a fitted sheet from the pile, and said, "I'll make your bed, if your shoulder—"

"No, I can do it. Actually, I should make yours, too. I have better reach. He leaned over the upper bunk and easily slipped the fitted sheet onto the mattress, a task that would have required Maria to climb up there. Then he held out a hand and said, "Top sheet, please."

She put it into his hand. In no time, he'd made the beds. She helped with the bottom bunk and then sat on its edge. "Bathroom's through there."

"Mm-hm." He sat down beside her. "They think we're in here making out, don't they?"

"They won't, if I go right back outside. But if I stay, yeah, that's what they'll think."

"Do you want to stay?" he asked.

"I really do," she said.

"Even knowing it can't go anywhere with us?"

She tipped her head to one side and searched his blue eyes in the dim room. "I think you're wrong about that. But yes, even knowin' you believe it can't go anywhere, I'd still *like* to stay. But I'm leavin' anyway."

He nodded slowly.

"See, I think it *could* go somewhere. And that means our first time together will be somethin' we remember for the rest of our lives. So, I sure as heck don't want it to happen in a bunkhouse with all my cousins a few dozen yards away."

He tilted his head like a dog hearing a new word for the first time. Like he was trying to figure her out. And then she said, "They won't think much at all if I'm only in here for ten minutes though."

"It's already been five," he said.

"Then we should be doin' more kissin' and less talkin', don't you think?"

All that puzzling left his brow, and he pulled her close and they kissed. His mouth moved over hers, all soft and hungry. She needed more of Harry than she was ever going to be able to have in this bunkhouse. Or in her aunt and uncle's place, either. She needed to get this man alone.

He moved his lips to her jaw, to her neck, below the ear, which made her want to tear his clothes off. Her breathing had sped up, and she put her hands on his chest to slow him down.

"I know," he said. "I know." He stopped kissing her, but his arms were still around her so when she rose from the bed, he did, too. He looked into her eyes like he was already in love and just didn't know it yet. God, his eyes were amazing. Sky blue. She wondered if it was logical to feel as much for him as she did.

But what she'd said outside was true. She'd been engaged

to Billy Bob so recently it could be measured in hours. Was she just reacting to the break-up by falling for the first man she saw afterward? Was this some kind of rebound fling?

Maybe it was a rebound fling. Maybe she should treat it as such.

"Maria?"

She was standing there face-to-face with him. His arms were around her waist and hers were around his neck, and she'd been staring into his eyes for what suddenly felt like a long time. She leaned up on tiptoe and kissed him again, a long, slow, tender kiss. And when she stood flat-footed again, she blinked slowly.

Oh, yeah, she thought. This was *definitely* going somewhere.

There was no way to oversleep in a bunkhouse full of early risers. Four of them had showered the night before, leaving four of them to take turns in the morning. There were two bathrooms, but Drew and Orrin got them first, leaving Harrison and Maria to trail behind.

He'd learned a lot last night. He didn't know what he'd expected of Maria's cousins, but he hadn't figured he'd find a celebrity and a scientist among them. He'd also learned why Bubba was the only one who called him Harrison instead of Harry. He was sensitive to the subject because he wanted to be addressed as Ethan. Harrison would make sure to call him that from now on. Not that he would likely be around much longer.

After his turn in the shower, Harrison went in search of Maria. He found her, fresh as a daisy, her mop of dark-red curls damp-dried and piled on top of her head. She was holding a coffee mug and standing in the open door, gazing outside, her back to him.

The place looked empty other than her. "Did they abandon us?"

"Left us a four-wheeler," she said. "But we'd best hurry. They're like vultures at breakfast."

"I bet." He came up to her in the doorway, seeing a steaming mug on the table as he passed and picking it up. "This for me?"

"Sure is. Bubba made it before he headed back." She shrugged. "I think they're tryin' to give us some alone time."

"Considerate of them." He sidled up beside her.

"Presumptive of them," she said. "I ought to line 'em up and smack 'em upside their heads."

"Oh," he said, and he heard his own tone. Confused, surprised maybe.

She left the bunkhouse, coffee mug in hand, and started walking toward the main house, ignoring the perfectly good four-wheeler sitting a few yards away, so he fell into step beside her.

After a few slow steps, without looking up at him, she said, "I been thinkin' about it all night."

"About... what?" He thought he knew.

"Us. This." She indicated the two of them with her hand.

"Oh," he said. "Me, too."

"My feelings are… well, I don't want to scare you, but they feel kind of…" She paused, tilted her head. "Different from past experience."

"Different, how?" He didn't mean to ask the question, but he'd been thinking something similar, and he wanted to know. Not that there had been many past experiences for him. But none of them had been like this. He didn't know what this was.

She sipped her coffee and kept on walking. Her steps were slow and easy, her jeans brushing through purple clover blossoms. They walked along a fence line, with horses grazing in the sprawling, wildflower-strewn pasture to the left of it.

"I don't know, exactly," she said. "Bigger maybe. No, that's not quite right. Deeper. That's closer."

"Deeper," he repeated, nodding, considering it.

"And I ain't fixin' to get my heart broke."

He hesitated to reply again. Words came into his mind, but he played them to himself first, then revised, and played them again.

"It's not that I don't *want* to… you know. I'm no blushin' virgin."

Her eyes and long pause told him a reply was required at this juncture, so he blurted, "Neither am I."

She grinned. "The way you talk about your life being all work, I gotta admit, I wondered if I was gonna be your first."

And then he was even more confused. "I thought you just said we're not going to... you know."

"Well, not *yet,*" she said. "*Obviously.*"

"Obviously," he repeated. He had no idea what she was talking about. She might as well have lapsed into Aramaic.

"It might not even be real," she said at length. "I did just ditch my own weddin' on Saturday. This could be some kind of... rebound reaction."

He nodded. "Did he break your heart?"

She snort-laughed, shaking her head. Some of her coffee sloshed over the rim of her mug. "I was disappointed about that beautiful weddin' goin' to waste, and not havin' the reception, and havin' to return all the gifts— which my mom and aunts have already taken care of for me." She ran her open palm over the fluffy tops of the tallest grasses alongside the well-worn path from bunkhouse to main. "I have a great family."

"Can't argue with you, there."

"I was disappointed about not marryin', I suppose. But not marryin' Billy Bob specifically? Not so much. When I could take stock, it felt more like relief. I didn't realize how much I wanted to call it off until I called it off, you know?"

"I do."

She raised her eyebrows high. "That's four times."

They'd stopped walking. They'd crossed more than half the distance to the main house. It was something to see, the Texas Brand, wide green meadows and pastures interspersed with brown patches and scrubby brush lots, stretching all the way to the sky in every direction. Cattle grazing as far as the eye could see.

And yet, she was way prettier. She fit this place as if it had been created around her, as her backdrop.

He took a deep breath, and said, "Just so we're on the same page, can you be more specific about what you mean by 'not yet'?"

"Well, aren't *you* eager?" She smiled at him like sunbeams, her cheeks blushing pink. "I'll take that as a compliment."

"It was," he said. "Is."

She sighed, and reaching over, clasped his hand in hers. "I don't know, exactly. Maybe… maybe when you decide to stay."

CHAPTER TEN

*B*reakfast at the Texas Brand with the whole family there was an experience like none before. Harrison's family had been just him, Lily, Mom, and Dad. And then it had been just him, Lily, and Dad. But lately, more like just Lily and Dad. He'd already broken his promise to his mom. And neither of them had called him out on it.

Oatmeal had always been the weekday go-to breakfast in his family. On weekends, kid's choice. Lily picked on Saturdays and Harrison on Sundays. Lily always picked pancakes. Harrison could never decide on a favorite. Every time he chose a breakfast, he was disappointed, thinking he should've chosen a different one.

Buyer's remorse.

There was no chance of that there. They served breakfast outside, at some of the tables they'd probably had on hand for the wedding reception. With the whole family present, there were too many to fit, even in the large dining room.

As they drew near the crowd, an older version of Willow rose from her spot and waved, "I'm Taylor," she said. "He's Wes," with a nod to the man beside her. "Willow's parents. Figured you could use a refresher." Her long dark braid had silver strands.

"Penny and Ben," said the blond woman beside them. Her husband was like a fair-haired version of Garrett. "Drew and Orrin's folks."

"Adam and Kristen," said the couple across from them, laughing at each other for speaking at the same time. Wow, the love between them was obvious in that shared laugh. "Childless cat people," Kristen added.

"Elliot, and my beloved Esmeralda," said a lanky man near a food-laden table, with a loaded plate in his hand. He was a paler version of Trevor. Same wiry build, same curly hair, only Elliot's was reddish brown. Beside him, Esmeralda had flowing black curls touched with frost, here and there. Garrett and Chelsea stood beside them— his hosts. From the orange juice turret, Baxter's parents reminded him their names were Jasmine and Luke. They both looked too young to have a biochemist for a son.

Maria and her cousins had a table to themselves. He bet it had once been the kids' table. Now it was the cool table, and Maria pulled him there.

"Thanks, for the refresher," Harrison said. "It helped."

Food was passed, and he marveled and piled way too much onto his plate. At one point he exclaimed, "There are home fries again!"

Maria laughed, clapping a hand over her mouth, maybe to keep the food in there.

So, they ate. There wasn't much talk for a while. Eventually, Garrett said, "They're forecasting rain end of the month."

"Hallelujah!" Elliot slapped his thigh. "It's about time."

"We've been trucking in water for the horses," Wes put in. "Speakin' of which…"

"Yeah, I was getting to that." Garrett set his napkin on his plate. "If everyone's done—"

There was a murmur of agreement, and people started passing their plates toward him. He got up. "Wait right here." Bubba and Chelsea both got up to help him, and then there was no more left to carry.

They were back in a flash, with freshly filled, jumbo-sized coffee carafes, one for each table. There were murmurs of appreciation as cups were filled.

"They were for the weddin'," Maria's mother said.

Everybody went silent, and every gaze shot to Maria. She was stiff, her head down. How he knew exactly what she was feeling, he couldn't have said, but he did. She was ashamed she'd put them all to so much trouble and cost them so much money for nothing.

He touched her shoulder on autopilot then tried to pretend he was brushing a crumb off it or something, which probably looked just as… intimate.

And then her mother, Jessi, smiled at him, and he had a flash of Maria in twenty-some odd years. "I'd much rather use 'em for this," Jessi said. "Thank *Gawd* you didn't marry that shithead Billy Bob, Maria Michele."

And it seemed the dam of silence and small talk was broken.

"Can you *imagine?*" Chelsea asked, "having to put up with *him* at family gatherings? I was dreading it."

"Manners like a billy goat," Garrett said.

"That's an insult to billy goats," Elliot put in.

Their kidding had the desired effect, because Maria lifted her head. She didn't look ashamed anymore. She looked relieved and a little bit playful. "Farts out loud and blames the dog," she said.

Laughter erupted.

Maria finished her coffee, leaned back in her chair, smiling at the chaotic chatter of her family around her. She said, "You know, there's still two free bedrooms, if you want to have your sister and dad come down."

"I told you before, I don't want to put them in danger." He'd sounded short, but before he could fix it, she was talking again.

"I just thought they might be in more danger *not* bein' here, what with Robert on the lam, and Carrie missin', and Solomon…" She shrugged. "But what do I know? You're the genius." She beamed at her aunts, but it didn't reach her eyes. "Breakfast was fantastic. Thank you." Then she got up and headed into the house.

When the door closed, there was a momentary delay before the chitchat resumed again, but as soon as it did, the youngest Brand, Drew, whispered, "This is where you go after her and apologize." She didn't lean in, or even look his way, just kept on stirring her coffee.

"Thank you for breakfast," he said, getting up. "I'm

uh…" He didn't have an exit line, so he just shrugged and headed inside. He credited the family with staying silent until he'd crossed the porch and stepped through the squeaky screen door into the living room. But he heard one or two laughs and a couple of "gol'derns" through it, all the same.

The big house was quiet, except for the snores of the hound dog and the rattling sounds coming from the kitchen. He headed that way.

It looked like a tornado had torn through a diner. Maria was in the midst of the mess. She'd taken off her button-down shirt. It hung over the back of a kitchen chair. She'd put on an apron to keep her tank top clean and was at the sink, rinsing plates, making stacks. The dishwasher was open and empty, so he walked up beside her, started taking the rinsed plates and loading them into the machine.

"I'm sorry, Maria. I didn't mean to snap at you out there."

"Yes, you did," she said. "I'd like to know why."

He managed to fit all the plates on the bottom rack, so he walked around gathering up smaller dishes to fill the top. It would take multiple loads to clean them all. Maria had moved on to washing the pots and pans. "It wasn't you," he said. "It's been a stressful time. One of my friends is dead, one is missing, a third might be responsible, and my life's work has been stolen. It's… a lot."

"It is a lot." She lowered her head. "But whatever we've got going on here is gonna require openness. Honesty. Flat out, nothin' held back. And I feel like… that wasn't it."

He'd filled the top rack and went to work on the silverware, because it kept him from having to look into her eyes. She was perceptive as hell, and she wasn't letting him get away with anything. He said, "I might've had the feeling you had an ulterior motive for wanting to get them down here."

"Like what?"

He shrugged.

She sighed, finished drying a pan, and hung it from a rack of them. "Like that they'd fall in love with it here, and never want to leave, and all your reasons not to stay would evaporate like mornin' dew in the hot Texas sun?"

Her accent made him feel like his brain was softening in that same sunshine. He fitted the loaded flatware rack into its spot in the dishwasher and closed the door. "Something like that."

She nodded, turning to lean back against the sink while the water drained, wiping her hands on a white towel. "That was a good guess. I *was* thinkin' that. But I was also thinkin' they'd be safer here. I wouldn't risk your family's lives just to try to land a man." She smacked the towel onto the counter. "I don't have to do anything to land a man, besides pick one. You know that, right?"

"I figured that out walking around town with you. Men aren't subtle."

"I'm set for life, financially. Got my business to add to the coffers, I'm educated—"

"— and smart, and drop-dead gorgeous," he said. He might as well go for broke. He had hurt her feelings. He'd seen his dad screw up and make it right with his mom a thousand times. "And you're funny and brave, and you're kind and compassionate, and you have velvet brown eyes, and when you look at me I feel it all the way to the bone." He moved nearer as he spoke, and by the time he'd finished, he was right up close. He pushed a loose curl off her forehead. "I'm sorry I was short with you. I might be a little bit shaken up."

"With all that's happened?" She asked so softly it was just warm breath across his lips.

"No. That's the weird part. I'm shaken up about this. Us."

"Why?"

"Because... it's impossible. And irresistible." Then he kissed her. She wrapped her arms around his neck and kissed him back.

A throat cleared, and they startled apart, Harrison turning automatically. Maria's aunt Chelsea stood there with the two empty coffee carafes. "Sorry," she said. Then she looked around her kitchen, and said, "Wow. Nice job. Thanks."

"We still have to wipe up," Maria said. She took a clean dishrag from the sink and began wiping down the nearby counter.

"Well, it's appreciated. And Harry, no pressure, but if you do decide you'd like your family close while this all shakes out, they're welcome. How many are there?"

"Just my dad and sister."

"Then there's room. Your call, though."

"Thanks. It's a thoughtful invitation. I'm going to call my sister and see what she thinks of the idea."

"Good. Now get outta my kitchen. You've done plenty."

Maria and Harry walked outside just as a horse came galloping in. Miguel, one of the newer ranch hands, slid off and approached Uncle Garrett, who rose to his feet, looking worried.

"We got a cow down in the north pasture. She needs a vet."

Maria scanned the tables, but she didn't see her mother. Her dad was gone, too.

"Jess got a call from the Stockwell place," Uncle Garrett said. "Horse off her feed."

Everyone else looked at her, too. She nodded with more confidence than she felt, and said, "I'll get my stuff. We'll take ATVs; it'll be faster than saddlin' horses."

"There's already horses saddled," Drew called. She was coming out the front of the stable with a pair of chestnut sisters, Thelma and Louise. "Orrin and I were planning to ride out. Take 'em, go on."

"I'll saddle up and come with you," Trevor said. "But don't wait, I'll catch up fast. Rusty's been teasin' for a ride since I got here." He nodded toward the green-and-wildflower meadow out past the stable, where several horses grazed. His horse Rusty, red with a shaggy mane, stood at the fence, looking back at him. In apparent response to all the attention on him, Rusty shook his mane and blew.

Maria turned to Harry beside her. "Will you come with me?"

"I wasn't planning to stay behind."

Trevor passed them on his way into the house and then came out again with a rifle. "I'm takin' one of yours, Uncle Garrett," he called. "Mine's in the bunkhouse." He didn't even pause in his long-legged stride toward the stable.

Maria took Harry's hand and ran around the side of the house where her van was parked, out of the way. Aunt Chelsea didn't like cars to stay lined up in front of the porch. Spoiled the whole point of the porch, she said, which was the view.

She opened the van, shouting over her shoulder, "Miguel. What am I treating out there?"

"Wolf, maybe. She's all cut up, agitated. Jake was fixin' to dart her when I rode out."

She grabbed the appropriate items, shoving them into a case that would fit in the saddle bags. Harry took it, and she packed a second, smaller one. Then they headed for the stables, where Drew was already strapping saddle bags onto one of the mares.

"I finally get to see you work," Harry said while they walked fast.

She blinked and looked his way, and those blue eyes were on her, and sparkling. "No fair. I haven't seen you work."

"It would be a good sleep aid," he said.

They shared a smile, and she marveled at how in sync with him she felt.

Drew opened the flap on the saddle bag as they approached, and Harry fit the bigger med pack in. Maria went to the other side to load the smaller bag and tied the flap down. Then she and Harry mounted simultaneously. Miguel rode out. Maria clicked her tongue and squeezed the mare's sides between her heels. "Let's go, Louise."

And they were off.

They followed Miguel at a gentle lope over a well-worn trail. When the terrain changed, they slowed to a walk.

Behind her, Harry said, "Why did we slow down?" He leaned forward, patting his horse's neck.

"The ground's uneven. There are loose stones. Smart to slow down. Gives the horses a breather, too," Maria said. She slowed just enough to allow more space between her and Miguel, so they could talk in private. "You've met my whole family now. Well, exceptin' the Oklahoma crew. I'm dying to meet yours, too, but this mornin', my only thought was keepin' 'em safe. I mean it."

He rode up beside her when the trail widened. It was still littered with boulders, but he did fine, giving Thelma her head and letting her pick her way through.

"I know that," he said. "I'm sorry. I just… I want to make sure you know that my family isn't the only obstacle."

"There's your career," she said, nodding slowly. "The one you think can only happen at some ivy league, yankee school."

"I just don't want to hurt you."

"And I don't want to be hurt. But… Jeeze, Harry, my aunt Taylor heads up the Archeology Department at a university only a half-hour's drive from here. And Baxter's doin' his research at another, even bigger school, same distance, opposite direction. You can have a career anywhere."

"I don't know if I have a career *left*."

"That's crazy talk. Anyone smart enough to come up with what you did is smart enough to do it again. Heck, you'll probably do something even bigger and better next time."

"I can't even think about next time until I get this time ironed out."

"You know what I think?" She didn't wait for an answer. "I think, even if you'd sold your solar tile for a gazillion dollars, you'd have gone on to invent something else. It's your art."

"My art." He smiled over at her, and she noticed how good he looked in that hat she'd bought him. "I've never thought of it as art before."

"It's creative, it's brilliant, it's destined to change the world, and it's what you were born to do. If that's not art, what is?" She reached toward him, and he reached back. They joined hands as the trail approached an open plain where wild roses grew. "I think you'll create more no matter where you call home, and I think it'll happen whether you get your tile back or not." Then she frowned and said, "Did you get hold of your sister? You haven't told me what she said."

"She hasn't replied yet," he said.

She nodded, looked ahead, where Miguel had already nudged his horse into a canter.

"This is the north pasture," she said several minutes later. Longhorns grazed, and ranch hands were gathered in a huddle around the fallen cow. She was white with red freckles. The hands' horses were tethered a few yards away.

"Is that a *road?*" Harry sounded surprised as he gazed just beyond the farthest edge of the pasture.

"The Texas Brand is huge," Maria replied. "This is one of three public roads that run through it. North Brand Lane." She dismounted, took one of the cases from a saddlebag and then went to kneel beside the cow. The hands dissipated, leaving only her, Harry, and Jake, the leather-faced foreman. "Trevor's a few minutes back," Maria said. "Did she collapse, or...?"

"I darted her," Jake said from beneath a dusty hat. Maria could not remember a time when he hadn't been foreman.

There was a rag tied around the cow's hind leg. Maria checked to be sure she was breathing okay, listened to her heart, affixed an elastic tourniquet near the wound, tying it tight, then untied the rag. Blood welled immediately. She tightened the band, and it stopped. Good, good. She turned to fetch the bigger bag, but Harry was behind her, kneeling with it already unzipped. "What do you need, doc?"

"The saline— looks like a bottle of water."

He handed her a large bottle of saline solution, and she rinsed the cut. As she dabbed blood away, cleaned out every particle, disinfected, and finally stitched each wound together, Harry remained nearby. He was quick to hand her whatever she asked for, providing she used a descriptive term rather than its official name. Their hands touched every time he passed her anything. The first time, accidentally. But after that he did it on purpose, and then she returned like for like. Like a lovers' game, woven into her work. And yet, they were not lovers. Not yet.

She wanted them to be.

When she finished the stitches, she sprayed the wound in Blu-Kote. "She needs to be isolated and watched, in case the wolf was rabid."

"What if it was?" Harry asked.

"She's vaccinated. But it's not 100%. We just need to wait and see."

"No bandage?" Harry asked.

"No, that blue stuff protects it. You can't keep a bandage on a cow." She turned to Jake. "Get a trailer out here to haul her to the barn. And have the men watch for predators. That was a bite. Something grabbed her from behind."

"We already found it," Jake said. He nodded toward a skin-and-bones canine lying dead a few feet away.

"You killed it?" she asked.

"Cow did," Jake replied with an admiring look at the unconscious animal. "She kicked and stomped it. Crushed the skull."

"Did it have young?" Maria asked.

"Lone male," Jake said.

"Okay. We can test the animal for rabies and know for sure. I'll need someone to take that carcass to the clinic. Wear gloves. No unnecessary contact."

"Got it. We can take it from here, ma'am," Jake said.

Maria nodded and Harry took her hand to pull her to her feet. While she'd been talking to Jake, he'd picked up the mess. He'd put the used tools and rubbish into a plastic zipper bag, before returning it to the case. She watched him walk to the horses, admiring him to her heart's content. It suddenly felt to Maria as if Harry was meant to be her man. It felt like he was the one. She hadn't thought *the one* existed for her. Hadn't thought she wanted him to. But now she did.

He put the case into the saddle bag, tied the flap down. His black eye had faded to a pale purple. He caught her looking at him and smiled back at her.

A gunshot cracked, the horse reared, and Harry hit the ground.

CHAPTER ELEVEN

*M*aria screamed Harry's name and raced toward him as chaos broke out all around her. The startled cattle were thundering away from the sound of the gunshot and directly toward them. The hands were running for their horses then racing to turn the panicked cattle. Then with a whoop, Trevor galloped by. Maria, still in motion, pointed in the direction from whence the shot had come, then fell to her knees beside Harry.

He was out cold. She looked toward the thundering cattle just as several riders managed to turn them. They'd need to turn them more, but she couldn't move Harry. She decided to trust the men and change the things she could. She opened his shirt. Blood pulsed from a well in his shoulder. She rolled him up to see the exit wound directly behind it, shirt still in place, torn and soaked with blood and dirt. Maria swore, and she never swore. She grabbed the med kit from the saddlebag and got to work to stop the bleeding.

Hoofbeats approached. Four more horses galloped toward them. Willow pulled Sundance to a stop. "We heard a rifle shot! You okay?"

"I'm good. Harry's not," Maria said. "Trevor went after the shooter."

"I'll go—" Bubba began.

"It's my job, Bubba. Stay and help here." Willow sent a worried look at Harry, then clicked her cheek, and galloped away.

Bubba slid off his horse, looped the reins around the saddle horn, and knelt beside Harry. "What can I do?"

Maria had rinsed the exit wound with saline, then alcohol, and packed the wound on both sides to stop the bleeding. "I don't know why he's unconscious," she said as she worked on the entry wound, doing all the same things.

"Hit his head," Bubba said.

She looked up at him, and he nodded at a rock sticking out of the ground a few feet from Harry's head. There was blood on it. She turned Harry's head, ran her hand over it, and felt the swollen spot in the back. "We need to get him back to the house."

She hadn't been trampled, she realized, noticing the hands and cattle not far away. The longhorns were calmer and the hands were talking gently from their horses, between her and the cattle.

Bubba looked toward the direction Willow and Trevor had gone. "Holy…"

Maria rose and looked, too. In the distance, Trevor was chasing after a man on horseback up a slight rise, swinging his lasso. He threw it, and as they watched, the lasso landed around its quarry, and Trevor gave a mighty yank.

The guy came out of his saddle so hard, Maria and Bubba winced.

"Jeeze, Lord, did he kill him?" Bubba asked.

"Willow's catching up, she'll deal with it. Let's get Harry back to the house."

Jake, the foreman, hollered from horseback, "Ambulance'll meet you at the main house." He held up his phone.

"They should be there by the time we are," Bubba said. He sent a worried look out toward where Willow had gone.

"She'll be all right," Maria said. "Willow can handle herself."

"I know, I just… Sometimes I feel bad I didn't join up like Uncle Garrett wanted me to." He picked Harry up with care, started toward his horse just as a four-wheeler came rumbling up.

Aunt Chelsea whipped off her helmet and said, "Put him behind me, Bubba. Maria, sit behind him on the cargo rack to hold him on."

Bubba set Harry upright on the ATV behind her, as instructed.

Maria climbed on behind Harry. She wrapped one arm around him and used the other to hang on.

They started off and she looked behind them. Willow was riding with her prisoner in front of her, his hands cuffed in front of him. Even Maria knew better than to cuff a prisoner in front like that, so she must have a reason. His head hung low. He might be unconscious.

Chelsea drove slow enough not to bounce her off, and then several of her aunts and uncles came riding toward them, thundering past.

"Don't they know Willow got the guy?" Maria asked loudly enough so Chelsea could hear.

"They'll make sure there aren't others. Your dad's on the way with deputies, too." Maria looked behind them. Bubba was riding along not far back, watching over them, scanning all directions.

By the time they got back to the house, an ambulance was waiting, as the foreman had predicted. Uncle Garrett was talking to the EMTs. Then finally, Chelsea eased the machine to a stop. Maria held Harry to her while Chelsea got off, and then the medics took over. They moved Harry with extreme care from the ATV to a stretcher and into the back of their vehicle. One of the medics jumped in with Harry and began checking him over.

"I'll follow you in," Maria said as the rear door closed. "Better get another ambulance for the shooter, Uncle Garrett. Trevor roped him right off his horse and last I saw, he wasn't lookin' too good."

"I'll drive you," Bubba said. "Somebody needs to keep you and Harry safe until Willow can send a deputy to stand guard. Wait here, I'll get the truck."

Harry was sitting in a little white chair, at a little white table. Both were made of metal in filigree swirls. He held an impossibly tiny china cup between his thumb and fore-finger, and his mom poured tea from a matching miniature teapot.

He looked up from the thimble-sized cup to her face. She was beautiful. Her angel blond hair had never seen a stylist and her smile could light a dark room. He looked into her big blue eyes last of all.

She said, "What are you so afraid of?" and she poured his cup until it was overflowing and wetting his hand.

He jolted awake, then thought it was another layer of the dream. He was still gazing into beautiful eyes. But these were velvety brown and full of emotion. Maria's eyes.

His senses were coming online one by one. He opened his mouth to ask what had happened, but what emerged was, "*Ow.*"

"Oh!" Maria jabbed a bedside button, making him aware he was in a hospital. Okay, that explained the pain.

"What happened?" he managed.

She leaned closer, laid her hand on his cheek. "You're okay. The bullet went right through. Only hit flesh."

"Bullet?" As the fog cleared, he remembered. There'd been an injured cow, and Maria had literally put the animal's flesh back together. She was amazing. He looked at her more closely. She still wore the same clothes. Damn, it felt good, her being there.

More pieces floated into place. They'd been by the horses. There'd been a gunshot and a sledge hammer had hit him in the shoulder. He couldn't have said which had come first. He lowered his head to try to look at his shoulder, from whence his pain seemed to radiate. It was covered in bandages

"You hit a rock when you went down," Maria said. "Knocked you out cold. They did a procedure on the gunshot wound, just to give it a good cleanin', remove damaged tissue, that sort of thing. It's gon' be sore."

"What about you? Are you okay?" he asked.

"I'm fine. Coward shot once and ran. Tried to, anyway. Here."

She filled a glass from a pitcher, then elevated his bed so he could sip from a straw. He nodded when he was up far enough, drinking like he'd been lost in the desert.

She was okay. He didn't see any signs otherwise and accepted it with deep relief. His last thought before he'd fallen was that the shooter could walk right up and shoot Maria if he wanted to.

"Trevor went after the guy," Maria said. "Willow right behind him, and Bubba stayed to help you. Trevor's the one who got him, though. Roped him right off his horse. Busted his clavicle."

"They got the shooter?"

"Yep, he's in a room down the hall with two Texas Rangers guarding the door. No ID on him and he's not talking, other than to demand a phone call and a lawyer. But they'll find out who he is by morning, Willow thinks."

"You have any theories?"

She met his eyes and held them. "I haven't had time to process any of this. I've just been scared you were fixin' to die." Tears welled in her brown eyes.

"Hey, no. I'm not gonna die." He pulled her in for a one-armed hug and got lost in the smell of her hair. She had the most amazing hair. He wanted wrap her in his arms, maybe pull her into bed beside him and the covers over their heads.

She was in danger, though. He was putting her and her whole family in danger just by being near them. He clasped her hand. "I don't think I'd better go back to the ranch with you," he said.

"I knew you'd say that," she replied. He could hear the argument in her voice before she even spoke it.

A nurse came in. "You're awake! Wonderful. The doctor's still here." Then to Maria, "We'll need to check him out, 'kay?"

"Yeah, got you, of course." Maria glanced back at Harry. She was smiling, but there was a tear on her cheek. Relieved he was okay? Sad he'd mentioned leaving the ranch? He didn't even know where to go. Home, maybe.

The thought of being 3,000 miles away from Maria hurt more than the bullet hole. She was almost through the door when he finally blurted, "Don't go home yet, okay?"

She looked back at him, surprised, and then she pushed the heel of her hand across her cheek and said, "Okay."

The "Family Waiting Area" was an alcove off one side of the unit, just past the patient rooms, which were arranged on three sides of the nurse's desk. Maria had a good view from there. The hallway-facing wall was glass. The rest, just a square room with chairs, three vending machines, and a TV. She lingered in the doorway while a medical team examined Harry. She was barely able to keep her eyes from the hospital room three doors to the left where two Texas Rangers stood outside the door. The man who'd shot Harry was in that room. She wanted to storm in there and give him an ass whooping he wouldn't soon forget.

Willow came up the hall with a tall, handsome man and a brown-haired girl in her mamma's pencil skirt and blazer, who introduced herself as "Special Agent Agnes Hofstadler, FBI." Her glasses were the biggest part of her heart-shaped face.

"Detective Connor Wynn, down from the New York State Police," the man said. He was as tall as a Texan, and bore a thick head of dark-brown hair, and Irish-green eyes that twinkled when he smiled.

Maria said, "Maria Brand Monroe," automatically invoking the power of her family name when faced with anyone who intimidated her. But these two showed no sign of recognizing it.

"We were hoping to talk to Mr. Hyde," Agent Hofstadler said. She was pretty, Maria realized, but hiding it. Probably wise in her line of work.

"He just woke up a few minutes ago," Maria told them. "But then everyone rushed in to check him over. I imagine you can talk to him after they get done."

From further up the hall, a voice was raised. "I'm his lawyer, and I *insist* you let me in!"

They all turned toward the prisoner's room to see a

short man with hair as thick and brown as a televangelist's and black-framed glasses, yelling at the Rangers.

"I've got it," said Detective Wynn, and headed that way to help them out. He looked at the lawyer's ID then nodded at the cops to let him in.

The doctor and two nurses exited Harry's room, and Maria said, "Let me go see if he's up to this, first, okay?" she said.

"He has no choice but to be up to it," said Agent Hofstadler.

"Just give me a minute." Maria went back into Harry's room, glancing down the hall where the irritated, jockey-sized lawyer emerged from the shooter's room and stomped, as if furious, toward the elevator.

"That was fast," Willow muttered to the agent and the detective.

"Hey," said Harry.

Maria went the rest of the way in, meeting his eyes with an encouraging smile. He was sitting up, his legs dangling over the side of the bed. "I need my phone. Lily and Dad have probably been trying to get hold of me. How long has it been? Can you get my clothes?"

She nodded, didn't answer the questions, and went to the closet. She knew the room better than he did, having been in it for nearly twenty-four hours.

"There's an FBI agent and a New York detective here," she said, handing him the stack. He frowned at the clothes, which were his, but not what he'd been wearing. "I asked Aunt Chelsea to bring them in for you. I hope you don't mind she went through your stuff. She took back the ones you were wearin'. The shirt will have to be thrown out, but that's up to you."

"I don't mind her going through my stuff. I just want to get out of here."

She slammed her eyes closed when he said that, so he wouldn't see the hurt. He saw it anyway, and rose from the bed, setting the clothes aside. He put his hands on her shoulders. "Maria, you could have been shot out there, today," he said.

Yesterday, she thought, and knew she had to tell him. "They're not after me, they're after you."

"But you were in the line of fire. Again. You were nearly mowed down by a feed truck yesterday." Day before yesterday, she thought. "The longer I stay near you, the more danger you're in." She caught his gaze, wondering if he cared as much as the tone of his voice and the look in his eyes suggested. He looked away. "All of you. Your whole family."

He set his belongings on the bed, pulled on the clean jockey shorts and jeans underneath the hospital gown. He undid the snaps on the the sleeves to get it off around his IV tubing, but then looked askance at the T-shirt, probably realizing he could not put it on over the IV in his arm. So, he stood there in jeans and socks, shirtless.

He glanced at Maria as if for help, but she didn't meet his eyes, because she was looking at his chest, and didn't feel an ounce of shame about it. She moved closer, put her hands on his chest and pushed until he sat on the edge of the bed again. Then she took hold of his hand, turned his arm and looked at the IV.

"I could take this out for you, but I think we should wait for the nurse. And she'll probably be back before Agent Agnes and Detective Hotty finish questioning you."

"Detective Hotty?"

"Dare I hope you're jealous?" She didn't give him time to reply, and said, "Good. But you don't need to be. I only have eyes for you, Harry. Now wrap a blanket around your shoulders or something. How do you expect anyone to think straight, when you walk around like that?"

He smiled at her and reached for his discarded hospital gown.

Maria turned and called through the open door, "You can come in."

Willow, Agent Hofstadler, and Detective Wynn entered the room and formed a half circle around the foot of Harry's bed.

Harry had put his hospital gown back on, sleeves snapped over his shoulders, and was sitting upright just like before, only this time the legs hanging over the side of the bed wore jeans and the feet, a pair of his own socks.

They introduced themselves, and Harry said, "Has anyone heard from my sister?"

"Can you tell them what happened, Harry?" Willow asked.

"We went to tend to an injured cow. Somebody shot me. Listen, I called my sister. She didn't answer. I texted her; she hadn't replied."

"It was one gunshot," Maria said. "From about a hundred yards away, near the road. North Brand, that is. He fled on horseback."

"And your cousin went after him?" Agent Hofstadler asked.

"Cousins, plural. But Trevor's the one who caught him."

"And how did the suspect wind up with a broken collar bone?" The short agent pushed her big glasses up higher on her nose, directing her question at Harry.

"I was unconscious at the time," Harry said.

"I didn't see that part," Maria said.

"Huh." The agent looked at her companion. He looked back, raised his eyebrows and shrugged, a whaddya-gonna-do sort of gesture. Agnes rolled her eyes and returned her attention to Harry. "How many people know you're staying with the Brands?"

Harry lowered his head. "The whole town," he said.

"Locals saw them together when he got hit by the truck," Willow said. "Everyone else saw the video of it. Dang, was it the same shoulder, Harry?"

"It was," he said.

Willow sighed and shook her head in a show of sympathy. "No question the hit and run was deliberate," she went on. "We found the truck abandoned off a side road in the middle of nowhere. It'd been stolen three towns over."

"We're gonna need to see those files," Agent Hofstadler said.

"I don't think they want me dead, though," Harry said.

"What makes you think that?" the agent asked. "Given that they just shot at you, I mean." It was impossible to tell if she was being sarcastic with her deadpan delivery.

"Solomon's death wasn't deliberate," Harry replied. "Everyone thinks all this is Robert, but even if it was, I know him. He would never have hurt Solomon. And he wouldn't hurt Carrie, either."

"But the guy who tried to shoot you, the guy in that room down the hall, isn't Robert," Maria said.

Harry's face didn't seem to register that. Maybe couldn't. He was clinging to hope. He looked around the room, and his gaze stopped then widened on the white board, which had that day's date in marker across the top.

"I've been here a whole day? Did Lily ever call back? Where's my phone?"

"I have it, I have it." Maria returned to the closet, took out a large plastic bag, and from it, removed his phone and his wallet. When she handed him the phone, he tapped his messages open, and searched. "She never texted back. I texted her yesterday, and she never replied. Lily never ignores a text. Not from me."

"I know," Maria said. "And I knew you'd contacted her. I told Willow yesterday. She had Ithaca PD send people to check on her last night," Maria said.

Harry looked at her. "And?" She hesitated and he said, "Maria?"

Agent Hofstadler said, "Your sister wasn't in her apartment. Her car and her handbag were missing, all of which suggest she left of her own volition. Her phone is apparently offline. We're searching for her, watching her bank transactions, and monitoring her phone pings."

"What about my father?" His words were nearly a croak.

"Your dad's fine," Willow said. "There's excellent security at his apartment complex and officers are checking in periodically, just in case. But there's no indication either of them are in danger."

"Except that my sister has vanished," he returned.

The PA system crackled, then "Code blue, five west," just as a herd of staff, some pushing equipment, stampeded past the open door toward the prisoner's room.

The three cops lunged out of Harry's room, Maria and Harry right behind them. Harry was still in jeans and a hospital gown, rolling his IV pole with him. Staff had flooded into the suspect's room as the Rangers, looked on.

"No," Willow said, moving that way.

"What the hell happened?" Agent Hofstadler demanded.

People were pumping the shooter's chest in between electric jolts, but nothing was working. Harry was still in the doorway of his own room, but he'd found his shoes. He shoved his phone and wallet into his pockets, and he was holding his shirt in his hand.

The commotion stopped. The people left the shooter's room, exited slowly, shaking their lowered heads. Dead. The shooter was dead.

"That lawyer," Maria said softly. "He did something to him."

Willow nodded. "He sure didn't die from a busted clavicle."

Harry whispered, "I have to find my sister. I have to go home and check on my father. I have to—"

Maria closed her hand around his. "We will."

Harrison had been discharged and was dressed in his own clothes by the time Willow, the Rangers, the FBI agent, and the NYSP detective had been ready to move the body of the shooter from the room where he'd died.

Willow, who didn't want the body out of her sight and who kept muttering "right under our noses" over and over to no one in particular, glanced back at him. "I have Uncle Garrett workin' on the fastest way to get you home to Ithaca to check on your family, Harry," she said. "Follow me. I don't want you out of my sight, either."

So Harrison, Maria, Agent Hofstadler, and Detective Wynn followed the dead man on a stretcher with a sheet over his face, into an elevator. They rode two levels down then exited into a dim concrete corridor. The solid metal door, gray and unmarked, led into the morgue. At least he thought it was the morgue. It was a small, cool room lined with medical equipment, and a single "corpse-drawer" in one wall. Just one.

He was terrified for his sister.

"Only one?" Maria asked, nodding at the drawer in the wall. Her voice trembled a little. She was not comfortable so close to a dead body.

"Even that barely ever gets used," the attendant said. He was a scrawny, sandy-haired young man whose jaw was the biggest part of his whole head. "Small town. The dead go straight to the funeral home most of the time."

"Well, this guy won't need it long," Agent Hofstadler said. "I'm shipping him to the nearest forensics lab, soon as I can arrange it. We just need to preserve evidence until then."

The attendant nodded and took hold of the drawer's handle to pull it open, saying, "I can't remember the last time we—" And then he stopped in mid-sentence, because the drawer was not empty. There was already a body in it, zipped into a body bag.

"Well, that's not right," the attendant said. "How could...?" He pulled the drawer the rest of the way open. Willow had to move the gurney with the dead shooter on it, to make room for the drawer to open all the way.

"Who is this? There's not supposed to be a body here. Where's the paperwork? Who the hell..." The attendant asked no one, as he unzipped the body bag and folded it open.

"Holy God," Harry said. "That's Robert!"

CHAPTER TWELVE

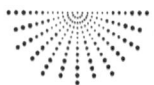

"Stay at the ranch," Maria said. "Just for tonight."

Harrison lowered his head, because he couldn't refuse her while looking into her eyes. And yet, when he wasn't looking at her, he kept seeing Robert again, lying on a stainless-steel bed, his skin gray-blue, a small round hole in the center of his forehead. So he looked at Maria again. "Robert didn't do any of it," he said and realized he'd said it a few times already.

They'd been sent packing. There hadn't been room in the tiny morgue anyway for that many living bodies and two dead ones. So they'd decided to return to the ranch for the moment. They were in Maria's van, and she was driving.

"I was sure Robert wouldn't hurt anyone, and Solomon was an accident," he went on. "But it wasn't Robert at all. He was a victim, too. And Carrie's still missing, and I can't find my sister. You..." He stopped talking, swallowed hard. "If you're near me, you're in danger."

"So, what are you fixin' to do? Head home and put your *dad* in danger?"

He opened his mouth, then closed it again. "I have to make sure he's okay."

"I know you do. I agree with you on that. So we're gettin' a private jet to fly you to Ithaca. No questions asked. No commercial airline. Nobody to follow you. As far as anyone knows, you'll still be holed up at the ranch."

He shook his head slowly. "Where are we supposed to get a private jet?"

"*Hon,*" she said, with a look that pitied his lack of knowledge. "My family owns one of the biggest operations in seven counties. We know people. Most of them owe one or more of us a favor. And some of those favor-owers have private jets."

He looked her way. "I keep forgettin'. You all seem so…"

"What? Hayseed? Redneck?"

"Down to earth," he said. "Relatable. I want to say ordinary, but the truth is your family is far from it."

"Oh," she said. "Thanks. I agree."

"The private jet's a good idea."

"Because if nobody knows you're goin' up there, you won't put your father in danger by bein' near him," she said.

He nodded.

"And so, by extension, I wouldn't be in any danger from your proximity, either."

He frowned at her, realizing she had tricked him with logic. "Not that it will matter, with you in Texas and me in New York," he said.

"Oh, no. I'll be in New York, too." She took her eyes off the road long enough to look right into his. "I come with the plane."

She came with the plane.

Harrison didn't have to spend the night at the ranch, because three hours later he was sitting in the most comfortable airplane seat in existence. It was one of six plush seats, in sets of two, facing one another. There was also a small sofa, full bathroom, a galley with coffee maker, and a mini fridge full of beverages.

"I had no idea private jets were like... flying campers," he said.

"It'd have to be a *nice* camper. This thing's amazin'." Maria was rummaging in the mini fridge. She popped the top on a Coke, ignoring the wine bottle with the gift card dangling from its neck. Harrison had been too curious not to read the card. "Always happy to lend a hand." It was signed, "Senator Mark Tompkins."

"Pilot said four hours," Maria said, nodding toward the closed and locked door between the cockpit and the passenger area. "There's a TV." She made that part a question.

He nodded and she located a remote and started flipping through the available selections. When they both said, "Oh!" at the same time, she was on *O Brother, Where Art Thou?* She looked back at him. "You love this one, too?"

He shrugged. "It's a good movie."

"One of my faves."

It had been his mom's favorite, as well. They'd watched it every year on her birthday. She'd loved movies. For a moment, his mother stood there in front of him, gauzy and beautiful. She was smiling and turning in a circle, holding the skirts of a long blue sundress she'd worn on one of those birthdays. Her head was angled downward, eyes up, smile bright.

Maria clicked play then returned to rummaging. She found a package of chocolate chip cookies, and returned to her seat, swiveling it so they both faced the screen.

When she offered him a cookie, he took one and a dewy can. Then he tried to focus on the movie but failed. And the cookie didn't appeal, which meant the world was off its axis. He checked his phone to see if Lily had replied, and then he tried to track her phone from his. He and Lily had convinced their father to enable this feature for them both by saying they were all doing it for each other, so none of them would ever be lost.

He'd never had reason to use it.

The app said his sister's phone was offline.

Maria slid her hand over his. It was cool from the Coke can, and he found that soothing, for some reason. He wanted to flip his hand over, interlace their fingers, and give a squeeze. But he didn't. He was trying not to lead her on. There was no future for them.

She took her hand away and returned to looking at the TV screen, munching her cookie, sipping cola. He set his drink in the cup holder untouched and willed the time to pass quickly. They were all alone. The pilot was behind a locked door and oblivious to them. The movie was playing with what might've been the greatest soundtrack of all time.

Maria fished a little packet of wet wipes from her bag and offered him one.

"Thanks." He wiped his fingers. She wiped hers. She put the packet back into her bag and came out with something else.

"Mint?" she asked

"Sure." He accepted the wintergreen Life Saver she pressed from the pack into his hand. She popped one as well. They settled back and watched the movie until his mint had dissolved to nothing in his mouth.

And then she got out of her chair and came to his. She sat on his lap, facing him, one leg on either side. "There's nothing we can do to help until we get there."

"I kn-know."

She pressed her palms to his cheeks and kissed him. Oh, man, how she kissed him. And before his brain finished processing the surprise of it and what to do about it, his body was already fully involved. His arms wrapped around her waist and his mouth joined them in the mutiny.

She sat up a little and said, "Is this okay?"

"Yeah. I mean, I thought you said not until I decided to stay."

"Yeah. I did say that. But now I'm kind of afraid you're never gonna decide it, and I'll have missed my one and only chance to be with you." And then she pulled her blouse off over her head, and there were a pair of perfect boobs in a pretty pink bra in front of his face.

"Uh-huh." He put his hands on them, bra and all.

She arched her back a little, pressing closer. She said something else, but his brain's language centers were no longer functioning. He pulled her closer and kissed her again. They undressed each other, trying not to part their bodies while they did so, mashing them back together immediately if they had to separate at all. And then they were skin against skin, and he was in heaven, and trying to go slow and savor every second. His forearm supported the curve of her back while he threaded his fingers through her glorious copper curls.

She was everything, his entire world in those moments. Every other thought was banished from his mind, and there was only her, her brown eyes, her soft lips, her warm skin, the sounds of her breaths, the pulse in her neck thrumming faster as he nibbled there. She moved with him, over him, taking him into her, and moaning when she did, and he wouldn't have known or cared if the plane had crashed. They moved together in wordless synchronicity. She lifted her mouth from his to look into his eyes as sensation crashed through her, and then she snapped her arms around him and held tight. He responded in kind, and he swore it felt, in those moments, as if they'd melded entirely.

Maria put herself back together in the restroom and got stuck in the mirror. Her eyes were round and full of something new. She wasn't sure what it was, but it was big. It was huge.

She knew, as she'd never known before, that Harry Hyde was meant for her. He was her other half. The one. This wasn't rebound from her failed wedding; this was the real deal. That hadn't even been close.

How had her family seen so clearly something entirely invisible to her? Billy Bob had never been the one. As Harry had told her, that never would have or could have worked.

Because it was Harry. It would always be Harry. She just had to be patient long enough for him to realize it, too.

When she returned, Harry had lowered the TV volume — at some point, he'd cranked it up to cover the sounds of their lovemaking. Hers, anyway. She'd really tried to be quiet, but...

She smoothed her blouse, returned to her seat.

"Touchdown in twenty minutes," the pilot said from a speaker nearby.

The hatch lowered, built-in steps gliding into place. Harrison looked out. There was a runway, a rolling meadow, and a man standing between two cars with his hands folded in front of him.

The pilot, who had opened the cockpit partition said,

"That's your rental car. That fellow will have your keys. Mr. Brand arranged it."

Harrison didn't bother asking which Mr. Brand. Maria could tell him who to thank later. Thinking of her, he turned. She was hauling her bag out of the little compartment in the back, where she'd stowed it. It was a big, soft-sided suitcase. He reached for it as she got close, and she shook her head. "You're injured. I've got it," she said. "What, you think your lovin' made me too weak to carry my own bag?"

"Your uncles and your dad would expect me to carry your bag," he said. They had not discussed what had happened between them. And they probably should, at some point. He didn't want her to think he'd taken it lightly. He didn't want her to think he didn't care. And he didn't want her to think it had changed anything. Even though it felt like it had changed everything all the way to the cellular level.

"My uncles and my dad are not you or me," she said.

All the same, he backed up to let her exit first, grabbing his own bag before he followed her down to the pavement. He came up beside her as they walked toward the two cars. They were both the same hybrid model, one green, one black.

The man in between said, "Mr. Hyde, Miss Brand," and offered a key to Harrison.

"Which one?" he asked.

The fellow nodded at the black car. Harrison looked at the key fob, popped the trunk, took Maria's bag and put them both in. When he closed the trunk, Harrison said, "Makes sense for me to drive. I know my way around."

The pilot got into the other car with the other dude, and they were already pulling away.

Maria said, "But is your shoulder up to it?"

"I'll steer left-handed."

He drove from the private air strip onto the nearest road, and then he stopped and looked at the GPS to figure out where they were, and to enter his dad's address.

"You don't want to go to your sister's first?" Maria asked.

"I do," he said. "I want to check things out, but then I figured, if whoever is after me already knows about her, they might be watching her place. Even if they already took her—"

"Don't think that," she said quickly. "But I think you're right. If someone *is* watching, they could follow us straight to your dad's. Good call."

He nodded and drove faster once they were on the road. They had a twenty-five-minute drive. And he ought to say something about what had happened between them, right?

He rolled his eyes at his inner turmoil. "That was some airplane, right?"

"Who *needs* something like that?" she asked.

"Well, today, we did."

"I s'pose that's a solid point." She made a face, and said, "I wish I'd taken a few snacks from the galley for the road."

"Dad always has food, and he gets his feelings hurt if people don't eat. He was a short order cook for twenty years, before he took over as manager of the same diner. But he wanted to be a real chef and started taking classes late in life. He even spent a month training in Paris while I was still an undergrad."

"That's amazing," she said.

"He was always putting some experimental new dish on the menu, only to have his heart broken when the locals just wanted their burgers and fries." He shook a finger her way. "But he didn't give up. He had to go slow. Keep all the stuff they were used to on the menu, and just introduce one new dish every couple of weeks. The ones that worked, he would keep in the rotation, the ones that didn't, he'd leave out. By the time he sold the place and retired, he had twenty-one different dishes taking turns on the menu."

"He found a way," Maria said.

"He still loves to cook." Harrison thought it was a good start at conversation. He should keep it going. "So, about what happened—"

"I chose to make love with you, Harry. It didn't come with strings."

"I know. I just want you to know that it... it meant something to me."

"Yeah?"

He nodded. This was going well.

"What?" she asked.

"Huh?"

"You said it meant something to you. So, what did it mean?"

"I..." He looked across at her, then back at the road. "I don't know, it just meant something."

She nodded, heaved a sigh. "It meant somethin' to me, too," she said.

He had the feeling that if he asked her "What?" she'd have a well-thought out and compelling answer. So he didn't ask her.

Instead, he glanced at the in-dash system and said, "Want to try to find us some music?"

She did, hitting the voice control, and saying, "Contemporary Country."

A smooth female twang came from the speakers with a catchy guitar riff behind it. It wasn't what he would have picked, but he liked it.

It kind of made him want to put that cowboy hat back on.

There was a security gate, with a round, smiling guard in a booth at the entrance to the apartment complex. He wore navy-blue trousers with an impressive crease, shiny black shoes, a white button-down shirt. Harry showed his ID, and Maria handed hers over, too. The guard checked them against their faces, handed them back, then walked away while speaking on a walkie-talkie. All Maria could hear was murmurs and static. He returned to his booth, hit a button, and the gate opened. Harry drove them through.

A pretty wooden sign said, "Elmwood," but did not elaborate.

As they drove over a paved lane, they passed dozens of

duplex units, all sided in cream with brown trim. Each unit had a small driveway and two-car garage. Similar lanes, all with tree names, split off in many directions, and she lost track of how many times they'd turned. There'd been Pine Street, Spruce Avenue, Willow Lane, and Oak Terrace. Harry didn't seem to look at the signs at all. He must know the way by heart. Eventually, he pulled alongside the curb in front of one of the units. "Not allowed to block the driveways," he said by way of explanation.

"I can wait here," Maria said, "if you want some time with him, before—"

"No, it's fine. I saw him a week ago, and we talk daily, up until all this, at least." He shrugged. "I didn't think it was safe to tell him we were coming."

"Just what everybody loves. Unexpected company."

He held her gaze for a minute, then he said, "I think you're right," and then he called his father on speaker. His father answered on the third ring.

"Hey, Dad."

"Harrison! It's great to hear from you."

"I can do better. Are you up for a visit?"

"You're here?"

"Right outside." Harry looked toward the house and Maria, following his gaze, saw curtains move.

"Who's that with you?"

The older man's tone had changed entirely. It was deep and, Maria thought, suspicious.

"Maria," he said. "It's her family who took me in down in Texas. I trust her."

"You sure?"

He frowned at the phone then at Maria. She shook her head, as lost as he was. As far as he knew, his dad had no idea about the intrigue and danger unfolding in his son's life, beyond that his car had been stolen and the solar tile with it. Then Harry said, "I'm sure, Dad. Listen, are you... um... alone?"

"If you're sure, bring her on in. I just put mixed berry tarts in the oven."

The man left the window then appeared in the open front door. He had hair that was fading to gray from a reddish brown, in a horseshoe pattern around a bald center, and a warm smile for his son. He wore loose gray warmup pants and a red polo shirt with an alligator logo on the breast.

Harry hit the lock on the car and walked with Maria right up to the door. His father hugged him, slapping his back hard. "Good to see you, son. Good to see you. Come on, come inside." He kind of herded them in then looked outside behind them before closing the door and locking it. Then he turned, smiling.

"Dad, Maria Brand Monroe. You met on a phone call. I've been staying with her family since the car was stolen."

"Hyram Hyde," he said. "A pleasure to meet you face to face at last."

"It sure is."

"Dad," Harry said. "I... I'm worried about Lily."

"Yes, I knew you would be by now. Sit, sit. Ah, my tarts!" He hurried to the kitchen, but then he started coughing when he got there.

Harry went to help, but his dad waved him away and

reached for a prescription bottle from amid a line of them on the kitchen counter. "Get the tarts," he managed between hacking.

So Harry grabbed a potholder and took a baking sheet full of golden brown, perfectly folded, triangular tarts from the oven. Each had red berry juice oozing and bubbling from teardrop-shaped cuts in the dough.

Hyram swallowed his pill and half a glass of water.

Harry said, "Jeeze, Dad, what's with the cough?"

"Bah." Hyram waved his hands. "I'm old. Deal with it." He nodded Maria's way. "There's fresh coffee made, cups in the cabinet above. My gosh, your hair is spectacular. Isn't it spectacular, Harrison?" Then he shuffled into the living room and sank onto the sofa. "Bring us each a serving and a cuppa Joe, will you?"

Maria met Harry's eyes, grinning. He mouthed the word "spectacular," and touched her hair, and the look in his eyes made her heart beat faster.

She found the coffee mugs and took down three.

Harry put a tart onto each of three dessert plates, and said, "Three tarts coming up."

"Four," his father called back. "You're not my only guests."

The two of them turned slowly.

The twenty-something woman with the platinum blond curls who stood beside Hyram, giving a finger wave, could only have been...

"Lily!" Harry dropped the plates onto the counter and was hugging her in two strides. "God, Lily, you don't know how scared I've been."

"I know. I'm sorry. I wasn't sure if it was safe to call." She broke the hug and clasped her brother's shoulders, smiling into his face, and then finally, she looked past him at her.

Maria smiled into sky-blue eyes just like Harry's. In person, the girl was the mirror image of the photo that had been hanging in Harry's car, the one of their mother.

"Hi, Lily."

"Maria!" Lily went in for a hug and said, "So good to finally meet you."

"What happened?" Harry was asking. "Why are you ignoring your phone and hiding out at Dad's?"

"Tarts, first." His father hadn't even got up. He was still sitting in a worn-out recliner.

"I've got this," Maria said. She headed back to the kitchen for one more cup and one more plate, filled them and delivered all four of each, using the baking sheet as a tray.

"Resourceful," Hyram said.

Since he was in his easy chair and Lily had taken the rocker, Maria had to sit beside Harry on the brown, microfiber sofa.

Everywhere, there were photos of them as a family, at every stage of life, with their mom, brilliant smile, sky-blue eyes, and fine, silver-blond hair falling in long waves. She was beautiful in every shot, at every age. She nearly always had one, skinny, beaded braid in her hair. Her face was makeup-free. She was always smiling. She seemed like the embodiment of light.

"So, Lily," Harry said. "Tell me what's going on?"

His sister nodded, sipped her coffee, and began. "I kept seeing this car, parked outside the apartment. Never in the same spot, but my place seemed to be the focal point. And then one night, this guy got out and came to the door. Rang the bell, smiled right into the ring cam. I called the police. They got there in under two minutes, but my *visitor* took off, soon as he saw the squad car turn onto my road. Knowing about Solomon, and that Carrie was missing, I thought I should get out of there."

Hyram picked up the tale from there. "She drove her car to the bus station parking garage, took an Uber here. And nobody is any the wiser. *You* didn't even know, until now."

"I think we should keep it that way," Harry said.

"I agree," his father said. "Did you notice *my* little ruse on the way in?"

Harry frowned. "What little ruse?"

"The road signs. I switched about six of them. You know, just in case. How did you not notice?"

"I know the way by heart, never look at them," Harry said.

"Well, the bad guys will. Ha!" Hyram slapped his knee, laughing. Then he started coughing again.

Harry's face went serious. "What's going on with the cough, Dad? I know you know. You have a prescription for it in the kitchen."

"Ahh." He waved a dismissive hand. "Same as always, just my asthma acting up."

"COPD," Lily said.

And her father's eyes went wide. "How do you—? What did you—?"

"I'm an RN now," she said. "And I can read labels. How long have you known?"

He shrugged. "It's not too bad unless I exert myself. It's complicated by my asthma and seasonal allergies right now, so that makes it worse."

"That's terrible," Harry said. "And you've been keeping it to yourself?"

"Trying to. Didn't want to be a burden on anyone. It is what it is."

"For Pete's sake, Dad."

"All those years smoking," he said. "But that's neither here nor there. What are we going to do about all this with Harrison's solar tile? Who do you think is behind this, Harrison?"

"It was Robert," Lily said to Harry. "The guy who stole your car looked like him, you said."

"That's what I thought, too," Maria put in, with a look Harry's way. The others looked at him, too.

Harry said, "Robert was found dead in Texas. He was shot in the head." His father and sister gasped in unison.

Then Lily reached across the coffee table and grabbed Harry by his wrist. "Are Dad and I safe here? Even with dad's… precautions?"

Harry met Maria's eyes, and she knew he wanted to say yes, but he couldn't.

CHAPTER THIRTEEN

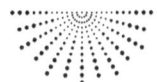

*H*arry's father only had one guest room, and Lily was already in it, but offered to share. Maria thought Harry tensed up a little, waiting for her answer. She hoped it was because he wanted to keep her close. "I'd never sleep if I put you out like that," she said. "Your dad's recliner looks perfect for me."

"That works," Harry said, almost too quickly. "I'll take the couch."

The look that flashed between Harry's sister and his dad was lightning quick, but Maria noticed it all the same. So did Harry.

"I'm going to move the car around back," he said. "No point advertising you have guests here." He was out the door before his face finished turning red.

Hyram chuckled to himself as soon as the door closed behind Harry. Then, shaking his head, he said, "Since I baked, I'll leave you younger folks to handle cleanup. It's past my bedtime. G'night."

When he was up the stairs, Lily and Maria went into the kitchen. There wasn't much cleanup to do. Hyram apparently rinsed and loaded mixing bowls and utensils as he went along. Maria washed the dessert plates, coffee mugs, and the carafe. Lily dried and put them away then wiped down the counters.

Eventually, Lily said, "So are you and my brother, uh...?" She lifted her eyebrows.

"Sort of," Maria said. "But I'll never leave Texas, and he'll never move there, so..." She gave a sad shrug.

"Because of your family, huh? He's been texting about them. And you."

Maria said, "They can be a lot," wondering what Harry had told his sister about them.

"They sound amazing," Lily said. "Kind, tough, loyal. Like a family straight out of an old western TV show."

"They are pretty great," Maria said. "But it's not just the fam. I'm taking over my mom's veterinary clinic. She's fixin' to ease into retirement while I ease into runnin' the whole shebang."

"But you could be a vet anywhere."

"I could. It would disappoint my whole town, but I could. I just... I don't want to." Maria lowered her head and tried to find words to convey her feelings. "It's the land, the place. Generations of Brands have lived and died there. The blood of my ancestors is in its soil. That place... it means somethin' me. It's the foundation of who I am. Takin' me away from Quinn, Texas would be like uprootin' a cactus and trying to plant it... well, here."

A soft footstep alerted her. Harry had returned. He

stood in the open back door with one foot in the kitchen, and she got the feeling he'd heard her whole speech.

"I'd love to see where you live," Lily said.

"I'd love to show it to you."

"It must be amazing to feel that connected to a place."

"It is." Then she added, with a look Harry's way, "It'll feel that way to my kids, too, and to their kids, if I have anything to say about it." She pulled the plug to let the dishwater out, wiping the sink as it drained.

Lily put the leftover tarts into a big airtight container then rinsed her hands, dried them on a towel, and said, "Guess I'll head up. Night, big brother." She hugged Harry's neck and kissed his cheek, and Maria pretended not to notice that she whispered something into his ear before she left the room.

"Your sister generally go to bed by 9:30?" Maria asked.

"Actually, she's a very early riser. But in this case, I think she was giving us our privacy. She asked me if we were involved," he said.

"Oh?" Maria busied herself rinsing the sink. "She asked me, too."

"What did you say?" He moved up behind her and clasped her waist in his hands.

"You first," she told him. The sink was long since clean. She took the towel from just to her left and dried her hands.

"I said yes, and it was complicated. She said complicated how, and I said when I figured it out, I'd let her know."

"And what did she whisper in your ear just now?" Maria

asked then quickly added, "You don't have to tell me if you don't want to."

"You want the exact quote?" he asked, and then he gave it to her without waiting for a reply. "'You're out of your fucking mind if you don't find a way to make this work.'"

Maria's eyes widened, and she turned around, so she was back-to-the-sink with him in front of her, close but not quite touching, except where his hands rested on her hips. "She said that?"

"She likes you."

"I like her, too."

"I can tell."

"And your dad's amazing. I loved all those stories about your mom. She was special."

"She was."

He was gazing down into her eyes. She said, "I don't want to fool around in your dad's house. It feels disrespectful."

"No means no," he said. "But I feel I must point out that we fooled around on a jet."

"I don't think it would've embarrassed the pilot if he'd known."

"Oh, he knew."

"But it would probably mortify your father."

"He would probably high five me in the morning. He was looking at you like his new favorite person."

She laughed softly, and he dipped in for a kiss. "Not to be pushy, but the car's right out back, and it's already nice and dark. And everyone in this community has been asleep for an hour already."

She pressed her lips to his and dropped her dish towel as they wrapped up in each other and kissed all the way out the back door, toward their borrowed, probably rented, car. He'd parked it up near a trash bin, so it was in shadow and all but invisible. When they reached it, she fumbled for the door handle behind her back while he kissed his way down her neck to her right shoulder, pushing her blouse aside along the way.

Maria's heart was racing. She'd never felt anything like the way her body responded to him. It had not come close to this with Billy Bob. She got hold of the door handle, shifted herself sideways, and opened it. They tumbled inside together, him landing on top, and grinding and kissing her with their feet still sticking out.

Lights painted the car's interior as someone drove by. She was only vaguely aware of whoever it was stopping and staying still for just a beat too long.

But then Harry's mouth was on her neck, and his hands were sliding under her blouse, and she suddenly cared very little about passing cars. However, before she even got her blouse off, it happened again. Same thing, only the car was moving in the opposite direction this time.

Harry stopped ravaging her and lifted his head. He met her eyes, and she saw a hint of alarm in his, then he straightened up off her, fixed his pants, reached for her hand.

She let him pull her out of the car and straightened her clothes while he closed the car door so silently it didn't make a sound.

Holding her hand, he led her around the side of the

house, for a better look. The car came back again. They ducked behind a shrub as it moved slowly, like a shark that smelled a seal. It stopped again at the street corner. Its headlights illuminated the street signs that read Maple Street and Poplar Place. A voice floated on the cool night air.

"This doesn't match the map. Where the hell is Oak Street?"

"*This* is Oak Street," Harry whispered. "Maple and Poplar are on the other side of the complex."

"Your dad's a genius. I see where you get it," Maria whispered. "It's them, isn't it? Whoever they are. They're looking for you."

"Or at least looking for my dad, just like they were looking for my sister."

The car turned right. Harry and Maria, still holding hands, slipped around and into the house by the back door.

"I'll get Dad," Harry said. "You get Lily. We have to get them out of here and I don't think we have much time."

Maria slipped into Lily's room, crept over to her bed, and gently laid a hand on her shoulder. "Lily," she whispered. "It's Maria. Wake up."

"Maria?" She sat up and reached for the lamp.

"No lights!" Maria said, covering her hand before she could turn the switch. "The bad guys have found us. Your father's trick with the street signs bought us a little time.

Get dressed. Grab what you need. We have to leave before they find us."

Lily was on her feet instantly, scooping clothes from a drawer into a big shoulder bag in one motion. She pulled on a pair of jeans and ran into the bathroom while pulling a shirt over her head.

"Try to stay away from the windows," Maria said. "I'll meet you downstairs. I have to grab my things. too."

"Okay."

Maria ran back downstairs to the living room, where her bag lay beside the recliner. She snatched it up, then grabbed Harry's, near the sofa. Lily came down the stairs, her steps soft on the carpet. Harry and his father came right behind.

"Okay, back door, my car."

"What about phones?" Lily asked as they moved into the kitchen. "I took mine offline."

"You think they're tracking our phones?" Harry asked.

"How else did they find you here?"

"Turn off cellular and wireless," Hyram said. "It in settings under—"

"I know how," Harry said. "Let's get to the car first, okay?"

Maria already had her phone in her hand, doing what his dad had suggested. Harry crept to the back door and opened it. Hyram went to the counter and grabbed the big container full of tarts, and when Lily sent him a look of blatant disbelief, he whispered, "What? They're for the road."

"I see their headlights three streets over, moving away from us," Harry said. "Now's the time."

He opened the back door wider and nodded to Maria. She took Lily's hand, and they headed out. Maria wanted to go fast and tiptoe at the same time and the result felt cartoonish. She expected piano sound effects as she crouch-ran to the car, passenger side. In seconds, Lily was in the back seat and Maria was in the front. She closed her door as soundlessly as she could. Lily did the same, but to Maria's ears it was loud.

Harry walked more slowly beside his dad. It felt like it took them forever, but it was only seconds, and they were in.

"Hand me your luggage," Lily said as her father settled into the back seat beside her. Maria took Hyram's bag and Tupperware from Harry and handed them over, along with her own, and Lily shoved them into the space behind the back seat, out of the way.

Harry put the car into reverse, and the headlights and backup lights came on, set to auto. He cussed softly and shut them off, then reversed and shifted gears.

Maria looked toward where that other car had been and spotted headlights closer than before, and heading toward them instead of away. She pointed, not saying a word.

"Take a right," Hyram said. Harry did so, and his dad, keeping watch of the other car's headlights as they all were, directed him. "Now right again. Then left." He kept directing, taking them further from the prowling headlights and around them, toward the exit.

Finally, they came to the gate.

It was raised, so Harry didn't stop. But as they rolled slowly past the gatehouse, Maria saw a pair of legs sticking out from its open door, shiny black shoes, navy trousers with an impressively sharp crease. Then they were pulling, unseen onto the public road. As soon as they'd rolled out of sight, Harry flipped the headlights on and sped up.

"I'll text 911 and Willow from your phone before we turn it off, Harry," Maria said. She took it from his shirt pocket, did just what she'd said. There was an immediate reply. "Willow wants to know where we're goin'."

"To the jet," Harry said. "Ask her to wake the pilot and have him meet us there. Then... back to the ranch. I think you were right. It's the only safe place right now." He met her eyes. "And I know you're trying very hard not to be delighted about that."

"I'm only tryin' very hard not to *show* it," she said. "But I'll be even more delighted when we get there in one piece." And then she texted Will, "We're coming home." She looked at the others in the car. At Lily, at Hyram, at Harry. Something made her eyes well up.

Harry glanced her way just then, saw her tears, and reached across to hold her hand. "You okay?"

She nodded. "I'm overtired. Or overwhelmed. Or scared or something." But those were not the emotions she was feeling. This was important, this night, this ride, this moment.

It was one a.m., West Texas time.

They'd flown four hours, but gained back two of them thanks to the time zone shift. During the flight, Hyram had discovered the small plane's galley and served them all coffee and perfectly warmed, leftover mixed-berry tarts.

The small jet set them down a few miles outside Quinn, where Willow and Bubba had brought Bubba's truck and Maria's van. Maria assumed six would be too many to fit comfortably in the pickup, despite its rear seat. Her van didn't have back seats at all.

Harry fetched the bags from the little cargo hold in the back, one apiece, and they debarked.

Maria was exhausted and nervous. She looked all around, but saw only rolling land. It was hot and still, and the cicadas were singing like mad.

Harry said, "Dad, Lily, this is Ethan Brand. The singer."

Lily's eyes widened. "*Country Kind of Love* Ethan Brand?" she asked, and Bubba lit right up. "Wow. Harrison, you didn't tell me!"

"Well, I've been a little distracted," he said. "And this is Willow Brand, Quinn County Sheriff's Deputy. They're Maria's cousins." And then to Bubba and Will, "This is my dad, Hyram Hyde, and my sister, Lily."

"So good to meet you both," Willow said.

Bubba just stood there for a second, smiling. Will

elbowed him, and he said, "Uh, yeah. Welcome to Texas. I'm your ride. This way."

Hyram and Lily followed Bubba. Harry walked Maria to her van, stood near the driver's door.

Willow came over, too, leaned on the van, and said, "Um, Harry, you care if I ride with my cuz? We need a word."

Surely, Maria thought, she could stand to be apart from Harry for twenty minutes. Besides, his folks would feel better riding with him.

"Sure," Harry said. Then to Maria, "See you at the ranch, then."

"Yeah, see you there." She wanted to lean up and kiss him, and she could see he wanted it, too. But instead, she leaned her head sideways to kiss the back of his hand where it rested on her shoulder. She was too tired to worry about who might see or what they might make of it, and she'd decided to go for broke with Harry, anyway. No point trying to hide it.

A few yards away, Bubba was already opening the truck's rear door for his passengers.

Lily got into the back, and then Bubba helped Hyram up into the front, passenger side. Willow muttered something and went back to the truck to talk to Bubba—but really to give her and Harry a moment.

He stood close to her. "Be careful out there."

"I'll have Willow with me. You be careful, too."

"I'll have your gigantic cousin with me." He slid his arms around her and pulled her closer then bent his head to kiss her. Apparently, he too, had decided not to hide what was happening between them.

"See you in a llittle while," she said.

"Yeah." Then he kissed her again. He went to Bubba's truck, passing Willow on the way, and got into the back seat beside his sister.

Maria went around to the passenger side of her own vehicle and got in, too tired to do more than ride along. Willow drove and followed Bubba's pickup across the meadow and onto the road. Then she punched Maria in the shoulder and said, "You did it, didn't you?"

"Ow! Did *what?*"

"*It.*" Willow wiggled her eyebrows as she steered the van back toward town.

"How... did you know?" Maria asked.

"You *did!*" She punched her again, but Maria caught her hand this time.

"*How?*" Maria asked again.

"The way you look at each other. The way he kissed you. That wasn't a *maybe we'll do it someday* kiss, that was a *we done it and we're fixin' to do it again* kiss. Plus, his eyes when he looks at you. Holy cow, Maria Michele."

"Yeah, well, it's not goin' anywhere."

"What do you mean, it's not goin' anywhere? You had sex."

"That was on me. He was tryin' to avoid it."

Willow looked her way, hat tipped back, eyebrows arched high. "Why?"

"He told me from the get-go that he could never live in

Texas, and I told him I couldn't live anywhere else. He didn't think it would be fair to take things any further." She shrugged one shoulder. "So, I jumped him on the jet."

Willow's laugh gusted full force, and the van veered a little. "*Dayum*, girl. I didn't know you had it in you."

"It's funny, isn't it? I was never all that eager for Billy Bob. It was more like I was doin' him a favor."

Willow's smile died. She swore a long streak under her breath then said, "You were gonna marry a man you slept with as a favor?"

"I thought it was me. I thought I just wasn't... you know, into it. Turns out, I just wasn't into him."

"But you're into Harry."

"I'm *so* into Harry."

They were driving away from town, out beyond the street lights.

"And it's not, like, a rebound thing? After your weddin' blew up?" Willow asked.

"I blew my weddin' up, and it surprised me, but I was relieved after. I'd been dreadin' it, and denyin' I was dreadin' it, even to myself. It was like I balled up my dread and shoved it into the back of my gut someplace. And when I left that church, it just exploded out of me."

"And all over Harry."

"Kind of. I ran him down on the Oxbow Trail." She laughed softly. "Poor Harry. What he must've been thinkin'."

They took the right onto the long, straight stretch of North Brand Lane. Willow said, "The fella that shot Harry was a local. Worked for Beckett Oil goin' on twenty years. Only things on his record were a few drunk and disorderlies and a speedin' ticket just last week. Nothin' to indicate why he'd want to shoot somebody he didn't know."

"Hired gun," Maria said. "Somebody paid him to go after Harry, and maybe the jerks who stole his car, and stalked his family were paid, too. But why? They stole the prototypes and made the patent disappear. They ruined the demonstration with the investors. What else could they want?"

"They stole the invention and are trying to kill the inventors," Willow said. "What does that tell you?"

Maria lifted her brows. "They're not tryin' to take credit for it, just like I said in the beginnin'. But they're not tryin' to profit from it, either. They're trying to stop it. Anything else of interest while we were away?" she asked to drown out the awful feeling in her stomach.

"There was a fire at the EV dealership on Main St.," Willow said. "Fire Chief Alex says someone set it."

"Jeeze," Maria said. "Never a dull moment around here, is there?"

"Not lately."

Ahead of them, Bubba's taillights vanished around a curve, just as a deer sprang out in front of them. The impact sent the animal airborne and the van skidding sideways. Willow yelled "hang on," and brought them to a stop in a cloud of red dust on the side of the road. "Holy mother, you okay, Maria?"

"I'm good, you?"

"Better'n him," she said nodding.

Maria followed her gaze to the deer, lying on its side and trying to raise its head. "Well, he picked the right person to hit him." She reached into the back for her large medical case and got out of the van.

CHAPTER FOURTEEN

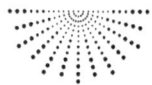

"*D*ad's been a wreck all week," Lily said. "But Ethan has him laughing out loud." She spoke softly, so her father wouldn't hear in the front seat of Ethan Brand's gigantic pickup truck. It occurred to Harrison that his sister would never call Maria's singing cowboy cousin by his unwanted nickname. She'd known him as Ethan Brand because Spotify knew him as Ethan Brand.

She was a serious girl, Harrison's baby sister. She always had been. She put her head down and did the work, whatever the work of the moment happened to be, from learning to write her name to earning her pin. She sat beside Harrison in the back seat, looking so much like their mom it was almost as if she was there, too, peeking out from inside her daughter's blue eyes every once in a while.

Ethan had been in lighthearted conversation with their father the entire time.

Harrison's initial impression of "Bubba" had been *big*. Then, talented, when he'd heard him playing by the campfire. And later, kind, when he was the only one who called him by his actual name. It turned out he was also a gentle and caring sort of man. He felt a little bad that it surprised him. But the big guy had talked Hyram right out of being scared and had probably lowered the older man's blood pressure while he was at it.

"I can't wait to see the ranch," Hyram said. "The way you describe it, it's obvious you love it."

"We're already on it, actually," Ethan replied. "This here road cuts right through Brand land."

"Amazing. Oh, if only it were daylight." Hyram was looking out his window, but it was hard to see much besides shapes in the darkness. "Do you take after your mom or your dad, Ethan?" Hyram asked at length.

"Oh, well, that's a whole other story, Hyram. A whole other story. My birth mother passed when I was knee-high to a grasshopper. Before she died, she left me on the doorstep of the Texas Brand with, she said in her note, the kindest family she'd ever met. They'd taken her in once, when she was in trouble. Helped her so much she named me after the head of the family. My mother's sister, my aunt Chelsea, came lookin' for me, and wound up stayin'. She married Garrett and they adopted me."

"That's a helluva story!" his father said. "Left on the doorstep!" Then he coughed for about a minute and a half.

Ethan hadn't mentioned his birth father, but Harrison had heard the rest of the tale from Maria. His birth father had murdered his mother and was serving life in prison.

That was probably the cause of the uneasiness behind his eyes. There were unseen depths to Ethan Brand.

Harrison glanced behind them, but he didn't see the headlights of Maria's van back there. He pulled out his phone to text her and tapped her contact, which was just her initials in a blue circle. He didn't have a photo of her to his name. He'd have to remedy that. When he thought of her, his heart twisted into a knot of pleasure and pain that was impossible to untie. They went hand in hand. He wanted to be with her, but he couldn't be with her, and it was killing him.

That was when something broadsided them out of nowhere. Lily screamed as they were plowed off the pavement and into some trees, and the truck crumpled inward around them. Harrison threw himself over his sister, and when the grinding stopped and he looked, the spot where he'd been sitting no longer existed.

Up front, Ethan got his door open, got out, and helped Harrison's father out behind him, picking him right up. "He's fixin' to ram us again," he shouted. "Everybody out, fast!"

The rear passenger door was mashed against a tree, impossible to open. Lily scrambled over the back seat, and jumped out of the truck through the open driver's door. Through the shattered passenger side window, Harrison saw a big black truck with an oversized, after-market bumper, surging toward him. He dove over the seat and out, as the killer rammed the truck again. Racing into the thick woods, he caught up to his sister, encircled her shoulders with his arm and kept running as the attacker rammed the truck yet again.

The revving and smashing continued. Ethan was up ahead, carrying Hyram piggyback.

Harrison still had his phone in his hand. He wondered if it had been an error turning it back on when they'd landed. Maria's contact was still open. He tapped the word AMBUSH and kept on running.

The deer let her approach, but when Maria got close, it sprang up, leapt away on three legs, then lay down again. She tried a second time, and the same thing happened. The third time, the animal kept on going, it's gait uneven, but rapid as it vanished into the woods.

She sighed, shaking her head. "This one's up to you, Mother Nature," she said as she turned. Willow was shining her phone's flashlight onto the front of the van. When she got close enough, Maria could see a small dent in the fender.

"It's fine," she said. "Just hope the deer is."

"Looked pretty peppy to me," Willow said. "Want me to keep driving?"

"Yeah, if you don't mind." She was exhausted, worried, and maybe it was just because she was tired, but she didn't feel very hopeful about things with Harry. Now that she'd spent time with his family, she didn't blame him for not wanting to move away from them. Or for wanting to keep his promise to his mother. It kind of made her love him even more.

Oh, dear Lord, I love him, she thought. I love him, and he's fixin' to break my heart. She couldn't even be angry about it. He'd been honest from the start.

Her phone pinged, and she picked it up.

Harrison: AMBUSH

"Oh, Lord, somethin's wrong." She showed Will the one-word text, and Willow stomped the gas pedal. "Tell the family he's in trouble," she said, then she told her own phone to call dispatch, while Maria texted. Dispatch answered, and Willow talked on speaker. "It's Deputy Brand. We've got trouble. Possibly another attempt on Harrison Hyde."

"Location?"

"North Brand Lane," Willow said. "Start looking around the five-mile mark."

"Dispatching deputies now."

They rounded a curve, and the headlights illuminated devastating wreckage. Maria thought her heart stopped. The smashed-in vehicle was red. Other than that, you could barely tell it was a truck. It was flattened against some trees. Willow shut the headlights off and stopped where she was, pulling off the road a good distance ahead of the scene.

Maria yanked the door handle, but Will grabbed her arm then pointed. Off the opposite side of the road from Bubba's ruined pickup, there was a large black truck with some kind of metal grill on the front. Willow opened the glove compartment and pulled out a handgun only she could have put there.

"No plates. Son of a gun. There's a shotgun in the back," she said. "I brought it along in case of trouble. Box of shells beside it. Get 'em. Load it. Move slow. I'll watch."

"If they were in that truck—"

"If they'd been in that truck, Harry couldn't have texted, right? Get the shotgun."

Maria scrambled into the back of the van and found the shotgun, an old Ithaca 20-gauge pump model. Not police-issue. A family heirloom. She loaded in four shells but did not chamber one. Instead she dropped the fifth slug into her pocket. Her forefinger brushed across the safety, ensuring it was on.

She turned, but Willow was gone, and she spotted her, creeping up on the passenger side of that black truck with her gun in both hands, its barrel angled downward. Maria got out of the van, using the side door. With the shotgun ready, she crossed the road to back Willow up, and moved to the passenger side of the black truck.

Willow yanked open the driver's door and checked inside. Maria did the same from her side. The truck was empty, so she moved to the back.

"Tailgate's down," Maria said.

"Ramps, too," Willow noted. "Had a four-wheeler in the back. Maybe more than one. Listen." In the distance there were faint motor sounds.

Maria crossed the road to Bubba's truck. The only door open was the driver's door, so that was where she climbed partway in. The truck had been compressed to half its width. There was broken glass everywhere, but she didn't see anyone inside. And she didn't see any blood. She looked over into the truncated back seat, but no one was there, either.

Her sigh was so heavy her neck went limp, and she dropped her chin to her chest. And then she saw the crimson puddle of blood on the floor.

"Maria?"

She backed out of the pickup, still carrying the shotgun. "No one inside, blood on the floor in back. Harry or Lily, they were the ones sittin' there."

"I spotted a little blood out here, too. They left a trail. Bad guy could've followed. Maybe not, though. He might not've seen it from his ATV. There's only a few drops here and there." She pulled out her phone. "No signal. You?"

Maria looked at her phone. "No. But there must be one nearby. Harry got a message out to me."

"Might have a different carrier."

"The family will spot that blood," Maria said. "But we might as well make it easy." She snapped a slender limb at eye level as she passed.

"Here, hold up here," Ethan said. "I think we lost him." He set Hyram on his feet in little clearing within the woods.

Harrison looked around. There was a low, stone wall

forming a boundary around gravestones. "This is a cemetery."

"Family plot," Ethan said. "Highest point on the property. Prettiest, too."

As he spoke, clouds moved away from the face of the moon, allowing its white light to spill down. The well-tended graveyard overlooked a small pond that reflected the moonlight. A couple of stone benches, and a birdbath had been placed near its edge. There was a small shed made of large stone blocks. Plants grew all around the pond and from every grave, old or new. Their buds nodded. Some of the headstones illuminated by the moon were centuries old. Some were much newer. And because the spot was elevated, and the moon was full, the view was stunning. Rolling meadows, woodlands, darkening layers of landscape. In the daytime, he thought, you could probably see the whole place.

"Well, I'll be..." Hyram looked around, blinking. "I've seen this place before."

"This is my mamma's spot, right here," Ethan said, laying his big hand on a rose granite tombstone. "Uncle Garrett had her moved here. Aunt Chelsea said it was what she'd want, to be where I was."

A lump formed in Harrison's throat. He started to say something, feeling a shared loss with Maria's big cousin, but the buzz of a motor cut him off, growing louder alarmingly fast. Lily released a shriek of alarm as an ATV burst from the trees, and she took off running. Harry and his father both lunged after her, but his dad fell, and then an ATV bore down on him. In the dark woods, the driver wouldn't see him to avoid hitting him, even if he wanted to. Harrison flung himself on top of his dad, wrapped his arms around him and rolled him out of the way, winding up in a thick patch of brush. The ATV roared past them. Ethan raced past them, too, trying to catch up with Lily as she screamed like Harrison had never heard before.

He lunged to his feet to go to her, but the ATV sped right at Lily, and the man driving it grabbed her, pulled her across the seat, and gunned it.

"No!" Harrison lurched after them as Bubba chased the machine on foot, but it was gone. And then a second ATV sped toward Harrison from behind, and he turned and ran right at it. Just before it smashed into him, he bent his knees and leapfrogged right over the hood and handlebars, smashing into the driver's head, helmet and all. He held onto the guy, taking him off the machine and onto the ground. Straddling, the guy's chest, he ripped off his helmet. "Where the hell is he taking my sister?"

The man didn't answer, and Harrison punched him in the face so hard it hurt his hand. He was like a passenger watching his own body acting without his consent. He drew back to punch him again, his entire body shaking. "Tell me, dammit!"

"Harry, don't!" That was Maria's voice, and it worked like cool water on his anger.

He turned his head to look at her. She and Willow had arrived, somehow, on the scene. Willow said, "I've got this," and pushed him off the guy then rolled the man over. Harrison looked at the guy's bloody face. He'd done that. None of this seemed real.

Willow cuffed the guy's hands behind his back. "Get up," she said, yanking until he was on his feet, then she patted him down.

Maria moved closer to Harry. It had taken her a beat. Maybe she'd been shocked, too, to see him pounding on another man's face. She hooked her arm around his waist, and he put his around her shoulders. She pressed so close to his side there was no space between them. She held a shotgun by its stock in her free hand.

Willow pulled a folded sheet of printer paper from the attacker's shirt pocket. She took it out, unfolded it, and then turned the sheet around so he and Maria could see what was on it. A photo of Harrison. Underneath it, an itinerary. "Brighton Private Airstrip to Texas Brand via North Brand Lane. 12:00 - 1:00 a.m."

He took it from her. "They knew exactly where I'd be," Harrison said.

"He ain't gon' hurt her," the handcuffed man said. His beard glistened with blood from his nose and split lip.

Willow spun him around. "Where's he taking her?"

The guy spit a mouthful of blood on the ground then said, "I want a lawyer."

Within a short time, there were cops surrounding the woodlot. So was every member of the Brand family. Harrison, Maria, Ethan, and Hyram had been driven back to Maria's van on a UTV. There were flares blazing and pulled-over police vehicles with lights flashing. Maria's mother, Jessi, ran to wrap her daughter in her arms. Then she turned to Harrison and Hyram.

"We're gon' find her," she promised them both. She nodded in the direction of the wreck, where the flashing yellow lights of a wrecker joined the strobing red and blue of the police cars. Then she looked at Maria and said, "I'm s'posed to drive you back to the ranch where it's safe. But uh… I heard that little Agent, Hofstadler— ain't she cute as a button?— sayin' the forensics team would arrive by noon. 'Til then, nobody's allowed to lay a finger on that truck that rammed you."

Harrison saw the way Maria's face changed. She looked right at her mother and there was no doubt in his mind that the two were having a private conversation nobody else was in on. Maria said, "They takin' it to the impound yard?"

"Seems likely," her mother said.

The wrecker was humming loud and lifting the front of the black truck. Then the driver made a few more adjustments, got behind the wheel, and towed the thing away.

CHAPTER FIFTEEN

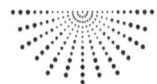

*T*he impound yard was an unpaved square lot with a half dozen cars, a couple of tractors, an ATV, and a cement mixer. Weed-tangled chain-link fence formed its boundary. The gate was closed and locked.

"Your dad's safe and sound at the ranch house, with plenty of folks watchin' his back," she said, nodding at her phone.

"Good to know. And *your* dad the chief deputy thinks we're *not* about to break into his impound yard, right?"

She made a face, then said, "If he doesn't, it's only 'cause he hasn't had time to mull on it yet. He raised me, after all."

Harry looked worried. In the dash lights, his brow was creased, his mouth, tight. "I don't feel like we have a choice," he said. "The idea of Lily being in that guy's hands—"

"I know. And I'm with you on that," Maria said. "Up ahead there's a spot to pull off. There, right there, see it?"

"I see it." He pulled her van off the road, amid some

small brushy trees that might conceal it a little bit. He shut it off but left the keys on the seat. They got out, and walked across the road, pulling on latex gloves taken from her veterinary supplies as they went. Maria jumped up onto the chain-link fence, near a pole, and climbed. In seconds she was landing on the other side and brushing off her hands.

Through the link, Harry gaped at her. She smiled. "Meet me at the gate. I'll let you in."

He shook his head then jumped onto the fence and climbed over, dropping down beside her. "I'm not gonna let you show me up."

"Yeah? Next time we'll race. See who's faster. This way." She led him through a half dozen vehicles and other items. "We have to avoid the camera. There's only one. See it? It's angled toward the front." And she pointed.

He nodded then said, "Why is there a barbecue grill in the impound?"

"Some locals were cookin' meth on it." Maria spotted the large black truck with the huge metal grill welded onto the front. Its bed was lined with wood planks and was wider than the truck. At the rear, there was a ramp, folded in at the moment, for loading and offloading the ATVs.

Harry opened the driver's door and climbed up, so Maria went around to the passenger side. She opened the glove compartment and found a plastic fork, some napkins, and the truck's manual. If there'd been a registration or insurance card in there, the police would have already taken them. She looked over the top of the visor. A pair of sunglasses fell down. Sighing, she put them back and checked the pocket attached to the door, which was filthy, and held several cellophane cigarette wrappers and an empty plastic ice cream bowl with a wooden spoon.

As soon as she saw that spoon, she remembered its flavor. Yuck.

She looked across at Harry. He was digging around underneath the driver's seat. So, she bent to look underneath the passenger seat, and whisper-shouted, "Ha! There's an envelope under here." She stretched her arm and got hold of a corner. "Got it!"

She pulled it out and climbed up onto the seat. Harry climbed up onto his as she looked at the envelope. He pulled out his phone, turned on the flashlight app to illuminate the address.

His face fell. "It's junk mail. Resident. Rural Route Twelve."

Maria said, "That's only a twelve-mile stretch. We're closer." She turned the envelope over. The back was covered in handwriting. She read it aloud.

"'Harrison Hyde, Texas Brand.' It has your description. See right here, tall, dark, and handsome."

He smiled, which had been her goal. Then she said, "It also says *First to provide proof of death gets 1 million cash.*"

He raised his eyebrows and whistled at the amount. "If they only wanted me dead, why take Lily?"

"Did they have a shot at you?"

She saw him thinking back. "No, I pushed dad out of the way, wound up in some brush. It was dark. They drove past without even seeing me."

"So they took whoever they could get. They'll use her to get to you, one way or another."

He pressed his hand to his forehead. She could feel his frustration.

"How could these guys have known we'd be on that particular road at that particular time?" he asked. "Who else knew? Besides your family, I mean. It can't be one of them."

"You trust my family that much?"

He looked into her eyes. "My mom used to say you can recognize good people. You can just feel them, she said. She could anyway. I didn't think it was very scientific, but even so, from then on, I always paid attention when I met someone new, looking for that sense. Never worked until now. With your family, I finally understand what she meant."

"*Harry*," she said, pressing a hand to her chest. "You're fixin' to make me cry."

"So besides them, who? The guy whose jet we borrowed..."

"State Senator Mark Tompkins," Maria filled in.

"And the pilot," he said.

"And the driver who picked up the pilot."

"And the crew who came to get the jet," Harry added.

"That's a lot of people."

Harrison drove slowly over the 12-mile stretch of Rural Route 12. It was a narrow, bumpy stretch of road in need of a fresh coat of pavement. There were not a lot of homes on it. Here and there, a trailer with a couple of outbuildings, or a two-story farmhouse at least a century old.

"I want to search them all," he said. It was killing him, thinking of his kid sister, tied up and scared in one of them.

"I do, too. But let's rule some out, first. Look, swing set, kids' toys on the lawn, we can probably eliminate that one." Maria had a notebook open and was jotting notes about every place they passed. "No vehicle in the driveway, that's a red flag."

"How about an ATV in the driveway?" Harrison asked, because he'd just spotted one, and his heart started beating faster.

She was still scribbling. "Well, that would be a —"

Gently, he closed his hand on top of her head, lifted and turned it. She looked where he was looking, at a small farmhouse with an ATV in the driveway. "Holy heck, Keep goin', keep goin'!"

"I am. I am." He drove past, and once out of sight, he chose the first spot where he could pull off the road safely. He did so in reverse, so they'd be ready for a quick take-off, backing up off the road as far as possible. Then he shut the car off.

"Should I call in the troops?" Maria asked. She had her phone in her hand.

"We should make sure." Because there was no way he

was waiting for help to arrive. Lily might be in there. He opened the car door.

Maria grabbed his arm. "Harry, this guy could be a professional killer."

"I don't think so," he said. "I don't think a pro cuts loose with rebel yells while repeatedly bashing an empty pickup truck."

She tipped her head sideways, her gaze shifting in the same direction she tilted. It was a peculiar thing she did when thinking, and it did something to his insides every time he witnessed it, even now when he was itching to run for the house. She said, "You're right, that wasn't very professional."

They started walking together toward the farmhouse. It was full dark and thick storm clouds had crept in to cover the moon. Insects whirred behind a cricket choir, and the air was thick and warm and heavy. It would be dawn in another hour.

"It seems to me like somebody put out a hit," Harrison said. "Made it a competition."

"That's what it sounds like from that paper we found. Somebody put a bounty on your head. And maybe not just yours."

"Maybe Solomon and Richard and Carrie, too," he whispered.

"But not publicly," Maria went on. "It's not like you could take out a classified ad. Whoever's behind this put it to a select audience of folks who wouldn't report it."

They stopped a few yards from the driveway. "I don't

see any cameras." Maria wished for more light. "The place looks abandoned."

"Let's circle around behind. There's scrub brush we can use for cov—"

The front door opened. They were in plain sight on the road, but it was pitch dark. Harry found Maria's hand with his own as he crouched low. She crouched, too. The figure staggered to the ATV, got on, and started it up. Its headlight came on, bathing the house. Something skittered underneath.

Harry and Maria backed into the nearest bunch of bushes, and in a moment, the ATV was turning in a tight circle, and roaring away, in the opposite direction from where they'd left the car.

"Let's go." Harry ran right up the driveway to the front door, ignoring Maria's whispered warning that the assassin might've left somebody behind.

But nobody challenged him as he tried the door and found it locked. He was about to kick it down, when Maria's hand clasped his shoulder from behind and she said, "Why don't we see if there's a less obvious way in first? Come on."

He was impatient, but it would only take a minute. It wasn't a very big house. So he went around the side, checking every window until he came to a basement hatch, angled low to the ground. There was no padlock on it. Its rusty hinges squealed into the night.

He froze, met Maria's wide eyes. She was motionless as well, partially crouched, ready to run. But they didn't hear a thing. "Okay," he said. "Flashlights." He held up his phone.

Maria took hers out, and activated the light, and then she followed him down into the basement. "We should close these behind us," she whispered.

"We'll be five minutes. In and out." He was already aiming his light into every corner and crevice of the cellar, and then mounting the rickety wooden stairway up. At the top, the door was closed, but not locked. It opened when he turned the knob, and he pushed it inward just slightly, peering through, flashlight off.

There was no sign of anyone. He stepped up into a kitchen. There were dishes in the sink, a towel on the rack, a bottle of dish soap, a pan hanging from a hook, potholders, a toaster. Someone lived there.

"We should split up," Maria whispered. "You take the upstairs—"

"Not on your life. Stay close to me, okay?"

"Okay." She looked around the kitchen, grabbed a meat hammer from a rack of utensils, and returned to position behind him.

He crept from the kitchen through a dining room whose table and chairs bore a thick layer of dust. The living room had a ratty sofa and chair, and a big TV on the wall. The recliner had a cup holder in which stood a beer can. There was an overflowing ashtray on a coffee table. A thin spiral of smoke rose lazily from a not-quite-extinguished butt.

"If he's living here, he probably didn't go far," Maria said. "We have to hurry." She tugged his sleeve toward the stairs, and they hurried up, flinging open doors, no longer being quiet. Bathroom, empty. Bedroom, empty. Bedroom—

"Lily!"

She was on a bed with a bare mattress and an old metal head and footboard, maybe brass. She was lying on her side, hands and feet bound, hair covering her face. The leg of her jeans was soaked in blood. She wasn't moving.

Harrison ran to her. "Lily." He rolled her onto her back, and she moaned. "She's alive."

"We need to get her out of here fast, before he gets back," Maria said. "Scoop her up and carry her out the back door. Come on, let's go." She reached over and pulled off one of his sister's slip-on shoes. "Sorry about this, Lily. I'll buy you a new pair."

They moved through the house rapidly, down the stairs, out the back door, which they left open, but Maria darted over to the hatchway door through which they'd entered and closed it. Then she threw Lily's shoe toward the farthest edge of the back lawn where it met with dark woods.

Maria rejoined Harrison and they headed for the car. "If he thinks she escaped, he'll waste time lookin' for her out there," she said.

"You're brilliant. I wouldn't have thought of that." He walked fast, his sister limp in his arms. "She's out cold, Maria."

"He probably drugged her," she said. "It can't be from blood loss, there's not enough."

The sound of the ATV's motor came then. Harry ran faster, but Maria sprinted. She got to the van ahead of him and opened the side door. The interior light came on. Harrison slid his sister into the back, lying her down on the floor, and then he and Maria dove into the front, slammed the doors. The lights went off.

The ATV was rolling up to the house. Harry started the van, pulled out, and drove away before the other vehicle's noisy motor shut off, heading away from the little house. He didn't turn his headlights on until they were clear.

"Perfect!" Maria said. Then she twisted in her seat, pulled out her cell phone and called Willow on speaker.

She answered on ring one. "Where the hell are you?" she asked. "Why aren't you at the house?"

"Well," Maria said, "We found a clue that led us to Lily, so we rescued her." Maria flashed a smile Harrison's way, and if he hadn't been driving, he'd have kissed her right then.

"You *rescued* her? Is she okay? Are y*ou* okay?"

"She's injured, and I suspect they drugged her. She's unconscious. Hang on." She put the phone into a cup holder then climbed over the seat to tend to Lily.

Harrison adjusted the mirror, driving and watching.

Hooking her finger into the tear in the Lily' jeans, Maria ripped them wide open, revealing a thigh sticky with blood, and a small tear in Lily's flesh that still trickled.

"She has a small wound," Maria said loud enough for Willow to hear on the phone. "From broken glass, probably. It's in her left thigh. She's been bleeding awhile, so she might need a transfusion."

"We're the same type," Harrison said.

"We're inbound to the hospital."

"Where was she being held? Was anyone else there?"

"Five-ten County Route Twelve," Harrison said. "One adult male captor. Has an ATV. Probably armed. And he probably thinks my sister escaped out the back door and headed into the woods behind the house, thanks to your cousin's quick thinking."

"Got it. I'll wake the doc, have him meet you at the ER, and then I'll wake a judge."

Harrison stayed by his sister's side, holding her hand, gazing at her face. It was as if he'd gone back in time a year, and it was his mom in the hospital bed. He'd refused to leave her then. He refused to leave Lily now.

She'd lost a little blood, but it turned out she was unconscious because she'd been doped with ketamine. And she still hadn't awakened.

He sat there, holding her hand, lost in his saddest memories, and starting to nod off. And his mom said, "She's fine, Harrison. Your sister's fine."

He startled awake, looking around the room. No one was there. The door was closed. Someone tapped on it before opening it. Maria came inside with a white paper bag in one hand and a larger, brown paper bag in the other. The sight of her rinsed the sadness from his brain. She'd been with him the whole time, but he'd been surprised to wake up and find her gone. He got up to greet her with a hug.

"Hey," she whispered. "I have sustenance and supplies." She held up the white bag. "Breakfast sandwiches. Two of 'em."

"Thanks." He took the bag, took out the sandwiches and offered one to her.

"Aunt Chelsea brought them." She looked at his sister in the bed, still unconscious. "Hey, Lily," she said, moving closer, leaning down to squeeze her shoulder. "It's Maria. I'm here with Harry and you're safe. Everything's all right."

"You think she can hear you?"

Maria shrugged. "Better I talk to her and she can't hear me, than not talk to her if she can, right Lily?" She gave Lily' a shoulder another squeeze. "What do the doctors say?"

"That she'll come around as soon as the drugs wear off. The IV's supposed to flush them out faster."

"Good." She pulled a second chair over nearer to his, sat in it, and opened her shoulder bag on her lap. From it, she pulled out a thermal jug, twisted off its cup lid, and filled it with hot coffee. "There's a machine in the waiting room, of course, but I thought you deserved the real deal, so I asked Aunt Chelsea to bring a Thermos."

"Holy, God, no wonder I lo... I mean, um. No wonder I'm lagging. No coffee. Heh-heh." Lame cover. He'd almost blurted, *No wonder I love you.* What was wrong with him?

No sleep. Murder attempt. Sister kidnapped. There was *a lot* wrong with him. He took the cup, took a sip. She screwed on the cap and set the coffee aside.

"Thank you," he said, and took another sip. "That's...

perfect." One more sip. Then, "What's the update? They get the kidnapper yet?"

"Not yet. He wasn't home when Willow went to his place. ATV was gone, too. Probably out lookin' for his escaped prisoner. Until she gets a line on him, Will decided it's best not to let on that Lily was rescued."

"Why?"

"Well, for one thing, if he's out lookin' for her, he's not out tryin' to shoot you."

She pushed his hair off his forehead. "We know who it is, though. Local fella, works for Beckett Oil, like half of Quinn County. Interesting thing is, so did the other fella. The one you uh— tackled off a moving four-wheeler like some kinda superhero. Once Willow arrests him, she'll get more."

"Well, what if he doesn't come back?" Harry asked. He'd demolished one sandwich and was unwrapping the second.

"Then at least he's not tryin' to kill you." She closed her eyes and gave her head a shake. Then said, "You need a shower."

He lowered his head and sniffed. "I stink?"

"It's nice and manly. Don't fret. I needed one, too. Aunt Chelsea brought us some clean clothes. They let me use a shower down the hall. I thought I'd let you sleep for a while." She set the brown paper bag on the bed. "You can use the shower right in here."

"That bathroom's for patients only," he said, repeating what he'd been told.

"Then you'd best be quick so you don't get caught. How often they come in?"

"Once an hour, need 'em or not," he said. He had not intended to sleep at all, so he'd been grateful for the hourly interruptions. If he slept, he was afraid his sister might die.

If he showered, she might die.

"When was the last visit?" Maria asked, shaking him out of his insane thought.

He glanced at the clock on the wall. "Fifteen minutes ago." His gaze slid back to his sister in the bed. And then her face changed into his mother's beautiful face, the last time he'd seen it.

"Then you have time. And I promise, I won't leave her side." She put a palm to his cheek. "She'll be fine. I promise. The drug'll wear off soon." Maria pushed his clothes into his arms. She'd taken the things out of the bag. There was soap and shampoo on top of the stack.

"Thank you."

"Are you okay?"

He wasn't sure. He looked back at the bed. Lily was Lily again. God, she looked like Mom.

For a moment, his mother appeared in his mind, her angel-hair flying as she twirled, laughing and holding his hands. In his mind she'd told him Lily was all right.

Maria pressed her palms to his chest. "Harry?"

He met her eyes. Could she see the tears in his? They'd pooled up a little. He blinked. "I'll be fast." And he went into the bathroom. He closed the door and set his clothes on the sink as there was no other surface and the toilet had no lid. He cranked on the water, adjusted the temp, and shucked his clothes. Then he took the products Maria had brought for him and got into the shower.

Beneath the spray, his emotions spilled over. He braced his hands on the wall and let them go. He couldn't name all the feelings that flowed with his tears. Grief for his mother, fear for his sister, worry about his father, and agony over his feelings for Maria. It was only when the well ran dry that he realized, he hadn't shed a single tear for his stolen invention.

When he left the bathroom, cleansed inside and out, Harrison found Lily lying just the way she'd been, and Maria in the chair beside her bed. He went to the bedside and took Lily's hand in his, and said, "I really wish you'd wake up, sis."

"I'm 'wake," Lily muttered, and he and Maria both jumped. "Jus' resting my eyes." Lily's voice was hoarse, her eyes still closed. She squeezed them tighter, frowning. "Why am I in bed?"

"You're okay," he said. He was aware of Maria catching her breath as Lily opened her eyes to a narrow squint, as if the light hurt them. "I'm here with you and you're okay."

Maria hurried to close the blinds. The light was already off. Then she came to his side, filled a water glass from a pitcher on the nightstand and handed it to him. She found the call button and pressed it.

Harrison held the straw to his sister's lips and she drank, and when he pulled it away, she said, "I remember now. Someone rammed the truck, we ran through the woods, and then… some guy on a four-wheeler grabbed me."

"Do you remember anything else?" Harrison asked.

"He jabbed me with a needle, like immediately," she said. "I remember being afraid I'd fall off if I passed out, but I passed out anyway." Then her eyes went wider. "What about Dad?"

"He's fine. Safe and sound at the ranch."

A nurse came in and said, "Well, it's good to see you awake, Lily." Then she made shooing motions at them.

Harrison took Maria's hand, meeting her eyes as they went through the door into the hall, probably beaming. "She's okay," he said.

"She's okay."

"Thanks to you."

"It was a team effort," Maria said.

He pulled her in for a kiss, and he was nowhere near finished when a throat cleared. They both turned to see Willow, in her uniform, smirking and wiggling her eyebrows at them.

"Shut up, Will," Maria said.

"She's awake?"

Harrison nodded. "A nurse is in with her now. Kicked us out. But she seemed good. Remembered what happened. Asked about Dad." He couldn't seem to keep the smile off his face.

Willow was smiling, too. "I'm glad. I wish my news was as good." She paused as another white-coated woman went past them into Lily's room. While the door was open, Lily caught his eye, held up the breakfast sandwich he'd left on the stand, and called, "Can I have this?"

He said yes while laughing, so the word had about four syllables. The door closed, and he got hold of himself. There were serious things going on.

"Let's talk where it's private," Willow said. "There's no one in the waiting room." She led the way, though they both knew it. Once inside, they didn't sit. They turned to face her, standing so close to each other they were touching.

Maria hooked Harry's pinky with hers.

"The guy who kidnapped your sister got away. But we know who he is. Kendrick Mason. The one we arrested is Cole Samson. And we'll get Mason eventually. The thing is, Mason, Samson, and the guy who took a shot at you—"

"The dead one?" Harrison asked.

"Yeah. Name was Bobby Green. They all had the same employer. Beckett Oil. Owned by Jimbo Beckett, one of the richest and most eccentric oil barons in Texas. And so did one of the guys we questioned in the windmill fire. I'm starting to think this little crime spree might be connected to the theft of your device. We need to pull this thread and see what unravels."

"And their connection is an oil company? Harrison asked.

"Jimbo Beckett might be crazy, but he's Texas royalty. I need more than a theory to justify questioning him," Willow said. "We found your sister's phone, in the woods, Harry. We were meant to find it. They'd texted a message from Lily to Lily. I forwarded it to myself." She tapped her own phone to show him.

> Lily: Harrison Hyde for the woman.
> Midnight, Lone Wolf Rock.

Maria grabbed his arm.

Willow said, "My notion is, you show up for the meeting. We have police surround the guy when he shows up, take him in, put him in a cell next to his buddy. Then we can play the two of them against each other. Lead one to believe the other's pointin' the finger and get 'em to tell us who's *really* behind it."

Maria said, "Yeah, Willow, you're forgettin' the part where this Mason character has no intention of trading Lily for Harry. He don't *have* Lily and he's fixin' to *kill* Harry!"

"Well, we're not gon' *let* him," Willow said.

Maria shook her head. "Things haven't exactly gone to plan so far. What if you *do*?"

"I'm going to do it," Harrison said. "I'll meet the guy tonight. But before I do, let's get my sister out of here. I'll feel better if she and Dad are together at the ranch before we do this. I know they'll be safe there. Whatever happens."

When he said that, he glanced at Maria. She looked into his eyes so deeply that he felt as if her soul was reaching out to his. And his was reaching right back.

Aunt Chelsea made a low-key dinner of biscuits & gravy with roasted sweet corn, fresh from the field. Uncle Garrett and Aunt Chelsea sat at either end of the oval dining table. Harry was between Maria and his dad with Lily and Bubba across from them.

The rest of the gang were around, watching out for them while that maniac Kendrick Mason, who'd kidnapped Lily, was still on the loose. They were just staying under the radar. Aunt Chelsea had probably asked for peace and quiet in the main house today. Hyram and especially Lily had needed the time to recover from the madness of the night before.

"You're a fantastic cook, Mrs. Brand," Hyram said at length. He'd been doling out compliments throughout the meal.

"Call me Chelsea," she said. "And thank you. That's high praise, coming from a chef."

"Oh, I mean it. Especially these biscuits."

"Well, if and when things settle down around here, I hope we can cook together."

He put a hand on his chest, nodding hard. "I'd love that."

They all got up and headed into the living room. Willow and Bubba stayed behind to clear the table, and as everyone found a place to perch, Maria smelled coffee brewing.

Ten years back, Uncle Garrett had a big picture window put in. Hyram and Lily were standing in front of it, looking out. The window faced the sunset, which was in progress, vivid orange, and painting the ground in brushstrokes of every shade from peach to red. Hyram said, "This place is…"

"It is, isn't it?" Lily slid a hand over her dad's shoulder.

Neither of them knew Harry was going to put his life on the line that night, and he'd asked Maria not to tell them.

Willow was taking all sorts of precautions, but Maria couldn't shake the sense of a dark shadow lurking over them all.

CHAPTER SIXTEEN

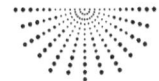

MIDNIGHT

"*I* hate this," Maria whispered. She was face down on the hard, dry ground lying under a desert camouflage net. Bubba was beside her, and they were under orders to stay put and not get shot. They were both armed, but only for self-defense, as they'd been reminded a dozen times.

Willow and rest of the deputies were at strategic locations around the area. Uncle Garrett and Maria's dad were directing things. Agent Hofstadler, Detective Wynn, and other officers were a part of the mix. The brown boulder known as Lone Wolf Rock was shaped like an upright, howling canine in an otherwise flat, brown landscape. Tufts of scrub brush dotted the area like the scattered toys of a giant's child.

Harry stood out there. He was wearing a bullet-proof

vest underneath his shirt, and it made him look twenty pounds heavier. He was wearing the hat she'd got him. She found it sexy as hell on him, because it was such a contrast, a cowboy hat on the head of a scientist. It emphasized his uniqueness. Maybe that was why she loved him.

She'd pretty much made peace with the fact that she loved him. It wasn't as if she could do anything to change it.

She looked around the area and then at her phone. "It's two minutes after midnight," she whispered.

"I know." Bubba's tone was as deep and low as an elephant's subsonic rumble.

"He was s'posed to be here at midnight."

"I know."

"He can't bring Lily to trade, like he said he would. We know that."

"Yep."

"He plans to kill him."

"Shhhhhhhhh."

The way he shushed made her think something was happening, and she shifted her focus from Harry to the area around him. The only places for a shooter to hide would be those patches of sage brush.

Wait, was something out there moving? There was a shadow in motion behind a patch of brush! Maria exploded out from under her tarp and tackled Harry flat to the ground just as gunshots exploded. He rolled over beneath her then saw it was her and rolled again, putting himself on top. Around her, the ground exploded in small, desert-brown puffs as bullets landed. It was chaos. Gunfire, people shouting, then roaring motors. Large black vehicles, jacked up with huge tires invaded, and one was about to run them over. It came so close she screamed, but it stopped almost on top of them, and its door opened. She tried to draw her gun, but Harry was on her arm, and then he wasn't. Someone was pulling him right off her and into the vehicle. "Harry!"

"Maria!" Their eyes locked in a frozen moment and everything he felt for her showed there in his gaze. He struggled and was bashed in the head with the butt of a gun. Then the car door slammed and the vehicle sped away. Other identical SUVs joined it, flinging desert dirt behind them, before they all sped off in different directions.

When he came to, Harrison was in the seat of a big vehicle. He looked around, disoriented, worried about Maria. But she wasn't with him. And this wasn't the same vehicle he'd been pulled into. It was a Limo-style SUV. He was in the furthest back seat, leaned sideways against the door.

On the seat beside him… "Carrie! You're alive!"

"More alive than ever, to be honest with you, Harrison."

He blinked. "What are you… what happened to you? Are you okay?" Again, he looked toward the front of the vehicle. The only other person inside was the driver, a large man who kept his attention focused dead ahead.

And then slowly, understanding dawned. He frowned and looked at his friend again. "Carrie?"

"Look— I was hired by a company to—"

"Beckett Oil?" he blurted, and then he wondered if he should've let on that he knew.

Her thin eyebrows, arched in surprise. "Where'd you hear that name?"

"His employees have been tilting at windmills all over west Texas. Literally."

She rolled her eyes. "Windmills, yes, and solar installations, and an EV dealer." She shook her head slow. "I know. The man's an idiot."

"Jimbo Beckett?" he asked. And when she nodded, "And yet you're working for him. What did he pay you?"

"Plenty, and a house in paradise, but that's not why I did it. He's getting John into a clinical trial, Harrison. A promising one, with real hope. And all he asked me to do was not file the patent and bring him the prototypes."

Even though she was saying it, he was having trouble believing it was true. "A clinical trial isn't a sure thing. You know that. Who'll take care of John if it fails, and you're in prison?"

"Prison? I have a mansion waiting on a tropical island with no extradition."

"What about the planet? What about our work?"

"What about my sick husband? Doesn't he deserve this chance?"

"Carrie, the climate—"

"Oh, come *on*. Someone else will do what we did. The

science is there. Others are working on it. Luckily for me, Beckett doesn't believe that."

"So, I'm just—"

"You're one remaining loose end," she said. "At least according to my crazy benefactor."

Harrison closed his eyes. "He's going to kill me."

"No, he's not."

"He killed Solomon," he said.

"Solomon had a heart attack." Carrie reached out to turn up the air conditioning. "Though Robert probably caused it. It wasn't deliberate."

"It was pretty deliberate when someone killed Robert, though," Harrison said.

Carrie flinched. Then she nodded. "Beckett found out Robert had fudged the data in a study he was part of, twelve years ago. Blackmailed him into helping. Robert didn't mean to kill Solomon. But Solomon found out I hadn't filed the patent and started asking questions. Robert was just supposed to scare him to keep him quiet. He was devastated when Solomon collapsed."

"But he left him lying there alone, all the same. Didn't even call for help."

She shrugged. "I don't know the details. Just that he came to Beckett, saying he wanted out. Taking your car was supposed to be his final act. Beckett told me he planned to let him go after that." She lowered her head. "I thought he had, but I overheard one of his muscle-heads talking about how cleverly he'd hidden Robert's body."

"In a small-town hospital morgue with only one rarely used drawer?"

She nodded, looking at him. "He dressed as a maintenance worker, rolled poor Robert through the hospital inside a trashcan. Found a body bag in the morgue, zipped him in, then planted him in the empty drawer."

"Why?" Harrison asked. "They had to know he'd be found there."

"The boss wanted him where he'd be found, but not for a few days," she said. "Who the hell knows why? Like I said, he's insane. When I realized he'd killed Robert I understood he must plan to kill you, too. You were the only one left, and you're too squeaky clean to blackmail and too upright to be bought. I got one of his thugs talking. Beckett has a bunch of good ol' boys on his payroll who do nothing but… solve problems. He told them whoever killed you would get a million, cash."

"Then why am I alive? Why am I even in this car right now?"

"Because of me, Harrison." She looked him right in the eyes. "I convinced him, I think, that there are more projects in the works than he can hope to stop on his own, and that he needs scientists who work in the field to tell him which pose the biggest threats to his precious oil-based lifestyle."

"That's stupid, there are hundreds."

""Shh!" She shot a quick look forward, toward the driver. He had earbuds in his ears. "Do not tell Jimbo that," she said. "Listen, this is not a smart man. But he's got billions and so far, he believes what I tell him. So, when I told him that his notion of sabotaging any renewable project that was getting close could work, he believed me. And when I told him it was a few more projects than I can monitor all by myself, and that I needed your help, he believed me again."

Harrison closed his eyes and shook his head. "And he's doing this in the misguided notion that it will preserve his oil business?"

"He's trying to preserve his way of life," she said. "He's a dinosaur looking at an approaching asteroid, and I think it broke him, Harrison. Broke his mind and broke his heart. He thinks he can stop it. He can't, and he won't, but he refuses to believe that. So…"

"You're cashing in."

"I'm saving my husband's life… and his mind."

"You scared your husband half to death. What was with the blood on the safe door? Huh?"

"I had to make it look real," she said. "Besides, he doesn't remember trauma for more than an hour anymore. But I can help him. I can give him back his life. I'm smarter than Beckett. I tell him what he wants to hear and do just enough to make it believable."

"Doing just enough o make it believable got Solomon and Robert killed."

"That was not my intent," she said, as if that made it right. "I advise you to take the same approach with him. Our species isn't gonna make it, anyway. I might as well get all I can out of life."

He shook his head slowly. "I refuse to believe that. There's hope— there's hope because of the very work we've done, and others are doing."

She shrugged and resumed driving. "Maybe you're right. But if there's any chance I can have my husband back, then that's enough."

"What about the solar tile?" he asked.

"What about it?"

"What did you do with it?"

She glanced out her window, effectively hiding her expression. "I crushed it and tossed the pieces into the river."

It was a lie and he knew it. She'd put thousands of hours into the solar tile, same as he had. There was no way she could bring herself to destroy it. Was there?

Maybe there was. Maybe he'd never known Carrie at all.

"I came to your wedding," he said, "We've been friends for—"

"That's why you're still alive, Harrison," she said softly.

"I'm not selling out to him. I won't."

She sent him a worried look. "Then I don't know if I can stop him from killing you. But I'm giving you a chance," she said. "You have to convince that filthy rich lunatic that he needs you alive more than he needs you dead. Understand?"

He wanted to shake her and realized he'd never known her at all. "Before I end up dead, I'm curious, how did your boss know about my flight home, that I was at my dad's, or what time I'd land?"

"I don't know. I heard him say Senator Tompkins owed him a bigger favor than he owed Garrett Brand. Could that have had something to do with it?"

Harrison thought of the gifts in the private jet's galley, the friendly, helpful note from its owner, the senator. It made him wonder aloud, "Honest people are few and far between, aren't they?"

"Endangered species," Carrie replied.

The family gathered at the ranch. That was what they did when trouble came. They pulled together. Most of the elders were out with law enforcement, searching. Drew and her mom, Penny, were working from Penny's home office. She had access to all her P.I. stuff there.

Maria was petrified— she felt as if her body had gone rigid and brittle. There was a low-level tremor that felt as if it was emanating from her soul, but for Lily and Hyram, she kept a brave face. They were in the living room, on the sofa. Blue Boy had taken up position on their feet, as if he knew they were in need of comforting.

Willow got off her phone call and said, "We've located every last one of those vehicles, abandoned in different areas. None were registered or had a lick of paperwork in them. They're running down the VINs, but they were bought for cash and delivered to a vacant lot where they were signed for by John Smith."

"It's Beckett," Maria said. "It has to be."

Every phone in the room chirped, and Maria pulled hers out to see a message on the family loop.

Drew: Attaching list of 5 closest Beckett-owned properties.

Maria opened the file. It was a list of addresses.

"That first one's one of his homes," Jessi said. "His whole family— kids, grandkids— are there every June. Unlikely he'd take Harry where there are so many people."

Bubba said, "I know the fourth one. It's a honky tonk out on Finn Road. I can check that.

"That one," said a voice from right close to Maria's ear, making her jump. It had sounded just like Lily's voice. Only it couldn't have been, because Harry's sister was sitting on the sofa across the room, petting Blue Boy. Maria looked around, but saw only family, none of them near her ear.

"I'm comin' with you Bubba," she said.

"We want to go with someone too," Lily said, the real one this time. Maria didn't even think about saying no.

"Second address is in town," Orrin pointed out. "Mom and Drew can check that out. I'll head in to back them up."

Baxter said, "I'll check the huntin' lodge on Wood Canyon Road. "Trevor, you can ride shotgun."

Willow raised her hands, saying, "Hold up, hold up. This is police business. We can't have the family just go charging in—"

There was a sarcastic laugh, from Aunt Chelsea of all people. Then she said, "Your uncle Garrett got that list too, hon. And he's been letting you lead this. Have you noticed? Showing you how good you are. And you are. But he's had your back the whole time and he has your back now. He'll share that list with the rest of law enforcement, don't you worry. And he'll do it quick, because he knows this family. Heck, he *raised* this family."

Willow shook her head. "Strictly recon, you hear? Don't approach or do anything until law enforcement arrives. I'll take some deputies out to the fifth address. Stay in contact! Hyram, Lily, you can ride with me."

Brands spilled from the house. Maria followed Bubba toward an ordinary blue pickup truck. He opened her door for her and kept walking around to the driver's side. She got in. "It's an okay truck," she said. "Rental?"

"Loaner. Mine's totaled. Insurance is replacin' it, but it'll take a bit to find one with the same color and trim package. I can wait."

Sure he could, she thought, but she knew how much he'd loved his truck. He pulled the sub-standard replacement into motion, and they drove out, part of a small parade passing beneath the familiar TeXas Brand arch, leaving a comet's tail of dust behind them.

One by one, they split off in different directions, until she and Bubba were on their own.

Seventeen miles later, they drove past the saloon. It was a slab-sided, one-story building with a roof that only slanted in one direction. Its front windows had neon beer signs, lit up 24/7, whether the place was open or closed.

It was closed just then, according to the sign hanging on the brown door that looked like it belonged in a country home. There were no vehicles in the driveway, but as they passed, Maria saw at least two parked out behind.

"Big SUV out there, and a pickup," she said. "I'm texting the loop."

Bubba turned the truck around in the road and started

back toward the bar. "I'll get as close as I can. We can sneak in from there, see if we can get a gander at our boy."

"If they hurt Harry, I'm gon' lose it, Bubba."

"Harrison," Bubba said. "He really wants to be called Harrison. And I really want to be called Ethan."

She frowned and looked at him. "Really? It's that big a deal?"

"It is," he said.

She frowned at him, and then said, "I apologize, Bub—Ethan. Dang, that's gon' take some gettin' used to."

CHAPTER SEVENTEEN

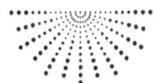

wo guys as big as the driver had been waiting when the SUV pulled around behind a country-style bar. They'd taken him by either arm and escorted him into the building by way of a back door, through a kitchen. Portholes in swinging doors provided a glimpse of the hardwood floors and bar top on the other side. Then they took him through another door off the side, into a small room with dark-blue paint, a wooden chair, and a single, small window set deep into the wall. Its windowsill was two feet deep, and it had bars on the inside edge.

The big dudes deposited him in a wooden chair, the only piece of furniture in the room. Then they left him alone and closed the door. Locks turned. He got out of the chair, walked around, tried the doorknob for the hell of it.

Someone thumped the door's other side and said, "Knock it off."

He went to the window, could reach through the bars far enough to touch the glass. But the window didn't have any opening mechanism that he could see, short of smashing through it. Which would do him no good anyway, due to the bars.

The door opened, and he turned. A barrel-chested man with Colonel Sanders hair, and the bolo tie to go with it came inside and closed the door behind him.

"So, you're the genius behind that little solar tile, are you? Smart fella. Smart."

"If I'm so smart, how'd I wind up here?" Harrison asked, looking around the room. Was there anything he could use for a weapon? Could he bring himself to bash an old man's head in, even if there were?

Was Maria okay? He thought she'd been okay. He flashed back to his last sight of her, lying on the ground, reaching for him, tears in her eyes. She'd better be okay.

"Winding up here might not be such a bad thing, son." The older man's use of the word *son* made Harrison's skin crawl. "I'm Jimbo Beckett."

"Charmed, I'm sure." His sarcasm went right over the old man's head, and he went on as if Harrison hadn't spoken.

"I've been fighting this battle for the better part of five years, now."

"Attacking windmills."

"Among other things." He sounded defensive.

Harrison told himself not to antagonize the guy. The only weapon he had here was his mind. He had to outsmart him, outthink him. Insulting him would not further that goal. Carrie had said he needed to give the crazy billionaire a reason to keep him alive. But her way wouldn't fool the man for long.

"You can't stop progress, though," Harrison said. "There are hundreds of scientists working on renewables. There are five teams right behind mine, working on the same technology. You stopping my team only delayed the inevitable by a few months. It's the way of the future. And it's a good way. Try to imagine it— limitless clean energy that doesn't destroy the environment."

"Limitless energy means I go broke. My wells shut down; my refineries sit idle. My businesses employ upwards of ten-thousand good people, young fella. What are *they* supposed to do?"

"There will be plenty of jobs in clean energy. They won't go away; they'll just shift from fossil fuels to renewables.

"Bah—"

"Sir, the warming alone is—"

"Lies. All lies."

Harrison lowered his head, realizing the notion of saving mankind wasn't going to be an effective approach with the oil baron.

"Carrie works for me," Beckett said. "She tell you that?"

"She mentioned it, yes."

"She says the job is too much for one person."

"What job is that?" He made himself sound interested.

"Keeping abreast of what's coming down the pipeline so I can try to steer it another way."

"Sabotage it, you mean," Harrison said.

Beckett shrugged. "Whatever it takes. But again, she says it's too big a job for one person."

"It's too big a job for one hundred people. The tech is coming like a hurricane over a freakishly hot ocean."

The older man waved his hands. "I told her you wouldn't listen. But she made me promise to try." Then he opened the door, and said, "Thing One, git in here. Bring your sidearm and a roll of that plastic from the storeroom."

A bolt of sheer self-preservation shot up Harrison's spine and emerged from his lips unplanned. "What you really need is a way to make fossil fuels harmless."

One of the big guys was right outside the door with a gun in his hand. It had a silencer on the end, like in the movies. Every part of Harrison's body went cold. He thought how devastated his father would be if he died. And Lily. He thought of Maria, and that he hadn't even said the words he'd been stubbornly refusing to let himself say, or even think.

Beckett held up a hand to stop the guy with the gun then closed the door and turned.

"Say more."

He couldn't say more, there was no such thing, and there wasn't enough crude oil in the ground to last much longer anyway.

Sure, but he doesn't know that. And if you told him that, he wouldn't believe you.

That had been his mother's voice whispering through his mind. For the first time, he wondered if it might be more than just his brain creating it based on memories and data.

"It's... just something I've been working on," he said, making it up as he went along. "The notion is, instead of *replacing* fossil fuels, we... take out the harmful parts."

The man's face changed. He looked the way he'd look if he'd been dying of thirst, and Harrison had handed him a glass of ice water. All the tension left, his brows rose and he said, "That makes a lot of sense."

It made no sense whatsoever. "I'm thinking the oil company with the patent on this would be way ahead of the game. Not just ahead of renewables, but ahead of all the other oil companies."

Beckett stared at him. Harrison held his gaze without blinking. He imagined Maria's uncles, staring down a black-hat in an old-west-style gunfight. He squared his shoulders, even pushed out his chest and lifted his chin. He would not blink or avert his eyes, because that was an honest cowboy thing. Right?

Abruptly, Beckett pivoted and left him, slamming the door behind him. Harrison got up, stretched his arms and walked around. It was working. So far, so good.

He paced, turned and paced back by the window, looked out and saw Maria's face, between her cupped hands, looking in at him.

He almost shouted her name and clapped a hand over his own mouth.

The door opened, and he jumped out of his skin, turning fully before he landed. Then he moved opposite the window, and Beckett, facing him, said, "You nervous about somethin'?"

"Yeah, I'm nervous. Shoot me." Had he really just said "shoot me" to a killer with a gun?

Beckett released a bark of laughter, though. "You're funny, I'll give you that."

"Can you really get Carrie's husband into that clinical trial, Mr. Beckett?" he asked to change the subject from taking lives to maybe saving one.

"I've done it before. No reason to think I can't do it again. Offer to fully fund somebody's next project, and they'll bend a few rules for you." He leaned out the door. "Carrie, git in here." And when she came in, he said to Harrison, "Tell your idea again, so she can hear."

Meeting her eyes, he repeated the ridiculous idea he had just presented to Beckett. Beckett was watching her face intently. It was creepy.

She listened, but he could tell she was also aware of Beckett's perusal. And it made her nervous. "I'd have to see your methods, Harrison, but... yes." She returned her gaze to Beckett's. "It could work."

"Then why didn't you tell me about this sooner?" Beckett asked.

"She didn't know," Harrison said before Carrie could have answered. "I've been keeping the notion to myself. You know, as soon as a new idea gets out, thirty people start working on the same thing, so..."

"Huh." Beckett looked at Harrison and then at Carrie. Then he said, "Still don't see why I need both of you."

"Sir," Harrison said. "It really does take a whole team to—"

Beckett left the room, closed the door. Harrison didn't

hear the locks turn this time. Carrie glared at him. "Great! Just great! Now he'll kill me and keep you!"

"No. Listen, if you can get outside, you can get away." He wasn't going to tell her his Maria was out there. He didn't trust Carrie not to betray him to Beckett to stay in his favor.

"What do you mean?" Carrie asked.

"Are they keeping you prisoner?"

She looked at the door. "He didn't lock the door, so no. Not yet."

"Can you walk outside freely? Make up an excuse to go get something out of the car or…?"

"Yeah. I can do that."

"When you get out, run toward the road out front," he said. "If you stay toward the east there are boulders you can use for cover. And keep your hands in sight."

She frowned at him, turned to the door, then turned back again. She pulled something from her jeans pocket. A key. "The prototype from the university is in a safe deposit box in El Paso. I don't know what Beckett did with the one from your car. I'm sorry."

Then she opened the door and stepped out into the kitchen. The big guy guarding the door said, "Boss said he'd be right back."

"I know. He told me to get that box out of the car by the time he gets here. I'd better hurry, he's not in a good mood." She headed for the back exit. The guard didn't try to stop her. He closed, but once again did not lock, Harrison's door. Harrison prayed Carrie would get out.

Less than a minute ticked by before Beckett was

coming in again, a bottle and three glasses in his hands. "Now, let's talk this through," he began, but then he looked around the room in alarm. "Where is she?"

Harrison shrugged.

Beckett turned to the guard. "Where is my scientist?"

"Went to get something out of the SUV, sir."

Beckett smacked the guy upside the head with an open hand. "Idjit! Get out after her and don't bring her back."

"Sir!" The guard hurried out the rear exit, and Beckett went in the other direction, out of the kitchen and into the front part of the saloon, roaring for his men and leaving Harrison's door wide open.

"Hey, wait!" Harrison followed Beckett into the barroom. The open bottle was on the hardwood, the glasses lying on their sides around it. An extinguished half-cigar rested in a glass ashtray the same color as the booze.

"Mr. Beckett," Harrison said, "I *need* Carrie, I can't do it alone!"

"Carrie sealed her fate when she sneaked outta here." Beckett went to a window, parted a curtain, and looked out. Harrison walked a few steps nearer, as careful as if he were approaching a coiled cobra, until he could see the three big guys walking around the parking lot in search of Carrie.

He willed her to hide someplace they'd never find her and prayed Maria was safe out of their sight. And then, right in front of his eyes, a lasso sailed out of the air and looped around one of the men. It fell to his legs then yanked itself tight. The guy's feet were pulled right out from under him, and he was dragged across the road and into the desert by a distant rider.

"Hell and damnation, the Brands are here!" Beckett said.

He pulled out his phone, and Harrison realized he would call for more men. More killers. And Maria was out there. He couldn't let him! He grabbed the bourbon bottle off the bar and smashed Jimbo Beckett over the head with it. The phone flew right out of the old man's hand, arching through the air and landing in the filled sink.

"Son of a—" Beckett, clutching the back of his bleeding head with one hand, pulled a gun with the other, and Harrison dove over the bar, crashing down behind it.

The gun went off, and off, and off, smashing bottles in the rack behind the bar. Booze and glass rained down on Harrison as he crab walked behind the bar from one end to the other, and then he switched direction and crept back to the beginning. He peeked out around the bar. Beckett was reloading while moving toward the other end. His back was to the exit. Harrison could make it out. Maybe.

He took a breath then lunged out from behind the bar, across the floor toward the exit. It was farther than he thought.

"Why you sneaky, son-of-a-varmint—"

Gunshots followed Harrison out the door. He ran for all he was worth, looking over his shoulder, turning fully when Beckett exploded out of the saloon, raising his gun. Harrison raised his arms defensively and closed his eyes, expecting to be shot. Then there was shouting and footsteps and shotguns cocking.

He opened his eyes. Beckett raised his hands and tossed

his weapon to the ground. Harrison looked behind him to see a solid wall of armed Brands, bearing various sorts of weapons, every one of them trained on the oil man. Maria stood front and center, Ethan on her left, and her mother, Jessi, on her right.

Maria met his eyes and smiled. "He hurt you, did he?"

"Not much." Behind the crowd of Maria's aunts, uncles, and cousins, Willow was putting Carrie, handcuffed, into the back of her SUV. Other police vehicles were arriving on the scene, sirens wailing. All three of Beckett's body guards were handcuffed and sitting on the ground against a boulder.

It was over.

Harrison walked toward Maria, and she smiled, lowering her shotgun.

Someone shouted, and Harrison turned instinctively as Beckett lunged at him with a big hunting knife raised over his head, yelling, "You tricked me, you no good, lyin' son of a—"

Maria fired.

Beckett howled, dropping the knife, and hopping on one foot, while holding the other up. There was a hole right through his boot.

Willow pushed through her family members with a pair of handcuffs and another deputy at her side. The Brands were putting their guns away, stepping aside to let law enforcement take charge. Ignoring Beckett's howls of pain, Willow cuffed him up. "We'll take it from here. If everyone's okay?"

She looked at Harrison and then at Maria just as Hyram

and Lily ran to him and wrapped him and Maria in their arms.

Harrison said, "I'm okay, Willow," over his family's heads.

"I'm way better now," Maria said. Then her family gathered around them both, everyone clapping shoulders, exchanging handshakes and full-on hugs that hurt like hell and felt great at the same time.

Ethan brought Harrison's hat over and put it on his head. "You dropped it out by Lone Wolf Rock," he said.

"Thanks, Ethan."

"You're welcome, Harrison."

After happy reunions and a huge family dinner, Maria and Harry sat on the front porch of the Texas Brand. It was late, full on dark and the bugs were singing up a storm. Everyone had gone to bed happy and relieved. She and Harry had taken a bottle of wine in an ice bucket and two glasses onto the porch with them.

She said, "I'm fixin' to talk to the real estate people tomorrow. See if they'll let me rent my place on Bluebonnet Lane while the mortgage processes through."

"I can help you move," he said. "Looks like I'll be here for at least a few days while all the legalities shake out."

"I'm glad." She didn't tell him her heart was breaking at the notion of it only being a few more days before he left her. She was determined to make the best of the time they had.

"Me, too," he said. "It'll be nice to see the place without all the drama."

"Well, it's usually pretty quiet. And hot. And dry."

"And beautiful in its own rugged way," he said.

She didn't want him to acknowledge her hometown's beauty. She wanted him to make it his own. His phone beeped, he glanced at it then his eyes lit. "Willow found the solar tile right where Carrie said it would be." He rose to his feet, scooped her up off hers, and spun her in a circle.

"Oh, Harry, that's wonderful!"

He set her on her feet. Then he opened the wine and poured. "Ethan's been sending stuff to my phone the whole time I've been down here," he said. "An article saying hot, dry climates are best for old men with respiratory issues. Another article about Texas Polytechnic being one of the world's top research facilities in the field of renewable energy. Stuff about the local nurse shortage. A link to apply for openings at the local clinic, and the hospital in El Paso, I presume for my sister. And MLS listings for houses."

"Also for your sister?"

"Yeah." He handed her a glass. "It's probably not cold yet, but still."

"I'm sorry Bubba's so— *Ethan's* so pushy. He doesn't get it."

"He totally gets it. He's hitting every reason I said I couldn't stay."

"Those aren't the reasons, Harrison. We both know that."

Surprise crossed his face when she used his full name. "We do?" he asked.

She nodded, holding his blue eyes with hers. "Your mom's the reason."

"My mom?"

"All your memories of her were in Ithaca. Your childhood was there. She's buried there."

He nodded and seemed to be taking in what she said.

"There's gon' be a big family barbecue Saturday. Gotta use up the rest of the food we bought for the weddin' reception. We can probably even eat the cake," she said, with a wiggle of her eyebrows. "But in the meantime, I think long showers, and comfort food, lots of sleep, and no pressure about anything. We can stay over at Bluebonnet Lane, just the two of us. Watch TV on the sofa and have a few of the most borin', ordinary days ever."

"Boring days sound good," he said, sliding his arms around her from behind and nuzzling her neck. "But let's not shoot for boring nights."

"Well, obviously."

She turned in his arms and lifted her head.

He pushed a hand through her hair, and said, "Don't give up on me, okay?"

And then he kissed her, and she wondered what in the all-fired heck that was supposed to mean.

"So?" Hyram said, two days later. He and Lily were sipping sweet tea with Harrison on Maria's front porch on Blue-bonnet Lane. The real estate agent had been happy to let her move in early.

The field across the way was a sea of bluebonnets, and the breeze was warm and gentle. Harrison was standing. Dad had taken the left rocking chair and Lily the right. The chairs had been Maria's first purchase for her new home. He'd helped her pick them out.

"This is nice, Harrison," Lily said. "I just love it here."

"Doc says the dry heat's the reason my cough is so much better," Hyram said.

Their enthusiasm for the place was helping him work up to the question he needed to ask them. "So you guys… would you be willing to… live here?"

They looked at each other, his dad and sister, grinning like Cheshire cats then they looked back at him. Hyram said, "What do you want to do, son?"

"Marry her," he said.

They both came right up out of their seats and were hugging him before he finished speaking. Then they let him go, and his dad was pulling something from under his shirt. A chain. With— oh, God— his parents' rings on it.

Hyram unhooked the chain, removed the engagement ring, and said, "Your mom wanted you to have this when the time came, if the girl was worthy. This one sure is."

"Thanks, Dad." He looked at the ring and tried not to tear up at the thought of his mother's ring on Maria's finger. But then he looked at his sister. "But maybe Lily should have it—"

"I get the wedding bands," she said. "Mom and I talked about this before she... moved on."

"If you're sure."

His dad refastened the chain, wedding bands still dangling, around his neck. He'd stopped wearing his wedding band because his finger had grown too thin to keep it from falling off. Harrison said, "I've been meaning to ask you something else, Dad."

"Anything, son."

"You remember that little burial ground? The family plot on the northern end of the Texas Brand."

"I do. It reminded me of a picture your mom drew once. She said it was a place she'd seen in a dream, right after her diagnosis. No gravestones, but the benches and the plants, the trees, and the pond. Even that little stone building— match the drawing to a tee. She said she thought that's what heaven must look like. Wait, I took a picture of that sketch." He took out his phone. "It was years ago, I hope I can..." He trailed off, scrolling for a long moment, while Harrison and his sister exchanged curious looks. Then finally, he said, "I *do* still have it. Here, see for yourself." He passed the phone.

Harrison looked at the photo of his mother's drawing and felt his brows arch in surprise. "It's almost identical. Even the vista." He showed his sister.

"I never saw a spot that matched it," his father said. "But that one sure did."

Harrison nodded. "Ethan's birth mother is buried there. Garrett moved her for him. Chelsea said that's what she would've wanted."

"Oh." Lily clearly knew where the conversation was going.

He forced himself to go on. "Do you think Mom—"

His dad interrupted. "I think your mom would want to be wherever we are," he said. "And I think she is, regardless of where her body rests. But I wouldn't object to moving her."

Lily sighed audibly. "That would make me feel *so* much better about wanting to move down here," she said. "And I hear the local hospitals offer nice sign-on bonuses, too."

Harrison raised an eyebrow. "Where'd you hear that?"

"Ethan keeps texting me listings."

"You, too, huh?" he asked, and they all laughed.

"I love it here, too, son," his father said. "I can find a place, and—"

"You'll stay with me," Harrison said. "Me and Maria."

"Or me and myself," Lily added, but she was smiling wide. Then she asked in her best Texas twang, "So? *Harry?* When you fixin' to ask her?"

"'Don't give up on me, okay?' What the heck did he mean by that?" Maria demanded.

Willow shrugged. "It means there's still hope, right? What else could it mean?"

They were at the Texas Brand. It was the weekend. There was a long picnic table packed full of food and the grill was still smoking.

"All week long," she went on, "we've been livin' like honeymooners out at my place. Oh gosh, I love it so much. Did I tell you?"

"Ten times," Willow said.

"I head to the clinic in the mornin', and I don't know what he does all day, but he makes delicious meals every night."

"His dad's been helpin' him cook," Willow said.

"And he's been stockin' the pantry. It's almost full. And it's just... it's just so *good*, Will. It's perfect. Except that he's leavin'."

"He say when?"

Maria glanced across the yard at Harry. He was chatting it up with Bubba and Baxter. The guys had really bonded. "He's doing a private demo tomorrow for several ethical companies that are truly working for the common good. This time, they're coming to him. Uncle Garrett said they could set up the demo out in the lower meadow."

"And?"

"And after that, I guess he can do whatever he wants. He'll get a big fat check, and royalties, which will be split with his partners' survivors, and probably offers from all his dream jobs at universities and research facilities and the like."

"Sounds like his life's right back on track, then."

"It is." Maria sighed, then deliberately changed topics. "What's gon' happen to Carrie?"

"She'll do some time. Less than she would have, because Harrison says she saved his life, at risk of her own."

Maria hoped Carrie's share of income from the solar

tile would be enough to get excellent care for her husband, John. The poor man.

Lily was weaving her way toward them. She was wearing a pretty sun dress and a big straw hat over her silver-blond hair, holding a longneck bottle of beer, and smiling as if it wasn't her first.

"Do you see my father?" she asked as she got closer. "Look at him!"

Maria looked where Lily pointed, to the horseshoe pit where the uncles were taking turns. Hyram was up, and his throws were impressive.

"It's the dry heat," Lily said. "His cough has all but stopped since he's been down here."

Willow raised her eyebrows very high and looked at Maria. Maria said, "Really? Wow, Harry didn't tell me that. Or, um, doesn't he know?"

"Oh, he knows," Lily said, and tapped her bottle to Maria's pop can.

"What does *that* mean?"

"Nothing." But she said it in that up-pitched way that meant something.

"Lily?"

"Oh, your aunt Chelsea needs a hand. Coming, I'm coming!" she called as she ran away toward Aunt Chelsea, who had apparently turned invisible.

"Well, what in the all-fired heck was that about?" Maria asked.

Willow shrugged. "Why don't you try to relax and enjoy yourself while they're still here? Maybe do what Harry said, don't give up on him. And let go of that need of yours to know exactly what happens next before it happens.

"I don't do that."

"You totally do that."

"You do," said Drew, who had sidled up beside them.

Maria frowned, reflecting. "Maybe I do. A little."

"Let's help clean up. It's gettin' dark. The boys are fixin' to start a bonfire."

Maria threw herself into helping out. They had it down to a science, these weekend family barbecues. Leftovers were boxed up and put away, dishes were rinsed and loaded, kitchen counters were wiped down.

The guys took care of washing down and folding up the outside tables, cleaning the grills, and starting a small fire, which was done with extreme care, due to the hot, dry conditions.

Maria was walking outside for the final stack of plates, when Harry stepped into her path. "Can I steal you for a minute?"

"From the dirty dishes? You bet you can."

He took her hand, led her along the path that wound away from the house and yards, and into the quiet of the shrubby woods. Far behind them, too far for sparks to reach, the little fire leapt and danced. And then there was music, far nearer.

Maria jumped, startled to hear Bubba— Ethan, she mentally corrected— strumming his guitar, a few yards behind them on the path.

"Well, what do you suppose he's up to?"

She turned toward Harry again.

"Everything's going to change for me tomorrow," he said. "But there are some things I don't want to change. So, I thought I'd nail them down now, tonight, you know. Just in case."

She tipped her head to one side. "What are you talkin' about, Harr-ison?"

He smiled. "You were right. I didn't want to leave Ithaca because of my mom, my memories of her. But the funny thing is, she's been with me ever since I came here. She likes it here."

"Yeah," she said. "I think she even whispered into my ear once or twice."

"I don't even doubt it," he said. "And the fact is, I can work anywhere. After tomorrow, I could probably even start my own lab. And Dad's breathing is better here, and Lily... I don't think I could get Lily to go north again if I tried. Look at her."

Lily was standing a few yards away, feeding a raw carrot to a mare called Ginger.

"So, what are you saying?" Maria asked, looking at Harry again.

"That I'm in love with you. Have been from— I don't know, maybe from the minute you plowed into me on that trail. And I know you just ran away from a wedding last weekend, but I'm kind of hoping you might want to try again."

He dropped to one knee. Female voices hummed a love song in perfect harmony, as Willow, Drew, and Lily all came walking nearer. Bubba came closer too, strumming his guitar, and in a moment, some male voices offered a harmonic baritone hum as Orrin, Trevor, and Baxter joined the chorus.

Harrison held up a ring. "This was my mom's," he said. And Maria's heart swelled to bursting. "Dad and Lily approve of me giving it to you. So, what do you say, Maria Michele Brand Monroe? Will you marry me?"

"You… you mean, you want to stay here? In Texas?" she said.

"I do," he replied. "Now you say it."

"I do," she said, "You're dang straight, I do!"

He rose to his feet and kissed her, picking her up off her feet. When he set her down again, she said, "And every fall, my sweet, sweet Harrison, we're going back to your hometown and takin' a trail ride through the foliage."

He kissed her again, and she tasted a tear on his lips.

Behind them, the youngest generation of Brands sent a cheer into the starry sky, and all was well on The Texas Brand.

ALSO BY MAGGIE SHAYNE

SMALL-TOWN CONTEMPORARY SERIES

The Texas Brand

The Oklahoma Brands

The McIntyre Men

The Texas Brand: Generations

THRILLERS & ROMANTIC SUSPENSE SERIES

Brown and de Luca Return

The Fatal series

Shattered Sisters

Danger After Dawn

PARANORMAL ROMANCE

Wings in the Night

The Immortals

By Magic

ABOUT THE AUTHOR

New York Times and *USA Today* bestselling novelist Maggie Shayne has published 112 novels and novellas for numerous major publishers. She also spent a year writing for American daytime TV dramas *The Guiding Light* and *As the World Turns*. But her heart was in her books, and she'd found it impossible to do both.

Now, she is excited to be publishing with dream-publisher, Oliver Heber Books and she's having more fun than ever.

Maggie lives in a century-and-a-half old farmhouse

with two waterfalls outside, in the rural hills of Cortland County NY with her husband Lance, who builds waterfalls for a living, and their dogs. There are always, always dogs.

Sign up for Maggie's NEWSLETTER!
Early looks at covers, new and upcoming releases, behind the scenes trivia, dog pictures, and sometimes a recipe!

MaggieShayne.com
Sign up at the top of the page.

[f] facebook.com/MaggieShayneAuthor
[o] instagram.com/MaggieShayne
[@] threads.net/@maggieshayne
[BB] bookbub.com/authors/maggie-shayne
[a] amazon.com/author/maggieshayne
[g] goodreads.com/maggieshayne